PARKER O'DWYER

White Hell

Copyright © 2019 by Parker O'Dwyer

All rights reserved. No part of this publication may be reproduced, stored or transmitted in any form or by any means, electronic, mechanical, photocopying, recording, scanning, or otherwise without written permission from the publisher. It is illegal to copy this book, post it to a website, or distribute it by any other means without permission.

Designations used by companies to distinguish their products are often claimed as trademarks. All brand names and product names used in this book and on its cover are trade names, service marks, trademarks and registered trademarks of their respective owners. The publishers and the book are not associated with any product or vendor mentioned in this book. None of the companies referenced within the book have endorsed the book.

First edition

This book was professionally typeset on Reedsy.
Find out more at reedsy.com

To my bean.

Chapter 1

The stars faded and disappeared as Rudy and Abby crossed from numbered country roads to the named streets and avenues of town. Within a few short hours, the sun would wake the world for another glorious day and their perfect night would draw to an end. The old farm truck's headlamps cut identical twin swaths of light through the moonless night illuminating the darkened houses of the sleepy Iowa berg. Rudy drove with one knee on the steering wheel, his left hand shifting and his right hand holding Abby's. Although his precarious driving position kept the Dodge truck within the proper lane, he was thankful Grisliness's pre-dawn streets remained empty.

"Did I disappoint you?" Rudy asked, choking on the question even as it crossed his chapped lips.

She withdrew her hand from his and used her nimble fingers to comb her red locks back into a simple ponytail. "Why would you ask that?" she asked. Rudy heard the smile on her face as each of her words turned up at the edges.

"You haven't said much." He turned the stereo off. Although Buck Owens proved the right choice for most occasions, the Bakersfield cowboy didn't fit the bill tonight. All the poets in the world couldn't write lyrics to match the buoyant feeling in his heart, not even the King of the Buckaroos.

Instead of watching the road for wayward deer, he stared at her patrician silhouette luminous in the pale dashboard light. Recent days had been unseasonably warm for November, but tonight the temperatures dipped near freezing. In their scramble to leave his grandparents' house, she left her wool peacoat behind and now dibbed his gray cable knit sweater. Although it was too large on her petite frame and the sleeves hung down to her knees, it suited her. With her light Irish features, she looked like a Gaelic princess in her father's fisherman sweater.

"Nervous?" she asked.

He nodded and laughed. "Not anymore."

This exchange was a common pattern in their relationship: he hinted at a small weakness and she teased him until he admitted her power over him. It was how she coerced him into asking her out a year before. The familiar banter comforted him and confirmed that the foundation of their relationship remained unchanged.

He fiddled with the heater controls. His father claimed the fan hadn't worked since the Carter administration. Rudy, however, prayed tonight he'd find a setting between freezing and sweltering.

Under each passing streetlamp, he glanced over at her and tried to gauge any change in her appearance. It was silly to think they'd been marked in some physical way. He did feel lighter – relieved in a way he couldn't put his finger on or give name to. She retied the thick black ribbon covering her ponytail elastic into a neat bow. Her placid features glowed angelic in the amber dashboard light.

"How are you feeling?" he asked.

She smiled. "Overwhelmed, but glad."

He frowned and whirled his hand motioning for her to keep talking and explain.

"Glad it was you," she said. She reached over and smoothed his rumpled hair behind his ear. He inhaled and moaned with the exhale and reveled in her touch: her soft fingers like silk on his skin and her

CHAPTER 1

affection radiant like the sun in late fall. "You could never disappoint me."

Rudy coughed into his sleeve. "I think I'm finally getting over this damned cold."

"I'm surprised your mom let you out of the house."

"Nineteen years old and she still treats me like an invalid if I get the sniffles."

Her hand slid down his shoulder and arm to caress his hand. She slipped her hand under his and intertwined their fingers. "How are you feeling? Your heart, I mean?"

"Never better." He lifted their clasped hands to his chest.

A scar, white and waxen with age, spread over his chest under his long underwear and moleskin shirt. Born with a hole in his heart, Rudy was subjected to multiple open-heart surgeries before celebrating his first birthday. Although the patch to his heart was successful, he continued to suffer from a murmur and occasional chest pain.

"What happens next summer when you leave for school?" Never one to live in the present and always looking to the future, he dared to ask the question gnawing at him since she started visiting colleges around the Midwest.

"Let's not worry about it right now. Can't we just exist and breathe and be happy?" She unbuckled her seatbelt and slid across the vinyl bench seat until she pressed into his side. She nuzzled her nose under his jawline. Her breath tickled his earlobe and his whole body responded with a quiver and goose bumps. "Nothing can ruin this night."

He kissed the top of her head and inhaled the exquisite combination of shampoo and her natural scent. "I love you."

"I love you, too."

She nestled her head into his chest. As always, she was right. This was a moment to savor rather than analyze. His anxiety about her college plan could wait for another day.

Rudy cut the headlights several yards before he pulled into her parents' driveway. No lights burned in the windows of the huge house. Maybe no one would notice she was out so late after curfew.

"I wish you were spending Thanksgiving with me," Rudy said.

"Aidan's back from Dartmouth. He got in this afternoon, but I didn't get a chance to see him. He's only here for three days and I have a million questions to ask him about college."

Although Rudy and Aidan graduated together, they were no more than acquaintances: a familiar face at a football game or a grunted greeting at a house party. Rudy craved acceptance from her family like he craved her affection. No matter what tactics he tried, her mother remained indifferent and her father didn't hide his outright disapproval. "I could stop over Thursday morning and say 'hello'."

"My dad's weird about having the whole family together for the holiday. I don't think that'd be a good idea."

"Could you come out in the evening? My mom'd love to see you."

"Your mom's the only one that wants to see me?" She tugged on his arm, her grin widening.

"My dad's sort of fond of you, too."

Abby ran her tongue out at him and made a pinched face. Rudy couldn't help but smile.

"My mom puts on a big show for Thanksgiving," he said. She was so good at teasing him, but every time he tried to return the favor it was an epic failure. "It's like a Norman Rockwell painting. I want you there."

"I'll see what I can do." Abby's whole face seemed to be pulled down when she looked at the hulking house and her lips hitched to one side. This fraught expression was nothing new when the topic of her family came up.

"I should go." She scooted away from him with her eyes cast down and shoulders rolled forward.

"Hey," he said.

CHAPTER 1

She looked over her shoulder at him.

"Come here."

She shook her head and looked down again.

"Please."

She looked out the passenger window, tears streaming down her porcelain cheeks.

"It's okay if you can't make it," he said as he shifted in the seat moving toward her. "It's no big deal." He wrapped his arms around her waist and pulled her delicate frame next to him. "Please don't cry." Her tears caused a searing pain deep within his chest. Her visible anguish manifested in him as literal heartache.

"I'm sorry." Her voice was nothing more than a whisper.

"There's nothing to be sorry about." He kissed her temple.

She turned and disappeared into his embrace. She wrapped herself around him. Her fingertips dug into his back pulling him tighter. Her ragged breath smoothed into a light rhythm matching his.

"Love you."

She looked up and smiled. "Love you, too."

He met her lips which tasted like her honey lip balm. Her soft tongue caressed his as they shared the same breath. He tangled his fingers in her curly tresses and ached for this kiss to last a lifetime, but he pulled back for a moment then kissed her on the tip of her pert nose.

She slid across the seat, then leapt from the truck. Rudy watched her walked up the driveway and round the backside of the house heading for the back door. The engine roared to life and he headed home with a warm heart.

Chapter 2

Abby strolled past her brother's Jeep parked in the driveway, keyed into the back door and eased the door open. Five hours past curfew, she didn't want to wake her parents, especially Dad. She leaned against the back door and prayed it wouldn't protest this one night. Instead, the door wheezed and shrieked when its swollen edges met the door frame. With all the house's Victorian charms, it needed some basic maintenance her father was too busy to do, but too proud to hire out.

She moved past the swinging door separating the kitchen from the formal dining room and navigated around the furniture in the dark. Mother kept an immaculate house, even though she only left the confines of her bedroom a few hours a day. The rest of the day was otherwise occupied with vodka and Xanax and romance novels.

At the base of the oak staircase, she slipped out of her loafers and stood on the ornate floor grate. Wiggling her toes in her striped Smartwool socks, the cast iron was still warm from the last blast of forced air from the furnace. As a young girl, she nestled on this grate below the coats and soaked in the warmth on cold winter days. Her daydreams were often interrupted by her brother's sobs floating out of the air ducts. She searched the house for the source of the cries without avail and eventually became convinced that the cries belonged to a sad ghost living in the room under the basement stairs.

CHAPTER 2

She tested her stocking feet on the first stair tread. The house seemed to be plotting against her and the tread squeaked. She pulled her foot back and shook it out. Like a gymnast preparing for her floor routine, she shook out her wrists and nerves and then climbed the stairs using the outside of the treads. Skipping steps, leaping like a gazelle in her stocking feet she made it up the two flights and stopped at her bedroom doorway. She fingered the holes in the door frame that one held the door hinges.

Without turning on the light, she plopped down on top of her down comforter, hugged herself and smiled. She ran her fingers down the coarse cable knit of Rudy's wool sweater. With her nose tucked into the collar, she inhaled slowly letting the scent of his body wash and lotion fill her nasal passages.

Her cheeks ached from smiling and her eyelids grew too heavy to lift. The last day of classes before the holiday break started in little more than four hours. Although the day would be an academic joke, she still needed some sleep.

She stood to step into the closet and change into her pajamas, but something bounced against the back of her head. She swatted it away with one hand and reached for her bedside lamp with the other. Her swatting hand made contact with the foreign object and tangled in its thick, serpentine mass.

In the dim light, a hangman's noose swung from a bolt drilled into the ceiling. She withdrew her hand from the noose's grip and covered her screaming mouth before she eked out more than a squeal. Borrowed from the canoe tucked in the garage rafters, the coiled marine rope was rigged through three massive eyebolts in the ceiling then down to a cleat on the wall beside the door. Small piles of broken plaster lie under each piece of new hardware.

She backed out of the room without taking her eyes off the noose. Her hands moved from her gaping mouth down to her chest in hopes of calming her galloping heart. She stumbled down the hallway toward the master bedroom, without the pretense of being quiet.

She rapped her knuckles on the solid oak door before pushing it open. Instead of the smoky smell her mother's Chanel perfume, the metallic scent of wet pennies tickled her nose.

Fractured moonlight filtering through the leaded glass windows formed mercurial pools around her mother's body propped up in bed. The quicksilver puddles flashed claret when she flipped on the overhead light, but mother hadn't spilled a glass of pinot noir. A scream rose in her throat only to be cut off by puke erupting from her stomach. Acid scorched her throat before splattering to the floor.

She grabbed a glass of water from the nightstand to rinse her mouth, but wretched again when the scent of lemon-flavored vodka invaded her sinuses.

Every opening on mother's wrecked face wept blood. She fumbled at the wall switch and turned off the light in the hopes she might blot her mother's eyeless grin from her sight and forget the severed ears perched on her father's unused pillow. There was too much blood, an impossible amount of blood.

She backed out of the master bedroom and bumped into her brother's bedroom door frame. Her trembling hand hesitated on the light switch, fearing what horrors hid in the darkness of this room. She swallowed the rising bile threatening to gag her yet again. She flipped on the overhead light and discovered half a dozen gas cans lined the rug.

Aidan. He had joked about setting the house on fire, talked about how fast it would go up in flames and how flammable it was from mother's stores of liquor, century-old timbers and layers of linseed lacquer on the oak woodwork. His eyes lit up as he fantasized about watching their home get swallowed in flames. Abby chalked it up to his odd and morbid sense of humor. The threat was no longer idle.

Backing out of the room, she tripped over her stocking feet and fell

CHAPTER 2

backward to the hall's floor. Crumpled into a ball and nursing sharp pains from her shoulder, she watched as the thin line of light from under the door to dad's study grew to fill the narrow space. Combat boots and heavy footsteps filled the hallway.

"It's about fucking time you got home."

The hulking shape of the man was unfamiliar, but the deep, bass voice belonged to her brother. He grabbed her by the hair, splaying fingers in her curly locks under her hair elastic and dragged her into the master bedroom. She screamed as she slid across the polished hardwood.

At the bedside, Aidan held Abby up by her hair, forcing her to gaze into mother's ruined face, empty eye sockets weeping blood. Abby tried to turn away but Aiden's unrelenting grasp and strong fingers pressed into her scalp wouldn't allow for movement.

"Isn't she prettier this way?" Aidan asked.

Mother drew in a deep, stuttering breath and her feeble arm reached out toward Abby's whimpering.

"So much prettier," he said while stroking mother's sweat and blood-soaked Auburn hair. That final moment of tenderness loosened his grip on Abby's throbbing scalp. She jerked her head forward to create slack between her hand and the stubborn elastic that held his meaty hand in place.

Aidan twisted his fingers into an underhand grip and dragged Abby out of the master suite. This time she kicked and fought grabbing at throw rugs and chair legs as she slid across the polished hardwood floor.

Past the bedroom's threshold, down the hallway and into Daddy's study she careened until Aidan smashed her head into the arm of the wooden rocking chair. Bright white light flashed behind her eyes then darkness pushed in from all sides until red blotted out the room. The painful blow opened a gash on her forehead. She held her bloody head as she turned around to discover Daddy's broken body.

Naked and hogtied on the study's Persian rug, Daddy looked up at her.

His pale blue eyes bulged and went wild as he tried to scream through the ball gag in his mouth. Tears and sweat ran in rivulets down his pale body as he tried to curl and cover his shame. The large, black plastic zip ties linking bound hands and feet dug deeper into this chafed and bleeding skin.

"Like what I've done?" Aidan asked with a wide smile. Each one of his brilliant, white teeth visible like the creepy Cheshire cat welcoming Alice to Wonderland.

Applying pressure to the gushing wound at her hairline, Abby looked away from Daddy to the Anthropology textbooks and field notebooks on the study shelves. Aidan grabbed her chin and forced her to face Daddy.

"I'm almost finished." Aidan smiled an odd, sadistic glimmer in his green eyes. "You should watch."

Abby turned her eyes back to the books, searching the titles for an escape—something to think about other than the brutal tableau.

Aidan grabbed her hair again and wrenched her head back to the violence.

"You will watch this!" His screamed and spittle rained down over her face. His pale, freckled face flushed bright red.

He released her hair and stomped across the room his combat boots echoing off the hardwood. He raised a knee to his inflated chest and stomped down on Daddy's face snapping his head to an impossible angle. Dad flopped in protest and then relaxed in death. Abby crumpled to the floor beside him. She caressed his sweaty and bloody hair. Aidan stepped closer and reached for Abby's head. Instead of having her head wrenched back again she glared up at him. A thick vein throbbed on the side of Aidan's rage-twisted face.

"Mother's injuries were inspired, don't you think?" Aidan asked. "Started with her eyes because she pretended to be blind. Then her lying lips and deaf ears."

"And for this fucking bastard." Aidan reared back his leg and drove

CHAPTER 2

his foot into the dead man's side. "I got to use all his favorite torture toys."

As she cradled Daddy's lolling head and fumbled at the ball gag's straps, Abby found a heavy metal object under dad's head. Her fingers traced the outline of a two-pronged form of rough iron under his head.

"Wanna know what I've got planned for you?" Aidan asked as he squatted down in front of her resting all his weight on his toes. Abby shifted Daddy's body, moving his weight away from her and off the metal stick. Her fingers explored its length for a handle.

"I've been planning it for over a year. Had to be perfect for Daddy's little princess."

Abby refused to listen to her brother's sadistic plans. She summoned all her strength and swung the metal fork at her brother's legs, wielding it like her favorite tennis racket. She misjudged the distance. Instead of knocking him off his feet, the fork jutted out from his leg. His yelp sounded like a starting gun and she sprinted from the room.

The next moment she was at the bottom of the stairs attempting to put her loafers on the wrong feet. She didn't remember her feet carrying down the stairs or the wails that followed her.

At the backdoor, she snatched her father's Volvo keys off the pegboard and pressed the garage door opener.

Behind the wheel, she tried to remember what Rudy taught her during her driving lessons: adjust the seat, fix the mirrors, foot on the brake pedal and ignition. She hadn't inherited her father's stature, so she was forced to move the seat up until her feet touched the pedals. With a white knuckled grip on the steering wheel, she backed out of the driveway, shifted into drive and headed west into the foggy night.

Chapter 3

The heretic's fork stuck out of his leg for a moment before it dropped to the floor bouncing off and marring the hardwood and splattering his camouflage pants with his own blood. Although he'd bathed the master bedroom in Mother's blood, the sight of his own appalled and further enraged him. Red spread across and down his leg. Sheer adrenaline and shock kept pain at bay while blood ran down his calf and dripped into his sock. Aidan shook his head to physically dislodge the shock of his sister's retaliation. Meek and naive and cowardly, she wasn't a fighter. Maybe he wasn't the only one that had changed in the past year and a half. He smiled and relished the new challenge.

He dashed down the stairs two at a time with a pronounced hobble. At the lower landing, out the leaded glass window, he watched his father's Volvo back out of the driveway. Through the window, the red flare of brake lights fractured and scattered across the landing to Aidan's smiling face. Abby was running to Rudy.

He skipped back up the stairs and back into the master bedroom. Mother moaned and reach for him when his footfalls reverberated off the floor and barren walls. He patted her thinning hair, more ash than strawberry blonde in recent years. He used one finger to pull errant strands of hair from the clotting blood on her face. She issued a low pitiful moan in response to the pulling on new scabs.

CHAPTER 3

He withdrew a butterfly knife from his cargo pocket. With a flourish he spun the knife between his fingers and buried the blade into mother's chest as she gasped for air. He twisted the knife and pointed the tip up into her heart. Her life drained away with the scarlet blood staining the white bedding and her head fell to her breathless chest.

Warmth flowed up his arm from her chest wound. At first he thought it was the blood seeping out over his fingers, but the liquid cooled in moments. The warmth was instead evidence that his retribution was justified as her life force warmed him with electric energy. He shuddered as he let go of the knife. The welcome validation felt like an orgasm without the mess.

Abby's head start could kill his mission, especially if she or Rudy called the police. Failure was a coward's end.

With the new energy coursing through him, he refocused on the hunt. He disagreed with his father on even the most fundamental ideas. On this one point, however, they agreed: police interference was a nuisance. Maybe, just maybe, he could use the nuisance to his advantage.

At the backdoor, he paused at the only landline in the house yet more evidence of father's controlling behavior. But Aidan was in control now. He lifted the receiver and dialed.

"911, what's your emergency?"

"You should come see what I've done. It's glorious."

"Sir?"

Instead of returning the handset to the cradle, he dropped it and allowed it to bounce and dangle on the short, springy cord as he ran to his Jeep.

Chapter 4

Highway six was a lonesome strip of two-lane blacktop connecting small farming communities as it ran parallel with Interstate Eighty across Iowa. The road was deserted this time of morning as most of the world slumbered or commuters chose the high speed and the convenience of the interstate. Abby liked the romance of this road, imagining Jack Kerouac rubber tramping his way across the United States. This morning, however, it was the quickest way out of town.

Although the Volvo was much easier to drive than Rudy's old truck, her hands shook and vibrated against the steering wheel. The urge to scream passed and her vocal chords relaxed. Tears would not come, but her lower lip quivered and her breath caught in her throat.

In the few moments she spent inside her parents' home, fog claimed the landscape. Thin, white puffs of mist clung to the road, filled in the ditches and tried to reach through the car's windshield.

With the lights of Grinnell fading fast in the rearview mirror and fog littering the highway, she pulled onto a county road and stopped the car. Removing her hands from the ten and two position she shook them out like she prepared to play the piano. The normal daytime chatter of public radio was replaced by classical music. The high-pitch whine of the violin sounded like her mother's dying breaths. She fumbled with the dials on the dashboard until the music ceased.

CHAPTER 4

Daddy's words echoed in her mind, "Ladies do not drive."

In this instance, she felt less like a lady and more like scared prey scampering for cover in a living nightmare. The night started like any dream – too good to be true. First they had dinner with Rudy's parents, played fetch with Zoe, then she enjoyed Rudy's affections. Her face flushed when she recalled his fingertips tracing the contours of her every curve. Just when she thought the dream was ending, the REM cycle over, it morphed into something horrific from which there was no waking.

She slumped over and hugged the steering wheel. Although it was cold and hard, she pretended the wheel was Rudy's chest and squeezed harder until the horn sounded. She jumped back with a yelp and noticed the gravel road for the first time – the road to Rudy.

She shifted into drive and accelerated, her body and soul ached for his comfort. With his arms wrapped around her, she'd forget everything — forget that home was now a house of horrors.

In her few driving lessons from Rudy, she'd never driven on gravel. The car felt like the back end was racing to get ahead of the front wheels. She tapped the brakes and fishtailed until the car rocked to a stop sideways in the road. The front end faced a deep drainage ditch while the rear bumper rested a few feet from a rotten wooden fence post.

She raised her face to the car's roof and closed her eyes to calm herself. The answer to madness wasn't more chaos, it was reason and logic. Aidan had finally snapped the tenuous tether that kept him sane and grounded. As his prey, his defenseless quarry, she could not – would not – bring the hunt to Rudy.

She opened her eyes, shifted the Volvo into reverse. Rocking the car back and forth several times, she righted her path and stopped again. She closed her eyes and bowed her head to the steering wheel as if in prayer.

"I'm sorry," she whispered. As the simple apology crossed her lips, relief washed down, her shoulders relaxed, the knot in her stomach loosened and her grip on the steering wheel slackened. "I'm so sorry." She wasn't sure who those words were intended for: Aidan, Rudy or God. She learned about fight or flight in biology and psychology classes. She understood the concept as dictated by teachers and textbooks. She recognized it on Discovery Channel programs of cheetahs hunting gazelles. This, however, was her first personal experience with the phenomenon. Fight or flight. Mentally and physically unprepared to fight or even confront Aidan, flight was her only option here.

She gave the gas pedal a light tap and the car rolled forward at a manageable speed. She pulled back out onto Highway Six and continued west, away from Grinnell, Rudy and life as she knew it.

Chapter 5

Few things are more ominous than a ringing phone at the cusp between deep night and the small hours of the morning. Garrison reached from under his drool-soaked pillow for his cell phone on the nightstand. His other hand splayed on the cold spot beside him.

"This is Gordon." The words slurred together to become one.

"Sir?" a familiar voice from the dispatch office asked.

"Yes, Rita."

"Officer Dykstra asked for your assistance at a crime scene," Rita said.

Garrison extracted his face from the sodden result of his slumbering exhalations and gazed at the clock: 2:34 a.m. "What's going on?"

"The 911 call was cryptic. Other than that, I'm unaware of the particulars, sir."

"What's the address?"

Garrison committed the details to memory, ended the call and sat on the edge of the king-size bed. The most painful part of his morning wasn't waking to the shrill ringing phone or anticipating the shit storm waiting for him, pain came with the first steps from the bed to the master bathroom — the first moments his stout frame stood erect on his aching feet. Flatfoot wasn't just another slur for his chosen profession. His arches no longer existed and no amount of orthotics saved him from this agonizing morning ritual. He stood on the threadbare woven rug and waited for the sharp pain to dull to a nagging ache.

In the small bath, he wet his hands and ran them through his salt and pepper hair. His dark brown eyes set in deep blue shadows met him in the mirror. He opened a drawer on Nancy's side of the double vanity and grabbed the Mary Kay eye cream. It was his ointment, but the pink packaging prevented him from keeping the tube on his side of the bathroom vanity. He dabbed little dots of the skin tightening gel around his eyes and rubbed it in with a feather-light touch. This whole routine would be a lot easier if they packaged the miracle goo in a gender-neutral color, like green or blue.

In jeans and a Chicago Cubs windbreaker, he exited the master suite. Garrison checked on Nancy as she slept in her sewing studio down the hall. Covered in the quilt his grandmother gave them as a wedding present, Nancy dozed in a wingback chair with the latest copy of American Patchwork and Quilting splayed on her lap. Her face grew more beautiful with each day of their twenty-five year marriage. Her cheeks were full and rosy with the weight she never lost after having Sarah. He liked her to carry a little more weight as it filled in her sharp angles.

They'd slept in separate rooms in recent years as Nancy's snoring worsened to the point that she'd rattle her reading glasses on the nightstand. Garrison swore to her that he could sleep through the end times, but she insisted on separate sleeping arrangements. He missed the weight of her in the bed and the scent of her hair after a shower.

He flipped off the overhead light and moved on to Sarah's room. The soft strains of Chopin leaked from around her door. He pushed the door open as far as he could before the hinges protested and woke her. Only her purple-streaked, blonde hair peaked out from her down comforter cocoon. Unlike his wife or the parishioners at the Grinnell Lutheran Church, he didn't care about the color of her hair.

He continued down the staircase lined with framed photos of family

CHAPTER 5

and friends. He paused at the last picture taken of his eldest daughter, Vicky, before she ran away. Her fourteen-year-old smile was strained and false in the school photo. He stroked the glass and said a silent prayer wishing her peace.

He smiled. Although unknown violence waited for him at a crime scene across town, looking in on his beloved girls felt like an affectionate hug and kiss before he left for duty. It was a ritual neither one of them knew about — a loving secret of a husband and a father. His time walking the beat in Chicago taught him to keep his affairs in order and always, always say goodbye.

Named after Josiah Grinnell, the town was formed around the junction of two rail lines as well as serving as a stop on the Underground Railroad. The town and its founders were strongly abolitionist and the culture remained liberal to this day.

The Flynn house was a few blocks west of the Grinnell College campus. Grinnell Police cruisers lined the block. He assumed the majority of the officers were roused by rumorous phone calls. A handful of officers congregated at the end of the driveway leading up to the stately house.

Enveloped in fog, the Victorian house loomed ominous in the breaking dawn. Above the portico, a turret reached for the sky like a church steeple, but offered no sanctuary. If a situation in the house required his attention, it was odd that only a single light burned in an upstairs room. Typically when he responded to a scene every light in the house and the neighborhood blazed.

Garrison walked up to the clucking men in the driveway — equating them with gossiping hens. Voss, Meijer, Jansen and Van Dusseldorp nodded as the detective approached. He referred to this set of colleagues as the Windmill Mafia — Dutch and proud.

"We called Sheriff Morris," Van Dusseldorp explained. "But he's visiting family in Wisconsin. He said we should call you."

The Grinnell Chief of Police was recently forced to retire after triple bypass surgery, leaving a very young and green police force. The city council was reluctant to hire anyone or appoint an interim until after the New Year, therefore, Sheriff Morris was left to run two departments.

"What's the story?" Garrison asked.

"We're not sure," Van Dusseldorp said. "Only Dykstra's been inside the house and he won't stop puking."

Garrison recognized the young man bent over the bushes lining the far side of the garage as the rookie relegated to the night shift. The greenhorn wretched and heaved into the dead foliage.

"You good, Dykstra?" Garrison asked.

The rookie raised his arm and flashed a thumbs up.

The rookie's vomit should have prepared Garrison Gordon for the carnage inside the house — like the foreshadowing of a hackneyed novel — but the grisly scene within was beyond even Hollywood's most sadistic imagining.

Chapter 6

Thick fog rose from the highway and flanking cropland like ghosts rising from unquiet graves seeking revenge on the living. They swirled and danced across the road and pressed against the windshield. Aidan slammed the older Jeep Wrangler's stick shift out of first as he turned onto the country lane leading to the Edwards' farm. Rocks pinged off the Jeep's body. He hated the toll gravel roads took on his beloved Wrangler, but if all went well at the end of the night, he'd never have to worry about such trivial things again. He pressed down on the accelerator with the tip of his combat boots daring the rising spirits to slow him down.

A year and a half of planning and his mission was nearly complete. The thrill of victory spilling into his bloodstream. The worst part of the ordeal was waiting for Abby to come home. In seventeen years, she'd never spent the night at a friend's house or missed a single curfew. Had he known she was going to ignore curfew, he would have taken more time to savor those last moments with Father. Watching the old man's face contort in pain and humiliation was glorious — a moment more gratifying than any orgasm.

Mother's life force coursing through Aidan's veins, like the moment before ejaculation when pleasure and adrenaline is infinite – better than any caffeine jolt, better than any recreational drug, like a wild animal released from his cage for the first time.

Sweat poured down his back as his emotions boiled over. Even with the windows down, driving fifty miles per hour through the mid-November night he sweat as much, if not more, than he would if he were recovering from a workout in the gym's sauna.

Not a single light burned in the windows of the Edwards' two-story farmhouse. A large floodlight hanging above the barn's double doors illuminated the driveway: a sleek Cadillac sedan and a sensible economy car and a battered farm truck sat outside. Rudy drove that old truck like a poet carries a journal or a mathematician carries a calculator. He was home, but no Volvo.

Plenty of time passed for Abby to drive the five miles from their parents' house to the Edwards' farm even if she got lost. There's no other place she'd go. No family. No friends. She had to be here.

Aidan slammed his fist into the dashboard. "Motherfucker!" He shook the steering wheel. "Where the fuck is she?"

Aidan switched off the headlights, shifted down into low gear and pulled down the long drive flanked by hundreds of acres of cornfields now desiccated by fall's deadening touch. He allowed the engine's idle to pull him down the drive without touching the gas pedal. He hoped the Edwards family was tucked away in bed.

At the base of the driveway, he pulled his Jeep around behind a small outbuilding. He killed the engine, reached behind the passenger seat and gripped the baseball bat. The worn maple felt good in his hand like he'd been born to play the game.

He stood in the building's shadow beside an animal pen. He tested the fence and climbed up on it to perch and wait for his sister's imminent arrival.

Sending the police to his parents' house was meant as a diversion as he tracked down his sister. If Rudy was foolish enough to call 911, the keystone cops would be slow to respond to anything after they discovered his artwork. She had to show up. It had to happen.

CHAPTER 6

His hands shook from prolonged adrenaline exposure and the strain of the evening's activity. From his perch on the fence, he started stretching out his corded muscles. Toes up. Toes down. Wiggle the fingers. Shake out the hands. Look to the left. To the right.

Something bumped against his leg. He ignored it at first, until it slammed against his ass and sent him sprawling off the fence.

Beside the animal pen, he regained his feet and performed his usual routine as if preparing to step to the plate. With the bat wedged between his thighs, he rubbed his hands on his camo pants stained with blood. He licked his left palm, tasted salty sweat and sweet iron and rubbed his hands together. With his left hand, he grasped the business end of the bat and with a twitch of his wrist he flipped the bat in the air for a half rotation and caught the grip with his right hand. He hoisted the bat to rest on his shoulder and stalked toward the fence.

A goat gazed up at him. Its white face glowed in the night.

"Are you fucking kidding me?"

The goat lifted its huge brown eyes up at him in polite disinterest.

Aidan lifted the bat from his shoulder with both hands, adjusted his grip and swung making contact with the side of the goat's head. She lifted her chin and let out a mournful bleat that echoed off the barns. Aidan reached over the fence and pulled the injured animal out of the pen and on to the driveway.

Next he lifted the bat above his head like he was hoisting a sledgehammer and drove it down between her eyes and her distress call ended. Her body went lax, eyes rolled back and her head fell to the ground. He beat her, slamming the bat into her head until it cracked open and sprayed him with brain matter.

He brought the bat down across her midsection hoping to spill her intestines, but the maple protested and cracked. His aching hands held a sharp splinter as the meat of the bat fell away. He considered the weapon for a moment and then drove it through the goat's belly.

Chapter 7

Impenetrable fog surrounding the truck stop reflected the light of the signs and gas pump flood lamps so it was wrapped in the cushion of phosphorescence. It looked like an oasis on a planet ravaged by disease and climate change. She wished that some unknown infection plaguing the planet were her only worry as her eyes flicked from the road ahead to the rear view mirror and the road behind. She expected the round headlights of Aidan's Jeep to materialize from mist and chase her down like the truck from *Maximum Overdrive*.

The twenty mile drive took her nearly an hour as she drove far below the 55 mile per hour limit on the desolate two-lane blacktop. Abby's every muscle ached from gripping the steering wheel and leaning forward to see the road through the fog as it shifted and coiled around the car like a snake ready to strike.

She pulled into the gas station and parked at the pump closest to the door. With her foot mashing the brake to the floorboard, she turned the key but it wouldn't come out. She pawed frantically at the key ring, but it wouldn't budge.

"Come on. Come on."

She released the brake as she leaned forward to see if there was button she was missing. The Volvo rolled forward. In panic, she smashed the brake back down the the floor. She looked around.

"Shit," she screamed and slammed her tiny fist into the steering wheel.

CHAPTER 7

Regaining what little composure she had left, she shrugged her shoulders several times to release the tension. Looking around the car for what seemed to be whole minutes, she discovered her mistake: the gear shift. She forgot the put the car in park.

In all her driving lessons with Rudy, he would reach across the bench seat of his truck and operate the gear shift mounted on the steering column. The Volvo's gear shift was located on the center console. She shifted it into park and dropped her head back to the headrest.

"God damn it. Get it together," she said to the car's ceiling.

The glove box only held the Volvo's thick owner's manual and legal paperwork. Breath mints, a spare pair of leather gloves and a small Leatherman multi-tool occupied the center console. Her father's meticulous nature left her without a single dollar bill aside from the five stuffed in the back pocket.

Before getting out of the car and sprinting into the convenience store, she scanned the parking lot for Aidan's Jeep. Although she couldn't determine the model of the car at the far edge of the lot, it was small and red; definitely not the boxy, white SUV.

The inside of the convenience store was old and dingy unlike the new pumps and signage outside. Flickering fluorescent lights revealed cracked linoleum tiles, yellowing shelves sparsely stocked with cheap snacks and a tiny soda fountain with a burned out light. A bored clerk lounged on a swivel desk chair with his feet on the counter while engrossed in the latest Stephen King hardback novel.

"Potty?" Abby asked as the heavy plate glass door slammed shut behind her.

Without looking up from the book, he pointed a tattooed finger to the back of the store where a hand-drawn sign marked the restrooms.

She thumbed the door's deadbolt to the lock position and pulled on the handle to make sure it was secure. The overwhelming scent of pine cleaner and bleach stung her nose and burned in her lungs. Vomit erupted from the deepest parts of herself before she could even take one step toward the toilet. She stumbled toward the toilet and filled the bowl with leftover steak, potatoes and bile. Puke scorched her throat with each violent heave. Then came the aftershocks of dry heaves. Her arms shook as she braced herself against the rim of the disgusting toilet. She rested her sweaty brow on her quaking forearms before she wiped errant vomit from her nose. Abby spat out the excess saliva multiple times before she decided the eruption was over although her stomach still churned.

After using fistfuls of flimsy paper towels to clean the obvious vomit off the toilet and floor, she stumbled over to the tiny sink jutting out of the wall. She splashed cold water to her face, then cupped her hand to sip the cool water. She rinsed the leftover chunks from her mouth and spewed them into the sink before gulping down several handfuls.

She tilted her eyes to the scratched mirror. A rash of red dots fanned out from her bloodshot eyes across her cheekbones. Petechiae. Tiny hemorrhages caused by the pressure of vomiting. It happened the last time she had the stomach flu, but this looked like someone splattered her face with red paint.

One last gulp from the sink and she turned to leave. A vending machine next to the door caught her attention. It didn't look like the feminine hygiene products dispensers at school. Instead it offered condoms in neon colors as well as novelties for three stacked quarters. But the sexual aids and prophylactics weren't what caught her eye. Papering the machine were fliers of missing, most no older than herself, all missing from stops along I-80 as it spanned the Midwest. Someone had slapped a fluorescent pink flier over the girls' faces asking, "Looking for a way out?" It listed multiple phone numbers for the National Human Trafficking Hotline.

She memorized the faces like they were yearbook photos of a school where she had just transferred. She imagined her own visage would soon share space on the sex vending machine.

CHAPTER 7

The clerk placed his book open upside down on the counter saving his spot deep in the novel. He stood and leaned over the counter, his hands supporting his chin as he watched her wander the aisles with her bucket of soda looking for another dose of sugar.

Hershey's Bars were three for three dollars. She snatched up three of them with almonds for protein. The man behind the counter crossed his thick, tattooed arms across his muscular chest. He rocked back on his heels and appraised her with a cocked head. His buzzed strawberry blonde hair reminded her of Aidan's new look.

"Rough night?" he asked.

She nodded and tossed her crumpled five dollar bill on to the counter. "How far away is Des Moines?" she asked. Her voice trembled and cracked.

She couldn't look up from the counter to avoid meeting his eyes like he was some wild animal and eye contact would provoke an attack.

"Bout forty miles if you take the interstate." He bent down to the counter to force eye contact. "Damn, girl. What are you scared of?"

"You." She grabbed the few coins off the counter and ran for the car.

Chapter 8

The Edwards' two-story house clapboard house stood silent in the fog as night gave way to the faintest glow stretching out along the eastern horizon. No lights turned on in response to the noise. Beating the goat, while deeply satisfying, only added to his aches, pains and and absolute exhaustion. His hands no longer shook, but felt dumb and clumsy. Killing the sad animal, however, didn't provide the same wellspring of energy he received with the death of his parents. The batting practice drained him. Covered in blood, sweat and brains, he needed a shower and his body required sleep.

He stripped off his ROTC tee shirt, used it to wipe off the organic matter splattered across his face and hair off and dropped it beside the battered goat before climbing into the Jeep. His eyelids drooped and head bobbed as sleep threatened to overwhelm him. He tried with great effort to keep his eyes on the unmaintained road ahead to avoid getting stuck in the deep ruts left when tractors and combines finished the harvest months prior.

He passed two houses with cars in the driveway and porch lights burning. A realtor sign poked out of the lawn of the third house boasting a newly reduced price. No lights. No cars. His home for the night. He pulled the Jeep behind the house and tucked it between the garage and a small utility shed.

He opened the back gate of the Wrangler and pulled out the bag he

CHAPTER 8

packed in his Dartmouth residence hall room days ago. When he jammed tee shirts and jeans into this battered duffel bag, he had planned a much different trip: a reconnaissance mission to lay the groundwork for his trip home over winter break. He planned to complete his mission during Christmas Eve dinner. The culmination of all his strategic planning over a year in a half, realized in one night. But his impulsiveness ruined the tableau he had planned.

He dropped his bag on the stoop leading to the back door. The doorknob didn't budge. Using his parent's house key for the last time, he rapped on the window of the door until the pane cracked and shattered into the house. He reached into the window bending his arm around the shards of glass protruding from the frame and thumbed open the lock.

The back door opened into a mudroom leading to a small kitchen. The house was no warmer than the ambient temperature outdoors. He flipped the light switch on to test the electricity. The exposed overhead fluorescents flickered to life for a moment before he extinguished them. The house still had juice running to it. In the empty living room, he turned the dial thermostat up to eighty. The forced-air furnace belched to life filling the space with the smell of burning dust.

He dropped his duffel bag to the hardwood floor. He picked through his clothes, touching them as little as possible with his filthy hands and found his toiletry kit. He wandered down the hallway in search of the bathroom. His footfalls echoed off the blank walls and pine flooring in the front room. The tiny bathroom was wedged between two modest bedrooms.

He was glad to find glass shower doors rather than an empty curtain rod, but the linen closet bore no towels. He checked the cabinet under the sink and in the bedroom closets to no avail.

Standing in the master bedroom he looked around for anything to use in place of a towels. Nothing but dusty white walls, shitty green carpet and hideous drapes. He grabbed the ends of the drapes and considered ripping the whole thing down, but this wasn't part of the mission. The drapes did not harm him, in fact they were about to provide him a great service. He dropped the drapes' hem and took them down as gently as he would a treasured artwork.

The water in the bathroom ran lukewarm. In order to save money while the house remained for sale in a volatile market, the owners turned down the water heater. He showered as fast as he did during field exercises. He performed a cursory wash of his scarred private parts and ran soap through his short hair while a cool trickle of water sluiced away the remnants of his triumph. He didn't avert his eyes from the drain until the last remnants of his mother, father and the goat washed away.

From his bag, he pulled out a gym shirt. With a pocketknife he cut the tee into one long strip of cloth and wrapped it around the puncture wound. Shock, the body's ultimate defense mechanism, had finally worn off and he felt the entirety of his injuries. He leg throbbed with each heartbeat.

After his chilly shower, he pulled down the heavy drapes from spare bedroom and made a makeshift bed in front of the heat register. The warm air washed over his naked body while he recited his usual bedtime incantation.

"I am an American soldier. I am a warrior," he whispered into his folded hands as he would a prayer. The Soldier's Creed comforted him as a Catholic might find solace in a Hail Mary. "I will always place the mission first. I will never accept defeat. I will never quit." Sleep descended as night pulled back its hood to greet the day.

Chapter 9

The backdoor to the Flynn house stood ajar allowing heat to escape onto the small back porch. Garrison and Voss entered with guns drawn and flashlights at the ready. He stopped at the threshold and scanned the expansive kitchen with the beam of light. He surveyed the space in methodical rows from top to bottom, like a camera taking panoramic photos stacked one atop another. The narrow beam of the Maglite allowed Garrison to focus only on the clues at hand, letting the flashlight to do the investigative work also had the added benefit of leaving the crime scene exactly as he found it.

The only thing amiss in the room was the phone receiver hanging by its coiled cord. Odd that the Flynns used a landline, let alone a corded phone. Most households switched to cell phones or at least cordless phones.

Satisfied with their survey of the kitchen, he stepped through the swinging door to the dining room. The light bounced off chairs and tables, but found no one hiding in a corner. Their sweep of the main floor revealed nothing more than empty rooms.

The two men climbed up the winding oak staircase to an empty hallway. No door hung in the door frame of the first room at the top of the stairs. Garrison held his breath before he turned the corner into an unoccupied bedroom. A noose hung over the bed from an eye hook in the ceiling and more hardware driven into a wall stud above the nightstand. A shiver ran down Garrison's spine.

"Why's it hung so low?" Voss asked with his flashlight trained on the chin-high noose.

"Judging by the girl's height," Garrison said, pointing his flashlight at a snapshot of the room's occupant. "It's meant to asphyxiate rather than kill outright by severing the spinal cord."

"Jesus."

In one last scan of the room, Garrison noticed a snapshot of the Flynn girl with Rudy Edwards, the youngest son of Garrison's best buddy. The couple wore formal attire: a form-fitting green dress for her and a tuxedo for him. Between the dress and her vibrant red hair, she looked like the mermaid from a Disney movie.

The next open door in the hallway led into an expansive master suite. White linens and a white comforter covered the four-poster bed all stained bright crimson by the ravaged woman propped up in bed. Her empty eye sockets stared back at him, blood clotted around her ears, her mouth spewed blood from where her tongue was removed and the thin handles of a silver butterfly knife jutted out of her chest. The Flynn matriarch, he presumed.

He moved to the room across the hallway, relieved to find another unoccupied bedroom. No door hung in the frame. This room was also immaculate except for a thin layer of dust that covered the books stacked on the floor next to a thin, twin mattress. The air was pungent with the acrid scent of gasoline. Half a dozen red plastic gas cans lined the rug in front of the bare mattress.

At the last hallway door, the tiny hairs on the back of his neck bristled as he steeled himself at the threshold before pushing the door open. The stench hit him first. It smelled like the overflowing latrines he'd encountered during Desert Storm: sweat, piss, shit and sheer agony. The lifeless, naked body of a man lay prone in the middle of the floor beside a set of crude, iron shackles, a riding crop, various silver instruments that looked better suited for a surgery suite and other devices he couldn't identify. The man's back bled from where he'd been lashed. A ball gag bulged out of his mouth. The thing that disturbed Garrison most was the odd metal device sticking out of the man's butt cheeks and his ass smeared with blood and shit.

"What the fuck is that thing?" Voss asked.

"I don't want to know," Garrison said. They backed out of the room into the hallway. "We're done here."

They retraced their steps down the stairs, through the house and out the back door. The rookie appeared to have regained his composure and Garrison pulled him away from the group.

"I'm sorry about before, sir."

"We all have our moments, Dykstra," Garrison said. "How far into the house did you go?"

"I—I—" Dykstra stammered.

"You're not in trouble. But I need to know where you went."

Dykstra nodded. "I entered the back of the house calling out for Mr. and Mrs. Flynn. No one answered. I went upstairs. Where ..." His voice quivered and faded.

"Go on."

"I saw the woman and the blood. I left and called in back up."

"Did you go into any of the other bedrooms?"

"No, sir."

"Good work. You did the right thing calling me."

Garrison put his hand on the officer's shoulder and guided him back to the group. The men quieted, looked up at Garrison and stood straighter.

"We need to call the Iowa Division of Criminal Investigation. They're better equipped for a multiple murder investigation. Next call is the the medical examiner in Montezuma. Better wake him up and ruin his day early," Garrison said. He knew he was mostly thinking out loud, but he was confident these men could handle the to-do list. "Dykstra, go check the garage and check with the DMV to see if any vehicles are missing."

The rookie ran up the driveway toward the detached double garage tucked behind the house.

"Voss, I need you to cordon off the entire property with tape. This place is about to be a zoo and we need to set a perimeter."

Voss stepped away, but stopped and turned back to the group. "Chief, what are we looking at here?"

A stiff western breeze pushed the fog to the east, chasing it out of town with a cold snap. Garrison looked down at his worn out Nikes, rubbed his temples and considered his words for a few moments. When he looked up he thought he saw fear and sorrow upon their faces. "Double homicide. The son and daughter aren't here. I need background. Did any of you know the family?"

Most of the men shook their heads but Van Dusseldorp nodded.

"Tell me what you know, Jack," Garrison said.

"The husband's a psych professor at the college. Don't know about the wife. The son goes to some fancy school out east. The daughter's in high school. Heard Dr. Flynn can be a real hard ass. Students are scared of him. He has a collection of torture devices on display in his office. He's a weird one," Van Dusseldorp said, shaking his balding pate.

"Just the two kids?"

"Yes, sir."

"Put out an APB on the kids."

"Anything else?" Van Dusseldorp asked.

"Talk to nobody. No press. Not your neighbors. Not your wives. This ain't pillow talk. Talk to no one," Garrison said. He pulled his cell from his jacket pocket and began alerting the world to the brutal fate of the Flynn family.

Chapter 10

The rising sun kissed the bellies of the eastern clouds tinting them red and vibrant pink. Pale fingers of light reached through the kitchen windows and massaged Rudy's tired, aching eyes as he waited for the coffee to steep in the French press.

A noise from outside caught his attention, it scratched at the back of his mind like the itch of a sore throat. He tilted his head toward the window, closed his eyes and tried to hear it again past the ticking wall clock. There it was. The screaming and bleating of distressed goats.

He left his empty coffee mug on the counter and grabbed an apple from a bowl on the kitchen island. He wedged the fruit in his mouth, pulled on his insulated work coat and headed out. The foul and fetid odor hit him as he crossed the driveway. The stink was more distressing than the goat's insistent cries. He broke into a jog and hustled around the small shed.

Alice lay in pieces outside the goat pen with a broken and bloody ball bat at stuck through her side. She was the best female in his flock: took in orphaned kids, kept the other goats in line and her offspring shared her sweet disposition. She was also the only goat he named among the hundreds he'd raised.

The rest of his herd bleated and rammed into the wooden fence rails. Their alpha was dead and they revolted.

Rudy wanted to grieve his loss, but he needed to calm the animals before they hurt themselves. He also needed to discover what happened to his sweet girl. She lay outside the goat enclosure that he designed with raised sleeping platforms, climbing structures and tall, escape-proof fencing.

In the barn, he pulled on a pair of heavy leather work gloves, tossed a spade into a wheelbarrow and returned to Alice's body. Her beaten body lay in three heaps with her small skull crushed. With a bobcat attack there'd be bite marks and torn flesh as well as paw prints. No cat tracks circled the body, rather the footprints of heavy lug sole boots marked the surrounding dirt.

What sort of sick bastard would come on a farm to beat a goat – with a bat, no less? He shook his head as he scooped her parts into the wheelbarrow. His shallow breaths shuddered in his chest as he tried not to cry. Being a farmer forced him into an intimate relationship with death, but some losses were harder than others.

He pushed the wheelbarrow away from farm buildings to the restored tallgrass prairie. He used the spade to dig a grave for the goat beside the resting place of his border collie.

He buried some animals here with ceremony, others he left by the creek for the predators to complete the circle of life. Ceremonies comforted the living and he needed comfort this morning. He placed her body into the hole, crossed himself. Whoever did this to Alice had no respect for life.

Pink cirrus clouds stretched out from the red ball rising in the east, while stacked along the western horizon thick gray clouds hung low with the weight of the incoming storm.

Chapter 11

Rudy poured feed into the small trough as dozens of goats bleated around him. A few of the smaller kids head-butted his leg, tugged at his pant legs or chewed on his shoelaces. He danced around the pasture as he tried not to step on the animals. He hadn't been able to sleep for more than two hours before waking for morning chores. Besides, someone had to feed the animals, gather eggs and milk the cow. Thoughts of the previous night with Abby played over in his head while the sun peeked over the horizon.

Abby laughed as Rudy fumbled with her buttons. Her giggles rang musical like spirited, buoyant notes played on a grand piano. She pushed his hands away and took over. He watched as her red lacquered nails slid her buttons from their cottony purchase. The flaps of her oxford shirt splayed open exposing the front of a pink lace bra and a thin line of freckled flesh from sternum to navel. She gazed up at him and smiled — pale pink lips hitched to one side in a playful smirk. Her eyebrows raised and eyes widened which sent tiny crinkles skittering out from the corners of her eyes. Rudy loved those little lines.

A car approached on the gravel lane and interrupted his reverie. Rudy held back some of the more aggressive goats so the little ones could get at the trough before breakfast was gone. His family lived at the end of a county road they shared with his grandparents' farmstead two miles away and another property he was in the process of buying. Even confused drivers did not make it this far into the corn often.

Zoe's shrill bark rose from a far off field. The Blue Heeler darted across the desiccated cornfields like a gray speckled bullet. She met the SUV as it pulled into the driveway. The crazy dog nipped at the tires and snarled like she was looking for a fight. The unmarked Ford Explorer belonged to the County Investigator. He assumed the officer was there to solicit his mother's help for the annual policeman's ball. Rudy returned to his goats. Each year she made gallons of her famous potato salad and peach cobbler for the fundraiser.

Some things could be counted on: mom baked for charity, dad worried about the fate of the postal service, the sky was blue and spring would come again. While those things never changed, after last night, however, he felt fundamentally different — relieved in some intangible way. He leaned against the fence post and wondered what Abby was doing at that moment. Was she thinking about him? Had she told anyone?

Heavy footfalls sounded on the gravel behind him. Rudy turned to find Investigator Garrison Gordon. The balding man looked fit and healthy in his dress uniform, although Rudy doubted the wisdom of patent leather on a farm especially around omnivores like goats and hogs.

"Good morning, Rudy," Gordon said as he removed his Pershing cap and tucked it under his arm. His bottom lip was tucked into his mouth as though he was biting back some truth.

"Dad's at the post office today," Rudy said. "Picking up some overtime to cover mom's Black Friday shopping spree."

"Yeah, he said I'd find you here."

Rudy's head snapped from his flock to Garrison. His father and Garrison were old pals. As the two men inched closer to retirement, they still went on adventure vacations together: gold-panning in Colorado, treasure hunting along the Gulf Coast and cowboy fantasy camp in Montana.

Rudy jammed his now clammy hands into his armpits. "What can I do

CHAPTER 11

for you, sir?" Rudy asked.

"Do you know Abigail Flynn?"

The question slapped Rudy across the face like the cold wind. Had Dr. Flynn called the police? Could he be arrested for keeping Abby out after curfew? That was absurd. Wasn't it?

"Abrielle," Rudy said.

"Excuse me?"

"Her name's Abrielle not Abigail."

Gordon ran his hand over his graying pate and asked, "When was the last time you saw Abrielle Flynn?"

"I dropped her off at home this morning." A looseness rolled across his chest like his heart dropped into his bowels. His intestines latched on to the hard-pumping muscle and wouldn't let go.

"What time was that?"

"Two. Maybe two thirty."

"That's awfully late to be dropping a girl off on a school night." Gordon said. He shifted the cap under his left arm and touched the hat's gold badge. "What did you do last night?"

"I'm not comfortable answering that." Heat rose to his face as he recalled Abby calling out his name in the dark, her lustrous red hair fanned out under her slender, naked shoulders.

"Son, how 'bout you answer the question."

"What's going on here," Rudy said. He took a step back from Gordon. His intestines catapulted his heart into his throat and rendered him mute.

"I need to understand why she got home so late."

Rudy picked up the kid that head-butted his leg and cradled it in one arm. The little brown goat nuzzled Rudy's neck. His coat was coarse and silken at the same time like raw cotton plucked straight from the boll.

"My grandparents are snowbirding in Texas. I took Abby there for..."

Rudy felt like he was going to explode from embarrassment and disintegrate into thousands of pieces of grain the goats would devour in minutes.

Chief Gordon stepped forward and stroked the goat as he fell asleep in Rudy's arms.

"What's going on?" Rudy put down the napping goat. He bleated and ran off. The men watched the goat find his mother. "Is Abby okay?"

"She's missing," Gordon said.

"She can't be missing. It was a late night. She's probably sleeping. Did her parents call you?" The words came out in a jumble like a spool of unfurling barbed wire.

Garrison drew a deep breath and said, "I'm sorry I can't tell you more." He placed his hand on Rudy's shoulder and slid it up to where his thumb rested in the hollow between collarbone, neck and muscle.

Rudy stepped away from the officer and mashed his face into his gloved hands. The work gloves smelled of leather and dirt as he tried to massage Gordon's words into his spinning head.

"Were you close with the Flynn family?" Garrison asked.

This question struck straight to the heart of Rudy's insecurities. "Her parents don't talk to me much. Doesn't seem like they have much to say to anyone."

"What about Aidan?"

"Aidan and I weren't friends in school. He hasn't been home for almost two years." He took off his work gloves and massaged his chest. "Matter of fact, Aidan called me last week."

"What'd he want?"

"It was weird. He acted like it was perfectly natural for him to call. Like we hung out last week. Forgot about it 'til now. He just asked me about Abby."

"Anything specific?"

"How she's doing in school, what colleges she's looking at and if she seemed sad."

CHAPTER 11

Garrison's mouth twitched to the side like he'd found a flavor he couldn't identify. "Was she sad?"

"Everyone's sad from time to time." Rudy pulled his ball cap down farther to cover his eyes.

"You didn't answer the question."

"She's sad a lot. Not depressed, just sad." Rudy considered Abby's sorrow. While it wasn't something she talked about, she wore it like a warm sweater in the depths of winter. Her shoulders sagged and her head drooped when she thought he wasn't looking.

"He say anything else?"

"He asked about his dad. I guess Dr. Flynn got passed over for department chair."

"I haven't been able to reach Aidan at school," Garrison said.

"He came back for Thanksgiving."

Surprise registered on Garrison's face. "He's here?"

"Yeah. Abby said he got back yesterday."

The two men surveyed the surrounding farmland. Rudy looked down the rows of desiccated corn stalks and down a sloping hill toward the horizon. At the bottom of the hill where carefully planned agriculture met wild prairie, a single doe bowed her head into a thicket of Indiangrass. Rudy watched her graze for several long moments.

"Any idea where she'd go?" Garrison asked. "Family? Or a friend? Anything she talked about?"

"Abby doesn't talk about family. If she's missing, someone took her."

"Ever been inside the Flynn house?" Garrison asked.

"Never beyond the front entry," Rudy said. He walked over to a wheelbarrow full of crab apples and dumped it onto the ground. He gave the pile of worthless apples a sideways kick to spread them around. "Sir, you're one of my dad's best friends. The way my dad tells it, you saved him from falling into a mine last time you went gold panning in Colorado."

"Your old man's a bit clumsy." Gordon laughed. "But what's your point?"

"You've gotta tell me what's going on." In his work gloves, he held his hands together in a pleading gesture.

"We don't know much," Gordon said. He took the cap from under his arm, hung it from the fence post and then ruffled his hair. "There was a 911 call from the Flynn residence this morning. Aidan said some weird stuff and left the line open. Now Abrielle and her brother are missing."

"Abby."

"Excuse me."

"She thinks she's in trouble if you call her Abrielle."

The Blue Heeler circled around the goats, narrowing the field each time she completed a pass driving the goats into a cluster. She nipped at Gordon's heels to move him into the fold, but Gordon stomped his feet startling Zoe.

"Dr. Flynn's Volvo is missing," Garrison said.

"Her father won't allow her to drive." Rudy said. "She doesn't even have a learner's permit."

Garrison's eyebrows furrowed in confusion. "Does she know how to drive?"

Rudy paused and pictured Abby behind the wheel of his old Dodge. "Yeah. I taught her."

Rudy tried to listen as the officer told him to call if he heard from Abby. His mind, however, ran through scores of questions. Each internal inquiry created a new path to darker more ominous places. He felt like he was falling from one bad dream into nightmares and horrors beyond his comprehension. The perceived motion made him nauseous.

"Can you tell me anything more?" Rudy asked.

Garrison pulled a roll of Tums from his pants pocket, dropped four of them into his hand and popped them into his mouth. "Abby's now an orphan and may be in danger. We've got to find her, fast."

CHAPTER 11

When Garrison's unmarked Chevy hit the gravel at the end of the dirt driveway, Zoe tucked her head between Rudy's legs and looked up at him with sorrowful brown eyes. The ill-tempered Blue Heeler hated everyone, but Abby. Zoe somehow knew that her friend was gone. She tucked her cold nose under his shaking hand and comforted him.

Chapter 12

The Grinnell Public Safety Building was awash with activity. Local print reporters as well as a television reporter out of Des Moines paced the sidewalk in front of the restored 1914 fire engine awaiting an update on the sensational story. Sheriff's deputies and police officers drifted in and out of the building as they attended the morning briefing before shift change. Even a few firefighters wandered over from their barracks in an attempt to get in on the latest gossip.

Although Garrison's main office was in the county seat twenty miles away, he often borrowed a conference room in the Grinnell police department. Garrison's job as County Investigator made him the chief law enforcement officer in the county. He worked with multiple agencies to prepare cases for court, ensuring that all investigative avenues have been explored and no possible defenses have been overlooked. He maintained the same authority as a sheriff with a smaller caseload and without annoying jurisdictional boundaries. Most of his time was spent working joint task forces investigating meth labs and drug trafficking, while the small Grinnell police department focused on a progressive and proactive approach to law enforcement by addressing smaller issues before they escalated. Grinnell was the largest town in Poweshiek County and sat at the intersection of two state highways and Interstate 80. This location kept him close to the larger investigations.

The desk clerk, Bretta, buzzed Garrison into the back offices. Bretta

CHAPTER 12

sighed as she held the phone receiver between her shoulder and ear. With low cut blouses, small skirts and high heels that defied the laws of gravity, Bretta was a walking lawsuit. She was initially hired as secretary to the mayor, but her level of incompetence got her demoted to running the police department front desk because no one wanted the hassle or threat of litigation of firing her.

"How's the weather?" she asked without pausing to hear the answer. She prattled on in a high-pitched whine. "They say we're supposed to get six inches of snow this weekend. It always snows the weekend after Thanksgiving and all those college students get stranded at the airport or worse they get in an accident or slide into a ditch because they don't know how to drive in the snow. They should really teach Driver's Ed during winter and not summer. They just don't teach 'em anything useful."

"I'll be in the conference room for awhile," Garrison said, cutting her off. "Please hold my calls and all visitors."

In his makeshift office, he dropped all the messages into the trash without looking at them. He assumed most of the messages were from the reporters he addressed moments ago. The Iowa Department of Criminal Investigation had taken over the investigation and would answer all future press inquiries. Multiple sightings of Aidan came in from around the state and the Grinnell Police Department was much too small to handle a large-scale manhunt.

Garrison leaned against the conference table and faced a bank of white boards, his back turned to the window overlooking a parking lot full of squad cars. He preferred a stark and barren workspace as compared to his contemporaries. The walls of dry erase boards called to mind chemistry lecture halls without the benefit of pupils. He'd worked for years to develop his process as he climbed up through the ranks of law enforcement in Chicago from deputy, investigator, chief deputy, until he accepted the position as an Investigator for the Poweshiek County

District Attorney. He left the Chicago homicide department to get away from the violence that he witnessed at the Flynn house that morning.

One of his white boards bore a mind map of the victims, suspect or people close to the case. On another white board he drew a timeline of the crime. An investigative to-do list was scrawled on a board beside the door. The final board was a list of questions about the case and a photo of the victims.

The white boards helped him remain objective about the crime as well as allowing him to wrap his mind around the logistics. He needed this exercise to put distance between himself and this case. Although he didn't know Aideen or Dr. Flynn on a personal level, Abby and his daughter were in the same grade and Abby took needlepoint lessons from his wife. Then there was the Rudy connection.

Garrison crossed to the timeline board and wrote Aidan's name as the accused.

"Hi, Daddy," his daughter's voice called from the doorway.

"Hey, Baby," Garrison said as he stood and crossed to his daughter. He wanted a hug. He also wanted to block her view of the white boards.

"I have a free period. Thought I'd check in on you."

"Check in on me?" Garrison asked. "Isn't that backwards?"

He wrapped his arms around her slender shoulders and pulled her into his chest. He lifted his head and tucked her head under his chin, breathing in the fruity scent of her shampoo.

The tension that had been building in Garrison since the phone woke him that morning was finally beginning to subside. Although she was a high strung, ball of energy, Sarah had a way of calming him on the worst of days and today certainly qualified. Violent deaths were uncommon of this small corner of Iowa. There was the poor Zywicki girl who never made it back to her dorm room at Grinnell College after the summer break. She was abducted after her car broke down in Illinois and later found dead in a ditch in Missouri. No one ever paid for the heinous crimes

CHAPTER 12

visited upon that girl. More recently a Grinnell College student, Paul Shuman-Moore, went missing early in the fall semester. After months of searching, following every lead and theorizing every scenario, Paul was found dead from suicide. He'd bound his legs and arms, jumped into the partially drained country club pool and drowned.

"Can I buy you some free coffee?" he asked leading her out of the conference room and away from the white boards.

In the break room down the hall, Garrison poured a cup of coffee for each of them and handed a Styrofoam cup to Sarah. She reached into a nearby drawer and pulled out several packets of artificial sweetener.

"Let me ask you something," Garrison said. He took a deep breath, gathered himself and asked, "If you were in trouble or if your mom and I weren't around, where would you go?"

As a young detective, Garrison learned to ask questions and let silence pressure an answer. People like nothing more than talking about themselves and by asking questions you reveal nothing about yourself. He used this tactic when talking to his daughter. He'd ask a question and she'd lay herself bare in her answer.

Sarah's brow furrowed and she stuck out her bottom lip as she considered his question. "Daddy?"

"Would you go to one of your girlfriends? What about Aunt Julie? Would you go to her?" His wife's sister, Julie, lived fifteen miles away in Newton. Single and childless, Aunt Julie was fond of her niece — sending cards and gifts each holiday, offering to take her on lavish vacations and planning extravagant birthday parties. "Where would you go?"

"I'd go somewhere quiet."

Her answer surprised him. Sarah was such a gregarious girl, it was hard to think of her as someone who'd seek solitude. "Why quiet?"

"So I could lose my mind. Without you or mom, I'd go crazy."

Although he was asking her to ponder tragedy, he hadn't considered her reaction or her grief and pain in the prescribed scenario.

"Girls are different, Daddy. With guys, it's all forward motion like if you stand still for a second you might actually feel something. You know, like an emotion," she said. "Girls do the feeling thing first, then maybe we'll act."

Through all her sociable bravado, she'd hit on something fundamental — wisdom wrapped in observation.

"Why are you asking me this?" she asked. "We've never talked like this before."

She was right. This conversation wasn't typical of their relationship. They'd tease each other, celebrate triumphs and accomplishments, but they did not discuss the uglier parts of life. Theirs was a bond built on good times.

"Something happened today." Garrison was reluctant to let his daughter in on the darkness dominating his day.

"I heard a few rumors at school."

"What have you heard?"

"Nothing much." She shrugged. "I know it has something to do with Abby Flynn."

"Why do you say that?"

"That girl hasn't missed a day of school since kindergarten."

He laughed.

"I'm serious. Each year they make a big deal about her attendance record."

Garrison finished his coffee and swirled the sludge that remained at the bottom of the cup while he considered how much to tell his daughter. She'd learn most of it tonight when the local tv news out of Des Moines reported from outside the Flynn house. Talking to his daughter in veiled euphemisms seemed insulting, so he chose to be direct without being alarmist. "Abby's parents were killed last night and she's missing."

Garrison watched as different emotions took turns controlling Sarah's face. Wide-eyed shock turned to brows furrowed in confusion to misty-

CHAPTER 12

eyed sadness.

"If I was Abby, I'd want to be alone for a long, long time. Just to be silent and push away all the bad things that must be going on in her mind." She paused, rolled her shoulders and stretched out her arms like she was trying to release all her tension. "I might just go insane and never come back. Crazy has got to be like a vacation on a beach in Hawaii compared to her reality. Thank God, I was so young when Vicky left."

The mention of his eldest daughter's name, made him gasp. Although he thought about her everyday, he hadn't talked about her for years. During the family's life in Chicago, Vicky rebelled against her beat cop father. Her defiance started small: shoplifting, truancy and cigarettes. Then it was smoking weed in the backyard, but that wasn't enough. She dropped out of high school sophomore year and started living on the street turning tricks to support her crack habit. Garrison and his wife did everything to help her. But each time they begged her to go to rehab her drug use escalated. Every day Garrison drove by the crack houses and low-rent motels where she'd hang out just to see that she was still alive. Then one day, she was gone. The vice squad found her body a week later during a sting at a no-tell motel. Her pimp had beaten her to death.

"What does this have to do with Vicky?"

"I was six when she ran away. Before that she was never around. She wasn't like a sister to me. When she disappeared, it was like you fired the girl that babysat me on Friday nights. I'm sad she's gone because I can see how much pain it caused you and mom."

They stared into their coffee cups for several minutes.

"My next class starts in ten minutes, I gotta get back to school." She stood and hugged him. "I'll see you tonight."

"Will you be home?" Garrison asked. It wasn't an idle question. He wanted her to be home and safe.

"I have a study group with Jessica."

"Can you have it at the house?"

"Sure, Daddy."

Garrison embraced his daughter once more before she returned to school and before returning to his white boards.

Chapter 13

On the cusp between Poweshiek and Jasper counties, the Edwards' combined farmland rolled across hundreds of acres encompassing prairie and Bur Oak savanna until it met the Cottonwoods lining Sugar Creek. Rudy stroked Zoe's head for a minute before she growled and sprinted away.

Rudy ran his hands through his hair, ruffling each of his multiple cowlicks until his own hair stood up like a rooster's comb. His mohawk didn't require any styling products or even conscious effort. By muscle memory, he reached into his coat for his phone, then remembered Abby did not have a cell phone. He gazed at Abby's photo on his lock screen, then balled the phone into his fist.

"Damn it!" He stomped his foot and sent several young goats scrambling for their mothers' comfort. He'd offered to get her a phone several times so they could text at night, but she insisted her parents would be angry. There were so many boundaries and restrictions because it might anger her dad. It took her six months to tell them she had a boyfriend and another three months before she introduced him to her mother. Now he'd never get the opportunity to impress Dr. Flynn.

He had to do something. He couldn't just wait for the next bit of news. No action was inaction. Whatever his next step, he had to get moving.

He hopped the fence in a single leap like a Hollywood cowboy, jogged toward the side door and entered the kitchen where Mom was busy preparing pie crusts for Thanksgiving Day's dessert bar and gluttony fest. In the morning, his mother, Sheila, would set up a foldable banquet table in the foyer and load it down with every type of pie: rhubarb, boysenberry, pineapple chess, mulberry and more. Although their Thanksgiving table had shrunk since his grandparents left for the Gulf Coast, Mom's pie production hadn't dwindled.

"Hey, ma." Rudy tried to ignore the tremble in his voice and sweaty hands that glued his palms to his jeans.

"What'd Gary want?" Sheila asked.

The Kitchen Aid whirred as it combined cold Crisco, flour and other secret ingredients to make Sheila's State Fair Blue Ribbon pie crust. His mother wore a vintage apron covered with flour. Even her face was smeared with batter.

"Smells good in here," Rudy said.

Evasion was the Edwards family team sport. Although his mother was a gold medal Olympian at dodging the question, she pretended to be unaware when others competed in her chosen sport.

"I'm making two black raspberry pies this year. One for you and one for Abby." She smiled. Due to complications during his birth, Sheila was unable to have more children, especially the daughter she'd planned for. During a childhood snooping session — an only child has a difficult time playing hide and seek on snow days — he found a box of baby clothes in various shades of pink. There was also a photo of his infant self in a pink onesie with frilly booties.

"Do her parents feed her? I swear that girl could eat us out of house and home." Sheila laughed at her own joke. It was true. Abby's table manners were impeccable, but she was as hollow as a chocolate Easter bunny.

"I don't think she'll be joining us for Thanksgiving dinner," he said. He pulled a small lunch cooler out of the pantry and filled it with an apple, leftover meatloaf, oreos and a few cans of RC Cola.

CHAPTER 13

Sheila's slender shoulders sagged in presumed disappointment. "That's alright. I'm sure she'll put a sizable dent in the leftovers this weekend."

Rudy forced a laugh. It rang false even to him. He waited to see if she caught on, but she smiled and loaded dough into the fridge. Pain flared behind his sternum.

"Do we have any Tums?" he asked as he pulled open the junk drawer.

"Got an icky tummy, sweetheart?" Sheila stepped over to a small cabinet and withdrew a bottle of extra strength antacid and threw it to him. "Eat a banana."

"Could I borrow your car this afternoon?" he asked.

"You know the rule."

Years prior, Sheila had spilled gasoline on her dress on the way to Mass. Bothered by the smell, other parishioners asked her to leave, When she tried to sneak out during the homily, she realized the gas had eaten away half her dress. His mom now refused to pump her own fuel. So anytime he or his father wanted to trade a pickup for the Cadillac SUV, they returned it with a full tank.

"I'll fill 'er up," Rudy promised.

"Will you be back for supper?"

"Naw. I'll grab something in town."

He gathered his lunch, duffel bag and keys in the foyer. "Thanks, ma!"

As he opened the door, Sheila called, "Tell Abby we'll miss her tomorrow."

It took everything he had not to sprint for the garage, but mom would be watching out the window. He hustled over to his truck to retrieve his Gore-Tex jacket. Abby's backpack sat forgotten on the passenger-side floorboard. He snatched up her pack and his jacket and headed for the Cadillac.

* * * * *

The town's founding father, Reverend Josiah Grinnell, relied upon insider knowledge of the Mississippi and Missouri railroad's planned route along an established Pony Express trail when he laid out the town bearing his name. The Flynn's Victorian house was built when the town was just a smudge on the map of the newly founded state.

Huge oaks and cottonwoods lined Broad Street covering the road like a canopy. One block away from the Grinnell College campus, the historic street was home to many of the college's faculty and staff as well as community and business leaders.

Crime scene tape was strung up like holiday garland around Abby's house. The yellow tape kept the onlookers off the lawn landscaped with ornamental shrubs, hostas and flagstone paths.

Rudy pulled into Merrill Park and used the small binoculars from the center console to watch as a plainclothes officer was taking notes from a paramedic behind an idling ambulance. The man's long lab coat peeked out below the hem of his blue parka. When the ambulance backed down the drive and lumbered down the narrow residential street without lights or sirens, Rudy realized that the man was the medical examiner or a tech of some sort. Rudy shuttered. Abby's parents—her dead parents—had left home for the last time. The police cruiser and unmarked Ford left soon after.

Acid crept up the back of his throat, burning his esophagus and gagging him. He grabbed the banana from the passenger seat, spilling Abby's backpack at the same time.

Nary an inch of the navy blue, canvas backpack wasn't covered by embroidered flowers, stars, butterflies and other doodles. The ornate bag was better suited to a hippy chick headed to a Grateful Dead show rather than Abby's East Coast preppy style. Abby carried her private world in her backpack. Along with her Chemistry textbook, lab book, research folder, Rudy found a small journal and sketchbook. Buried at the bottom of her pencil case was a stunning pocket knife with a mother

CHAPTER 13

of pearl handle and sterling silver detailing. Rudy'd never seen the blade before, but if Abby carried a knife it would be this ornate.

Her pencil case didn't hold a single writing instrument, instead it looked like a miniature first aid kit: alcohol swabs, iodine scrub and Band-Aids in multiple sizes. Rudy tucked the pencil case back into the backpack.

He cracked open the well-worn notebook. Abby didn't go anywhere without a small journal. It was more than a simple diary, more like a scrapbook of her everyday life: funny overheard quotes, receipts, stats from tennis games and research notes from her sociology class. Her chosen project dealt with women in homeless shelters escaping abusive relationships. She'd glued several clippings from the *Des Moines Register* into her book. Next to a profile of a Des Moines woman transitioning out of a shelter and into an apartment. In the margin Abby'd written and decorated a single word: *brave*.

Instead of following the police's lead, it was time to connect the dots on his own. In chess, luck favored bold and calculated moves. He shifted the car into gear and left the park.

Chapter 14

Deep shades of gray and dissipating fog pressed at the conference room windows like the day's gloom was animate and desperate to snuff out the fluorescent lighting.

"Thank you for your assistance," Garrison said into the phone receiver before replacing it to the cradle.

He looked down to the legal pad of notes on the conference table. He'd traced the letters ROTC over and over with his pen so that it leaked through to the yellow pages below.

According to Sergeant Major Ken Brogan, Aidan was their top performing recruit: best scores in military science courses and excellent marks during field training exercises. Garrison circled the words "natural aptitude" on his notepad. After a tour as an MP during the first Gulf War, he knew those officers and enlisted men with a "natural aptitude" for military service were often crazier than a shithouse rat. Garrison witnessed first hand that the Army encouraged pathological behaviors in training and field exercises, while feigning shock when the media criticized these practices.

Between ROTC and academic scholarships, Aidan enjoyed a free ride at Dartmouth, without the control or obligations of his parents' money. And according to the high school guidance counselor, Abby recently turned down early acceptance at UC Berkeley. Both very prestigious schools. Meanwhile either one of them could have attended Grinnell

CHAPTER 14

College – a damn fine school by any measure – without the burden of tuition or scholarship applications thanks to Dr. Flynn's tenured position. They had to be running from something. This exceeded the typical teenage rebellion.

Garrison swiveled in his desk chair to face the white boards and perched his wiry frame on the edge of the seat. He'd filled every board to capacity without any revelations. Now it was time to stare at the boards until something — an answer, a question or new consideration — floated to the top of his muddy and murky mind. The more he stared at the puzzle on his white boards the more he was convinced a big piece was missing.

His eyes bounced from Abby's picture to the small section of the mind map she inhabited to the ultimate question: Where is Abrielle Flynn? The more he stared at Abby's photo the more she began to look like Vicky.

Grinnell police officer Benjamin Dykstra peeked his head around the corner. Most of the officers in the small department knew better than to disturb the investigator in his ritual. But if Dykstra had something on his mind, he wasn't deterred by Garrison's mood or unconventional investigation methods.

Benny, as the officer was more affectionately known, disappeared from the doorway. Garrison would have bet dollars to doughnuts that Benny hid outside the conference room door thinking of how to interrupt Garrison's concentration.

"Speak now or forever hold your peace," Garrison said.

"How's it going?" Benny asked, stepping into the room. "I can comeback, if you're busy."

"I could probably use a break," Garrison said. He pulled off his reading glasses and dropped them to the desk. "Shit's just not adding up."

"You're telling me. You had me looking into the girl, but it's strange. She's got no social media, no cell phone, no driver's license. I don't get it."

Benny looked up at the white boards, scanning each one, until his eyes stopped at the small box marked "possible motives."

"Can't find a motive?" Benny asked.

"Aidan doesn't profile as an arsonist." Garrison rubbed his eyes with both fists before replacing the glasses to their perch on his nose. "Most arsonists have a low IQ, an absent father and a domineering mother. Those indications are contrary to everything I've learned about the boy. And the murders themselves are baffling."

"I don't follow, sir."

"The way he killed his parents was specific and very symbolic, while hanging his sister seems uninspired, like killing her was an afterthought, a means to an end." Garrison stood and began to pace in front of the white boards.

Benny nodded in agreement but his face displayed confusion in a furrowed brow and frown.

"And what was his plan after setting the house on fire?" Garrison asked

"Don't most family annihilators kill themselves?"

"Self-immolation? You see that more in protests or martyrdom."

"Maybe he thought he was a martyr," Benny said.

Garrison shook his head.

"You think we're looking for the wrong guy?" Benny asked.

Garrison pursed his lips and tilted his head to the side as he studied the officer. He shook his head. "We missed something. Maybe at the scene. Fuck. I don't know."

Benny danced from foot to foot like he either had something on his mind or needed to pee. "I was wondering about the Flynn house," Dykstra said. "What'd they do with the old wine cellar."

"What wine cellar?" Garrison asked. His head snapped up and he met Benny's eyes for the first time.

Benny's frown deepened and he shook his head. "They must've torn it out." He continued to shake his head and started clenching his fists lost in a thought he couldn't reconcile.

"Spit it out." Garrison asked.

"That wine cellar was a part of history." He slapped a hand down on Garrison's desk. "My dad worked really hard to get that house put on the Register of Historical Places so no one could alter it. He even tried to get the historical museum to buy the house. He'd roll over in his grave knowing the wine cellar was gone."

Benny's dad was one of the original curators of the Grinnell Historical Museum. After Benny's mom died in childbirth, his old man became obsessed with local history and lore. He redirected every conversation to some arcane scrap of history. Garrison once commented on the darkened skies and ended up getting a lecture on the 1882 tornado that destroyed over half the town and college campus.

"What are you talking about?" Garrison was amazed that Benny got this upset over a wine cellar rather than the grizzly murders committed upstairs in the same house.

"My dad took me there when I was studying prohibition in high school. He talked the former owners into letting us take a look around."

"Tell me more," Garrison encouraged.

Benny took a deep breath. "During prohibition the town doctor owned the house. He built a room hidden behind a shelf in the basement for a liquor still so he could still use alcohol for his patients."

Garrison thought about his cursory search in the Flynn's basement, but couldn't remember anything out of the ordinary. "Tell me how to find it."

"Honestly, I'd rather show you."

Garrison wasn't fond of Benny. It wasn't that he disliked the officer, rather he couldn't stand how he blustered about his family's prominence and influence. In Garrison's estimation, if you had to brag about something, it did not really exist; like couples that draped over each other in public but required police intervention for domestic disputes at home.

Garrison, however, held out hope that the wine cellar would fill in the gaps of the jigsaw puzzle or at least shed some light on where the missing pieces might be.

Chapter 15

Rudy circled the area a few times before he pulled the Cadillac down the alley. The houses on Broad Street shared an alleyway with College administration building on Park Street. Rudy squeezed into a parking spot behind the Center for Religion, Spirituality and Social Justice. From the car, he walked two blocks up the alley and ducked between two shrubs not marked by crime scene tape. He ran to the back porch thankful the tall privacy bushes blocked the backyard from the neighbors' view. From the porch, he entered the Flynn's immaculate kitchen.

Contrary to his parents' house where the kitchen was the heart of the home, this room looked like a page of a modern design portfolio. Ceramic canisters, wooden cutting boards and scores of cookbooks lined the counter. He moved through the dining room into the living room.

At the top of the stairs, he skipped over Abby's bedroom to save it for last. In the master suite, a four-poster bed was dressed in mountains of white eyelet lace etched by rivers of blood. He understood that Dr. and Mrs. Flynn were dead, but he hadn't expected to find remnants of the crime. This was an impossible amount of blood.

The door at the end of the hallway led into an expansive study. A foul concoction of bodily fluids pooled on the Persian rug in a putrid cocktail. Although there was no direct evidence of violence in the room, his imagination filled in the horrific gaps. Rudy closed the door without taking another step into the study.

The next room stood in stark contrast with the rest of the house. Rather than furnished from a showroom, Aidan's bedroom looked like a monk's cell or maybe a high-end sanitarium. A vintage wind-up alarm clock sat atop stacked books next to the bare, stained mattress. No photos or art adorned the stark white walls. Anyone would go insane attempting to live in these quarters. The room contained the strong stench of gasoline, like petroleum was seeping from the blank walls. Again, Rudy closed the door before the smell overwhelmed him.

When Rudy stepped from the hallway into Abby's room, he felt like he was falling down Alice's rabbit hole. A noose hung from the ceiling beside Abby's double bed. His heart leapt into his throat and throbbed there until he was able to swallow it down with his fear. The knot was perfect, like whoever tied it had practiced for years. Such attention to detail belied madness and demonstrated planning and preparation.

Rudy stepped around the noose and sat on her bed. As he scanned the bookshelves and personal mementos, Rudy wondered where Garrison would look for clues: not clues regarding the murders, but insight into Abby's whereabouts. He tried to imagine Abby's room like he did a chessboard. Often viewing at a chessboard from the opponent's perspective helped him gain an offensive strategy.

He leaned back to lie on her pillow, closed his eyes and tucked his hands behind his head. His fingers found a small book tucked into her pillowcase. He withdrew the book. The small, black Moleskine journal was two-thirds full of her meticulous scrawl. Initially Rudy felt guilty reading her diary. His remorse, however, was tempered by the words. The pages were full of factual accountings of her day like a scientific field journal rather than a glimpse into her personal world. When he tucked the journal back into her pillowcase he discovered a stainless steel letter opener shaped like a blunt knife.

This couldn't be the first and only notebook. He flipped over onto

CHAPTER 15

his belly on the bed and leaned over the edge so he could peer under the bed. He ignored the organized plastic bins of embroidery supplies and instead grabbed a scuffed shoe box. He flipped open the lid to find a dozen similar notebooks with dates written on the spines. Half the books contained the same perfect writing while the other half looked like the lab book he was forced to keep in chemistry class with dates, times, measurements, weights and other notations. Although they were bizarre, the notebooks weren't leading him to her location. Snooping for details about her private world wasn't his aim. He put the books back as he found them and laid back down.

The books lining the shelves were alphabetized within subject areas. The bed was made with hospital corners. Even the trash in the metal bin next to her twin bed was neat: pieces of paper folded into fourths rather than crumpled into a ball for shooting practice.

Car doors slammed outside followed by muffled voices. Rudy assumed the neighborhood would be full of rubberneckers and looky-loos for the days and weeks to come. Grinnell considered itself cosmopolitan and progressive; however, it was not immune to idle gossip and morbid curiosity.

As Rudy reclined on Abby's bed trying to read her bedroom, searching for his next move, the front door slammed and voices filtered up the stairs. He rolled off the bed and peeked out a window overlooking Broad Street. Garrison's familiar SUV was pulled up to the curb out front.

"Shit."

In two swift strides, Rudy stepped into the closet and crouched to the floor. Abby's shoes were piled to the side of the closet floor to make room for a mound of blankets and pillows. He curled into Abby's nest and found comfort there.

Chapter 16

The day was steely and gray like an old nickel. It was how Garrison felt—dull and worn around the edges. During the short drive from the public safety building to the Flynn house on Broad Street, they passed by a bucket truck hanging Christmas decorations from the light poles in preparation for the Jingle Bell Holiday Celebration.

"Where do you think she is?" Benny asked as they took the short drive across town.

"If I knew that, she wouldn't be missing." Garrison took a deep breath, tried to settle his nerves and take the annoyance out of his voice. "She took off at about 3:30 this morning. She could be hiding in this supposed wine cellar or she could be halfway to Canada. We have no idea how much money she has or what other resources she might have."

"You're confident we'll find her?"

"What other choice do we have?"

They pulled up to the Flynn house. The yellow crime scene tape encircling the property was starting to sag as the west wind tried to blow in winter's first storm.

"I always thought this house would be the perfect setting for a horror movie or a really good ghost story," Benny said. The officer looked like a kid staring up at a theatre's marquee plotting how to get into see the latest rated-R slasher film.

CHAPTER 16

"Movie's over," Garrison said.

Inside the back door, Garrison noted that the telephone receiver was dangling off the hook. Although it bore fingerprint powder, no one thought to return the receiver to the cradle. Garrison considered hanging it up, but refrained. When Abby did come home, she wouldn't want to deal with the answering machine. Better to leave the line dead.

Garrison led them through the kitchen to the basement stairs. He did not want Benny wandering the rooms where the murders took place, did not want to satisfy Benny's morbid curiosity or send him on another puking jag.

The stairs led them down into a laundry room. This room was as immaculate as the rest of the house. A large front-loading stainless steel washer and dryer were tucked under a granite countertop that ringed the room with a large basin sink for stain soaking, an ironing center and wall mounted drying racks for delicates. Beyond the laundry room, was a well-stocked pantry. Built-in shelves lined with canning jars encompassed the room. Hundreds of Ball jars held everything from tomato sauce to peaches to homemade blueberry jam. One set of shelves held bins of potatoes, onions and other root vegetables.

In contrast to all the canned goods, a modern Bang and Olufsen digital receiver rested on a shelf. Garrison waved his hand in front of the unit and it lit up. He tapped play on the touchpad. There was no sound despite the counter ticking off the seconds of an audio track entitled, "Baby Don't Cry."

"It's still here!" Benny stepped over to a shelf laden with gallon-size jars of various types of flour, rice and sugar. The officer's face lit up with a huge grin as he felt under some of the shelves with one hand. Garrison was baffled. There was nothing here, nothing but a years worth of pasta sauce and salsa.

"Got it," Benny said. His hand slid a board to side and the shelving unit swung into a chamber beyond the pantry.

"What the hell?" Garrison said.

Benny pushed the shelf back as far as it would go and started to step into the hidden room when Garrison stopped him.

"Hang on a moment," Garrison said. His trepidation about what lay in those hidden rooms palpable. His temples pounded and his ears filled with the sound of blood rushing to his confused brain. Garrison inhaled to a slow count of seven, held it for seven seconds and exhaled to another count of seven. After two more repetitions of the breathing exercises his doctor prescribed, the roar in his ears subsided. "Benny, why don't you go grab the camera from your vehicle? We need to document what we find. And bring some gloves."

Benny bounded up the stairs. Garrison continued with his meditative breathing and rubbed his temples. The cold sweat prickling his forehead faded. Cop's instinct told him that he was about to cross into another world like Dorothy stepping from her wrecked home into the realm of Oz.

When Benny returned with camera in hand a few minutes later, Garrison had regained his composure and a better grip on his equilibrium.

After pulling on nitrile glove, they crossed the threshold between the dry storage pantry and the hidden room. Inside they encountered was a mix of exposed brick foundation, an oak wardrobe and mahogany wine racks. Instead of various bottles of port or rare vintages of merlot, the wine racks were full of different torture devices similar to those Garrison first learned about in the Medical Examiner's preliminary report. Ball gags of assorted colors and sizes filled one cubby meant for chardonnays. Riding crops of different compositions and lengths hung from hooks on the wall.

"Is this a naughty kitty dungeon?" Benny asked. "Like a bondage playroom?"

"They weren't here to play. Think less dominatrix and more Guantanamo Bay."

CHAPTER 16

"Holy shit."

Each compartment intended for wine contained a different instrument designed to evoke nightmares: floggers, spreader bars, leather bullwhips, paddles, canes, cat o' nine tails, handcuffs and black-out hoods. Benny snapped photos of each shelf while Garrison noted the empty spaces and the spots where the instruments used in Dr. Flynn's murder once occupied.

"Jesus. What the fuck is this?" Benny asked.

"I don't want to speculate," Garrison said. "Don't think about it too long or it'll make you sick."

"What are we going to do with all this stuff?"

"That isn't our decision. If a crime was committed in this room, the perpetrators are most likely dead."

"That just seems wrong. Someone should pay for this depravity."

"What punishment can we dole out? Dad was tortured for hours before his heart gave out. Mom was mutilated and stabbed through the heart. The daughter sees her family dead and runs away from everything she knows and possibly loves." Garrison stopped pacing and turned to face Benny. "Hasn't there been enough punishment?"

Benny looked to his scuffed boots.

"That doesn't include her boyfriend, Rudy, who must be out of his mind with worry and grief." Garrison resumed pacing, but with a purpose other than nervous energy. He searched for access to the second room. "That doesn't include the entire Grinnell community who will grieve this loss and gossip about this for years. While being objective about the job and the crime, you also gotta remain human and look at all the wreckage."

"I'm sorry, sir. I was mistaken."

"Where's this second room you mentioned? The one that contained the whiskey still."

Benny stepped over to the oak wardrobe and opened the double doors.

The hooks inside the large closet were hung with lengths of rope. Benny knocked on the back of the hulking piece of furniture before giving it a shove. The back panel swung into a space beyond.

Garrison was impressed with the ingenuity used to create these hidden spaces. Although sworn to enforce the law, a criminal's attempt to evade apprehension fascinated him. These rooms were beyond detection, completely invisible in plain sight. Built to hide illegal hooch, they now hid truths beyond comprehension or prosecution.

As the back of the wardrobe swung open the wailing sound of a crying baby leaked from the room. Benny and Garrison rushed into the room.

"Where's the baby?" Benny shouted.

"It's the sound system." He pointed to speakers recessed into the ceiling. The walls were painted high gloss white. The white reflective walls in combination with high power LED lights were enough to disorient and nearly blind the two men.

Garrison shouted. "Turn it off."

Benny ducked out of the white room. In a minute, the crying stopped and Benny poked his head through the door..

"Stay there," Garrison said.

"I thought you said this wasn't a crime scene."

"Let me rephrase. I don't want to disturb anything and awaken the devil." Garrison spun around and motioned for Benny to hand him the camera.

Garrison took a photo of the enormous metal birdcage made of black powder coated steel hanging in the far corner of the room. Wrist restraints hung from the top of the cage, which was only tall enough to allow its victim to sit or squat.

"I imagine that a dungeon would be dark and damp and infested with bugs and vermin," Benny said. "Not like this."

Across the room was a stockade made of brushed steel. The simple construction made the device more terrifying. The h-shaped construc-

CHAPTER 16

tion had metal restraints welded to each end to hold wrists and ankles in a spread and vulnerable position. Welded to one end was a metal locking collar.

Garrison closed his eyes and looked away. The sheer humiliation of being chained up like an animal would be enough to shatter anyone's ego. He knew, however, the intent of this contraption went far beyond debasement. The stockade was the first stop on a long and ghastly trip to degradation. He imagined he could hear the devil stirring below his feet like a snake awakening for the hunt.

"Did you hear that?" Benny asked.

Garrison shook his head, not because he didn't hear the noise rather he didn't believe Benny heard the same thing.

"We need to get the crime scene guys back out here. They need to document this."

Garrison turned away from a metal chair with bonds similar to the stockade, except the foundation had been replaced with a toilet seat. He hustled into the pantry. To imagine what happened in that chair would fully awaken the slumbering beast.

Chapter 17

Aidan rolled over in his cocoon of drapes as afternoon light slanted in through the mini blinds. His morning erection woke him as the intentional scars down the shaft forced his penis into a c-shape pulling away from his body. The scarification and hard-on served as a daily reminder of his father's horrific abuse. No matter how much time he spent at the gym or running ROTC courses or studying military science, his erection was one part of his manhood he'd never reclaim.

After relieving himself in the bathroom he studied his naked form in the mirror. The mass of scar tissue etching thick, white tracks that crossed his entire torso to below his knees used to look pathetic as it clung to his pale, gaunt frame. After a year and a half of physical transformation, he wore the scars as a shield – a warrior's mantle – against the world. Father was finally witness to this great transformation as he met his end.

Beyond any textbook or classroom lessons, Dartmouth and ROTC taught Aidan that his true strength lie in seeing through the tremendous load of bullshit he'd been spoon-fed since birth. Father maintained that the family was holy and ordained. Father, therefore, had the right to rule as he saw fit, like the divine right of kings. He preached this philosophy with the fervor of a zealot or charismatic cult leader. Unlike the feudal system, however, he chose his daughter to ascend to the throne. He groomed Abby to be queen while Aidan remained his whipping boy.

The great revelation came slowly during his first semester at Dartmouth. His psychology seminar class on family dynamics opened his eyes. Family is an antiquated construction passed down from agrarian societies where survival depended on the cooperation of the entire extended family to work the farm. Feudal systems were even crueler: birth order and surname determined the entire course of a life. Aside from the need of a support structures like food and shelter, a child born today doesn't require their family for more than seven, maybe eight years. Although their brains aren't fully developed until their early twenties, children don't need the family structure to survive and mature to adulthood. Besides, seeking a parent's love or approval was a ridiculous pursuit and crippled so many otherwise functioning adults.

Most nights as he drifted off to sleep, he fantasized that he'd been shipped off to boarding school, maybe Culver Military Academy in Indiana. He never suffered under the hands of his father and never sought affection from his absent mother. Aidan thought of his mother less as the woman that bore him, but more like the vacuum of deep space between galaxies: dark, empty and altogether worthless. At Culver, he was the football quarterback and rowed crew and made dean's list. He was popular and dated a perky, blonde cheerleader. He and the cheerleader fucked like rabbits because his penis wasn't mangled.

His sister. His fucking perfect sister. That spoiled cunt could not live into adulthood. The way she'd been coddled and spoiled doomed her to a life of helplessness. She would never be as well-adjusted as Aidan. She didn't understand the cruelties of the real world. She couldn't and wouldn't survive.

Killing her would be an act of mercy and a public service. Women marry their fathers and perpetuate the cycle of abuse. With the type of hero worship his father fostered, Abby was certain to complete the cycle. If he followed this logic to its conclusion, maybe he needed to take care of Rudy, too. If Abby loved him, Rudy had to be just like Father.

Aidan splashed water on his face and washed away thoughts of the past. Focus on the mission. It was only half done.

He paused in front of the full-length mirror behind the bathroom door. He moved and flexed like a body builder in competition. He admired his muscle mass and definition in his arms and thighs. He turned away from his reflection, looked back over his shoulder and rose up on his tip-toes. His calves contracted and turned into upside-down heart. He grinned. Narcissism was a new trait born from hours a day in the weight room. He bench pressed and deadlifted like his life depended on it, because it did. Like a butterfly from chrysalis, he was reborn from fragile weakling to alpha male hero.

Energized and refocused, he strode into the kitchen. Inch by inch, he walked the gas stove away from the wall scuffing and scarring the peeling linoleum floor. He crouched behind the stove. A thick layer of dust and cooking grease covered the gas line. Without a crescent wrench, the fitting almost didn't budge. Almost. Natural gas shushed out of the pipe filling the space between the wall and oven.

This was a mistake. If he flicked his Zippo now, he'd burn the shit out of himself without major damage to the house. The small farmhouse wasn't part of the mission. Although he'd love to watch the place explode, he replaced the fittings.

It wasn't time for fire. Not yet.

Chapter 18

Abby pawed at her sodden face to wipe away her tears, instead she raked her ragged nails down her sunken cheeks and neck. The pain was a welcome wake up. Her fingers paused at her pulsing carotid. The throbbing skin would be so easy to break. If only her nails were longer, she could do some real damage, but piano lessons and tennis lessons and needlepoint lessons required short, manicured fingernails. She suffered these lessons to become a fine lady and keep Daddy happy.

Instead of scratching the tawny freckles off her face one by one, Abby wriggled out of the Volvo's trunk space through the lowered back seats. Although not an ideal bed, she made due with the Pendleton blanket kept in the car for emergencies and used a towel from Dad's gym bag for a pillow.

Running low on gas and cash, she'd pulled into the downtown Des Moines parking garage for a nap and a place to hide among the masses. Once a manufacturing hub, the city kept up with the times and transformed itself into the Hartford of the Midwest. The city was now the third largest insurance hub in the world. At sunrise, she'd lowered down the backseats, wedged herself into the trunk space and forced her eyes closed to end the waking nightmare and give her racing mind a rest from the horrors, both real and imaginary.

She clambered over the front seats and settled into the passenger seat.

This perch was as familiar as her own bed. She'd spent hours here as her father chauffeured her to and from school, various lessons and volunteer hours at the library. She flipped down the visor and opened the vanity mirror.

The gash on her forehead had faded to a small line of dried blood just above her hairline. Her eyes were bloodshot from too little sleep. Her lips chapped and cracked from where she chewed on them – a habit lost since childhood and rediscovered in the last hours. Her cracked and bleeding mouth reminded her of mother's lips missing around her bloody, gaping maw. She shook her head, trying to dislodge the images from her mind.

She dropped open the glove box and riffled through the owner's manual, vehicle registration and insurance form. Nothing useful. Pulling open the console between the two seats she found a few practical trinkets. She emptied the coin tray into her hand and stuffed the few dollars into her jeans pockets. Next she tucked nail clippers, tiny Maglite, half a pack of gum and Daddy's aviator sunglasses into the pocket of Rudy's cardigan. She held her frigid hands to her eyes like an ice pack for a moment before climbing out of the car and strolled to the stairs.

From her perch in a parking garage above Des Moines' Grand Avenue, she could see the river to the east and the downtown skyline to the west. The peak of the Principal building, shaped like a citrus reamer, did little to quell her hunger.

The elevator mechanism wheezed and coughed when she called the car. When the doors slid open, the floor of the elevator was rippled and buckled. Abby opted for the stairs. Cinder block walls radiated the winter chill while the glassed in stairwell acted as a solarium trapping in autumn's fading heat. The stairwell reeked of vomit, human waste and strong disinfectant. Down three flights of stairs, she emerged into the skywalks, a system of modern hamster tubes connecting downtown office buildings, hotels, convention space and miles of industrial carpet squares.

CHAPTER 18

She breathed in the forced air heat. The warmth was seductive after a morning curled in the back of her dad's car hiding from reality, the world and the breadth of her fear and grief. Although she'd taken many advanced math classes, calculating the probability of running into her homicidal brother in the office buildings was beyond her reckoning. She was certain he hadn't followed her into Des Moines, but she was being hunted.

She scanned the hallway, wondering which direction would bear food. A five-dollar bill was tucked deep into her jeans pocket with the coins. It wouldn't buy her much food, maybe enough to satisfy her rumbling stomach. With no breadcrumb trail, she followed the music.

Several twists and turns later, she rounded a corner to find a woman strumming a guitar with an upturned cowboy hat full of crumpled bills in front of her. The woman's lustrous black hair fell halfway down her back in a thick, elegant braid. She sang a Van Morrison cover with a raspy voice best reserved for late night radio. Abby stood while she finished "Moondance." The acoustic guitar's pick guard was engraved with an intricate rose and a single rose was tooled into the soft leather guitar strap.

"Have a seat, honey," the woman said, indicating the floor next to her. "You're making me nervous."

Abby sank down to the floor next to the guitarist, thankful the first voice she heard after waking from her nightmare was kind. The woman launched into a rousing rendition of "Sweet Caroline." During the chorus, she reached over, caressed Abby's cheek and tapped the tip of her nose with a playful wink of her dark brown eyes. While the woman strummed, Abby scanned the skywalks for familiar faces. Her heart raced as she imagined Aidan rounding the corner with fire in his eyes and coiled rope in hand.

The woman played with passion, it radiated in her brilliant smile and in how her head bobbed in time with her strumming fingers as she held the guitar. She paused her singing and took a long pull from a battered water bottle.

"That's the problem with the holidays."

Abby's brow furrowed and lips pulled together in a question.

"Everyone's more generous, giving fives instead of ones." She pointed to the bills in her hat. "But half the world took the day off work to prep for tomorrow's gluttony."

She pulled the hat to her and collected the bills, ironing them out on her dirty denim clad thigh.

"What about you, Red? You got somewhere to be tomorrow?"

Abby shook her head as tears flooded her eyes. In all her grief, she'd forgotten about Thanksgiving. The looming holiday reminded her of Rudy's pleas to spend the day together. Deep pangs of loss and guilt tightened in her chest.

"Everyone calls me Rose," she said with her hand extended. Her handshake was firm, but warm. "I'll call you Red."

Abby smiled.

"Come on." Rose pulled on Abby's sweater sleeve. "I'll buy you a cup of soup."

She stood, flipped her hat up onto her head and slung the guitar across her back with the detailed strap intersecting her ample breasts. She could have walked off the cover of a best-selling country record, except for the cloying scent of days old sweat.

Rose walked with a spring in her step like she hadn't a care in the world other than guitar strings and the chords to every folk song ever written. Abby stutter stepped as she peeked around corners, glanced over her shoulder and scanned faces expecting her personal boogeyman to pop out at anytime.

Chapter 19

Baxter's deli served food cafeteria style with different lines for soups, salads and sandwiches. Abby assumed the place was normally bustling with professionals from nearby offices. Today, however, secretaries, lawyers, insurance executives and accountants occupied only three tables.

They walked up to the soup counter. Rose squinted up at the menu board with eyes shrouded in wrinkles like she'd spend too many days gazing into the burning sun. Abby stood with her back to the counter looking out the glass front of the restaurant.

"What'll it be today? Chili or tomato basil?" Rose asked indicating a chalkboard with the day's selection of soups. Abby jumped when Rose tapped her shoulder. "I wouldn't suggest the chowder. The clams are chewy and overcooked. Yuck." Rose ran her pink tongue between her teeth. "The Wisconsin beer cheese soup is to die for, but you gotta get here early for that. They always sell out."

"Chili, please," Abby said to Rose, her voice low and shaky.

"No use telling me." She pointed at the young man behind the counter. "Order for yourself."

Abby turned her back to the skywalk entrances to address the clerk. "May I have a bowl chili, please?"

"Anything to drink?" the man behind the counter asked.

"Coffee."

Rose paid with busker dollars and joined Abby at a small table in the corner of the restaurant. She sat with her back against the wall and her legs stretched out across the booth. From her vantage point, she surveyed the whole restaurant as well as anyone wandering the skywalk outside. Abby wrapped her hands around her paper coffee cup to warm herself. She wished the bitter liquid would trickle down into her soul and warm the cold and dark places that didn't exist yesterday. Holding onto the coffee also had the added benefit of giving her trembling hands something to do.

"Tell me something, Red," Rose said, cocking her head at her new friend.

Abby nodded.

"Who was it?" Rose asked.

Abby furrowed her eyebrows and shook her head, baffled. "I don't understand."

"In my family, it was my uncle." Rose's high, trilling laugh was sardonic. "Jesus, I sound like such a cliche. Dirty Uncle Sal coming to get me in the middle of the night and playing peek-a-boo with my private parts."

Abby shook her head with her mouth agape.

"You picked the gunslinger seat in an empty restaurant." Rose indicated their surroundings. "Who abused you?"

"Not abused." Abby gulped. "Just scared."

Abby looked down at her hands folded in her lap. Her shoulders slumped forward as she slouched farther down in the booth.

Abby bit down on her bottom lip in an attempt to hold back the tears.

"You got someplace to spend the night?" Rose asked.

Abby shook her head and scratched at an invisible spot on the table. She couldn't spend another night in the Volvo. It was getting colder and she didn't have gas money. She was loath to admit for the first time in her sheltered life she didn't have a place to lay her weary head.

CHAPTER 19

"You'll come stay with me." Rose said like the decision was already made and not up for debate.

"You live around here?" Abby asked

The downtown area was being redeveloped and gentrified from dilapidated retailers to high-end lofts. The local news reported record high rents even in historic hotels turned into tiny studio apartments. Although generous to a fault, Rose didn't seem like she could afford loft-living.

"Something like that."

Rose smiled like Abby was a puppy with a favorite shoe in her mouth.

Rose stood and gathered her guitar case and messenger bag. "I got a tent. It's not much, but it's mine. You're welcome to it. I got an extra sleeping bag and pillow."

"Are you sure?"

"Supposed to be colder than a witch's titty tonight so an extra body in the pile will be nice."

"The pile?"

"Relax. It's just an expression."

"I guess I don't get out much." Abby glanced around searching for Aidan. She quickly considered her options: following her new friend or fending for herself in the trunk of her dead father's Volvo.

"Come on, Red. Let's get out of here."

Abby stood and reached back to grab her coat before remembering she didn't have one. She spotted a knit cap sticking out of Rose's pocket. "May I borrow your hat?" she asked.

"Sure," Rose said and handed over beanie.

Abby pulled on the hat and tucked all her hair up into it. She ran her hands along the edges several times to ensure all of her bright red tresses were hidden.

Chapter 20

The angular, yellow metal sculpture of the head and beard of a wheat plant outside the Franciscan Outreach Shelter and Homeless Services building was a tribute to Norman Borlaug, the father of the green revolution and Iowa native. The sharp corners were softened by a thin layer of freezing rain that glittered in the growing gloom. The shelter was an island at the far corner of downtown Des Moines, a block from pricey lofts and hundred dollar a plate hipster diners with cryptic names like Obsidian and Fluid. The shelter was mentioned by name in Abby's journal and included notes from interviews. Rudy entered the homeless shelter with Abby's bag slung over his shoulder. Its straps hugged him and gave him comfort. An elaborate and colorful mural of crop fields marked the front entry. The art may have been a way to make the shelter more palatable to its downtown neighbors. The modern facility looked more like a high-end gym rather than the largest homeless shelter in Iowa.

"Hello," the lady behind the counter said. Elaborate braids with strands of vibrant pink, purple and yellow drew attention to the smooth dark skin framing her round face. "Help you with something?"

"I'm looking for this girl," Rudy said. He snatched off his ball cap and handed her a sheet of paper he pulled from Abby's backpack. He had stopped by Kinkos before searching the bus station, airport and youth shelters. The Kinkos clerked helped him download a photo of Abby from

CHAPTER 20

his phone and print it on a flier with his phone number.

"Pretty girl."

"Have you seen her?" Rudy asked with his ball cap between his trembling hands. He ran a finger over the raised Chicago Cubs logo, tracing the C methodically like his mother might meditate with a rosary. Rudy leaned forward over the reception desk and watched the woman's lips with tangible hope.

She shook her head. "Sorry, love. A girl like that would stick out around here." She handed the flier back to Rudy, but he refused it with the wave of a hand.

"Anybody else I could talk to? Maybe they saw her out on the streets or something."

The lady considered it for a few moments as she ran her long acrylic nails through her braids. "You might want to ask Otto. He knows all the street people."

"Where would I find him?" he asked.

"He's serving lunch in the cafeteria." She pointed down the hall.

"Thank you, ma'am," he said as he headed in the direction she indicated.

"Ya can't miss him."

Rudy followed the farmland mural around a curving corridor into the dining room. The space confounded Rudy's expectations. It looked more like a hotel convention space than what he expected of a soup kitchen: open modern spaces, natural light filtering in from banks of windows and skylights with tables, countertops, chairs and flooring all in coordinating shades of blue. Dozens of people gathered around various tables and huddled over steaming plates of spaghetti and garlic bread.

A large man danced behind the serving line. His shiny head bounced to the beat of the music drifting in from another room. He shook the ladle in his left hand like a maraca and hoisted the tongs in his right hand like a drum major's baton. The hulking man could have been Arnold Schwarzenegger's younger brother with bulging biceps, ripped abs that showed through his Slipknot tee shirt and no neck supporting his clean-shaven head.

Rudy joined the serving line behind two men their shoulders slumped like they were shielding themselves from hurricane winds. The men grabbed plates and waited to be served by the staff.

"Grab a plate," the taller of the two men said. "How else you gonna get fed?"

Between his Semper Fidelis hat and camouflage jacket, Rudy guessed he was former military. His lack of teeth, however, indicated a life of drugs since his discharge. Rudy waved him off. He tucked his hat into his back pocket and waited with hands folded in front of him and head bowed like he was waiting in line for communion. Finding her would provide him better nourishment than any meal: spiritual or otherwise.

"Plate?" the large gyrating man asked when Rudy reached the head of the service line.

"I'm not here to eat." Rudy shook his head. "The lady out there said you might be able to help me."

The man stopped dancing and looked Rudy up and down. He was suddenly self-conscious in his faded Levis, Carhartt twill shirt and scuffed Ariat boots.

"Otto?" Rudy asked.

"That's me," Otto said. His voice had a deep bass quality like Issac Hayes.

Rudy tried to hand him a flier. "Have you seen this girl?"

Otto exhaled through his nose in annoyance and stepped away from the pans of pasta, marinara and bread. He handed off his ladle and tongs to a petite woman, pulled off his vinyl gloves and shed his apron. When he stepped from behind the hot table, Rudy was able to take in the man's full breadth. Otto more resembled a refrigerator rather than the former

CHAPTER 20

governor of California.

"Why don't we step into my office?" Otto said and indicated a nearby empty table.

Rudy sat down and waited for the man to squeeze into the space between table and seat at the picnic-type table. Tattooed on one his beefy hands was the number eighty-eight and on the other was the number fourteen. These numbers baffled Rudy as he tried to decipher meaning from them, but assumed they were of a personal nature.

Otto motioned for Rudy to hand him one of the fliers. Otto squinted as he studied the photo. "How long has she been missing?"

"A day."

Otto held the photo up next to Rudy's face. "And you're her brother or boyfriend?"

"Abby's my girlfriend."

"What makes you think she's here?" Otto asked. Weary skepticism heavy in his voice.

"She was studying homeless populations in Des Moines for a college paper. Your name was in her research notes."

Otto's eyes widened. "She's a college student?"

Rudy nodded. He didn't want to squabble over Abby's status as a high schooler taking college classes. He also didn't want to debate anything with Otto for fear that the man would either crush him or refuse to help. Otto's deep set brown eyes held Rudy in place and warned against dishonesty.

"What makes you think she wants to be found?"

The question hit Rudy in the chest like Otto had slugged him. He was so focused on his need to find her, his need to bring her home, his need to know she was okay, he'd failed to consider what Abby might need or want.

"She's scared," Rudy said.

"We're all scared of something."

"You don't watch the local news, do you?" Rudy asked. The murders were the top news on all the local news stations. Rudy was certain his photo would start showing up on the news soon enough. He rubbed his left arm as it tingled like he'd been leaning on his funny bone too long.

"Shit, son. I don't watch the news. I get enough reality right here." Otto lifted his meaty hands and indicated their surroundings.

"She went home and found her parents murdered. I have to find her before her brother kills her."

Otto looked at the photo one more time before setting the flier on the table. He lifted his massive hands to his face and rubbed his temples. As he massaged his head, his massive biceps bulged and his grey tee shirt rolled up his arm to reveal another tattoo. The heavy script used to say, "Hate." But the E had been blacked-in so that it now looked like "Hat" with a giant period at the end. It took Rudy a few minutes to connect all the dots or rather all the tattoos to realize that Otto was or used to be a neo-Nazi.

The large man steepled his fingers and held them under his nose. He closed his blue eyes and drew a deep breath. On the exhale, he said, "I haven't seen her."

Rudy stood up, zipped up his coat and gathered the fliers. "Thank you for your time." He headed for the door. Although he wasn't sure where to go next, he was certain he wouldn't find help here. The big man wasn't forthcoming or inclined to help.

"Did you say she's from Grinnell?" Otto asked.

Rudy perked up. He hadn't mentioned their hometown. He spun around. "Yes."

"I spoke to her," Otto said.

"What? When?" Rudy asked. He crossed the cafeteria back to Otto in two long strides anxious for Otto's revelations.

"She called a few weeks ago, curious about the women that we help here. I encouraged her to come volunteer, but she said that wasn't

CHAPTER 20

possible."

Rudy found another dead end where he thought he'd found the right path. "Thank you, again." Rudy pulled on his ball cap and dipped the bill to Otto and again headed for the door.

"I told her about the homeless camps around town and that spurred another flurry of questions. She seemed really interested."

"Is there anything else?" Rudy asked without turning around this time.

"You want my help?" Otto asked.

Chapter 21

Saul's Pawn Shop sat two blocks away from the Polk County Courthouse and next to Rubenstein's Bonds. A single block of businesses designed to profit off the criminal misdeeds and misfortunes of others lay adjacent to the Des Moines' downtown bar district on Court Avenue. Aidan had followed Rudy into downtown, where he went into businesses posting fliers like he was looking for a lost puppy. The idiot didn't have the first clue where to look for his girlfriend. Aidan almost felt sorry for him. Almost.

Aidan had other priorities right now. He needed cash. He had depleted all his resources buying gasoline to light up his parents' house and now barely had enough change to buy a gas station soda. He knew better than to use his debit or credit cards.

He dropped the Jeep's tailgate, shifted aside two coils of nylon rope and pulled open the Pelican 1740 case. He'd customized the long case to hold his collection of assault rifles, handguns and tactical combat knives. He stroked the Bushmaster Model XM15-E2S .223-caliber semiautomatic rifle, the same beauty used in the Sandy Hook Elementary School shooting. This beautiful weapon wasn't meant for the deeply personal mission of family vengeance, it was reserved as a last resort. Stuffed into a nook at the back of the case was the gallon-size Ziploc bag he needed for this errand.

As he flipped up the tailgate, his combat boots lost their purchase on

CHAPTER 21

the icy asphalt. He danced a little jig while hugging the spare tire and maintained his upright position.

Inside the pawnshop, Aidan wandered to the back of the narrow shop and waited while the clerk was on the phone. Guitars hanging by the neck lined the back wall, from a beat-up acoustic to a stunning powder blue Les Paul to a pink toy ukulele. Glass display cases of modest and gaudy gold and diamond jewelry ringed the large room. Glassy-eyed taxidermy animals watched Aidan negotiate the cramped space.

He lingered over the gun display. He stroked the glass case like he was stroking the stainless steel of the polished weapons.

"You got a permit?" The clerk asked.

Aidan shook his head. "I'm not looking for a gun."

"Can I help you find something?"

He withdrew a Ziploc baggie of jumbled jewelry from his backpack and put it on the counter. "I'm looking to sell these."

"Who'd you rob?" The clerk laughed through his crooked teeth.

Aidan's eyes widened for a moment, but recovered. "My grandma died a few months ago and now I gotta buy a plane ticket back home for Christmas or my mom'll blow a gasket."

The clerk studied him for a minute sucking on his yellowing teeth. The clerk unrolled a bit of black velvet across the glass display case and began sorting the jewelry by metal and type. He then pulled a jeweler's loupe from a drawer and examined Mother's twenty-fifth anniversary solitaire and her enormous diamond earrings. Aidan leaned across the counter intrigued by the loupe.

When Mother left the house, a rarity, she preferred to be draped in gems. While visiting the grocery store or downtown for a cup of coffee, her gestures became exaggerated to call attention to the sparkles adorning each thin finger. She flipped her auburn hair over her thin shoulder to display her earrings and necklace. Diamonds and emeralds and rubies were father's payment for staying stoned on vodka and Valium and ignoring the atrocities committed in the basement.

When Aidan leaned in closer, the clerk looked up from father's wedding ring. "Can I get a little space?" he asked.

"Sorry, man."

"Go play a guitar or something." The clerk flicked his hand brushing him away.

"Restroom?" Aidan asked.

The clerk looked him over again as if determining if Aidan was worthy of using his urinal. "In the back."

Aidan returned to the back of the store, passed the guitars and stepped into the tiny bathroom.

* * * * *

Abby only half listened as Rose babbled about the weather, history of various buildings and the best places to get coffee as they meandered through a labyrinth of skywalks and down to the street. Being on the street made Abby uneasy. Death could come from any direction. She pulled the stocking cap further down on her head and checked for flyaways. She knew her hair was a beacon announcing her location and her identity.

On the sidewalk, they walked as close as possible to various several office buildings and closed storefronts to avoid treading on the layer of ice sheeting the cracked pavement. Near the courthouse, Rose paused at the door of a tiny pawnshop. "Hope you don't mind. I gotta stop in here for a second."

In the growing gloom and freezing drizzle, a large neon sign with "Loan" written vertically cast the street in an eerie red glow, while a "Cash for Gold" sign blinked in the window.

When they entered the musty shop, Abby was overwhelmed. She didn't know where to look. Her eyes flitted to the collection of taxidermied

CHAPTER 21

heads looming over the glass cases that encircled the cramped room. She watched out the window at passers-by looking for her brother's angry face.

Rose waited for the clerk to look up from a pile of jewelry. Abby remained at the shop's front, watched commuters scurry by the doors. She studied each face trying to read their expressions, wondering if her fear was visible on her face.

"Can I help you?" the clerk asked with a loupe stuck in a squinting eye. When he looked up, he smiled and his yellow teeth shone ear to ear. "Hey, Rose."

"Did my strings come in?" she asked and her eyes lingered over the spread of jewelry before her.

Abby turned her attention away from gazing out the plate glass window and she wandered over to a display case of knives. She missed her cutting kit at the bottom of her school backpack. She longed for the feel of sharp stainless steel across her skin.

"Not yet. Mail from the West Coast is delayed by the storm."

"Well, thanks anyway."

"I expect a shipment on Monday."

"Cool. See you then." Rose waved, then she and Abby stepped back on to the street.

* * * * *

Aidan stepped out of the bathroom as the front door closed with the jingle of brass bells. He stayed at the back of the store, foregoing the guitars and violins in favor of a saxophone that caught his attention. The Buescher New Aristocrat alto sax had a lovely dark patina and the engraving on the bell was beautiful. He picked up the horn and tested the keys. If the mouthpiece had a reed, he would've played.

He never learned much more than the scales before Father pulled him out of lessons and sold his sax. Another case of items caught his attention when he put the horn back on its stand.

"Isn't it illegal to sell military medals?" Aidan asked peering into the case.

"I don't sell them," the clerk said. "Some down on his luck veteran will come in here looking to sell. I'm a sucker and buy 'em."

Aidan marveled at all the ribbons and medals displayed in a rainbow of valor.

"I'm afraid I can't offer you much for all this. You'd be better off selling it on EBay or Craig's List."

"What can you give me?"

"Two-fifty."

Aidan looked down at the thousands of dollars in glittering family heirlooms on the counter and glanced back at the case of military items. "Two-fifty and you throw in a few of those medals."

"Deal."

Outside the pawnshop, he stuffed the folding money into his pocket and pinned the medals inside his jacket next to his heart. He pulled the hood of his sweatshirt over his head and studied the passersby before returning to his Jeep.

Chapter 22

Otto extracted himself from the cramped cafeteria table and guided Rudy down an administrative hallway to a small office. Otto had to turn sideways to squeeze through the doorway. The room resembled a storage closet more than a functional office except for a flimsy pressboard desk. Toiletry items, survival supplies and children's books lined the industrial metal shelves.

"What's your name?" Otto asked.

"Rudy."

"I'll call you Cowboy."

Rudy opened this mouth to protest, but thought better of it. He needed the big man's help and squabbling over his name wasn't going to soften him up.

As if understanding Rudy's concern, Otto explained, "The homeless respond better to nicknames. They're less personal and less intimate. It also discourages identity theft." Otto withdrew two cheap backpacks and set them on the desktop. The desk looked like it would crumble if Otto sneezed on it. It didn't look sturdy enough to support the man's elbows while he pounded on the keyboard of the antiquated Dell desktop. "Put on your white hat, Cowboy. We're heading into Indian Territory."

He filled the bags with provisions from the boxes on his office floor. Neat packages of Mylar thermal blankets, travel toothbrushes, hotel-sized bars of soap, packs of tissues, granola bars and wet wipes filled the two packs. Then he reached into the bottom desk drawer and pulled out two flask-sized whiskey bottles

"You need to understand our battle here. The homeless are not a throw away population," Otto said.

"I would never think that." Rudy tucked Abby's backpack onto a high shelf before pulling on the bag laden with supplies.

"Each person has a different story and deserves dignity. That's what we try to provide here but our resources are tight. There are over twenty-three thousand homeless Iowans, six thousand in Polk County alone. This isn't a place you come to escape bullshit your first world problems."

"I understand."

"Do you?" Otto asked. He gave Rudy a stern look. "The people you meet today deserve your respect. If you show them anything less, you're on your own."

"Yes, sir." Rudy didn't appreciate the lecture. Otto made some incorrect assumptions about him. He worked hard for everything he had and gave generously to Saint Mary's Catholic Church back in Grinnell. He wasn't blind to those in need. Although the farm was doing well now, that wasn't always the case. After a bad flood year, his under-insured parents sold many of their belongings to make ends meet and keep food on the table.

"Good. We'll head over to the river first."

When they exited the building, Rudy headed for his mom's car tucked in a spot at the back of the full parking lot. The lights flashed when he clicked the unlock button on the remote.

"We walk," Otto said. "If we roll up in a Caddy, we'll look like a couple of assholes."

Otto tightened the straps on his backpack and headed south. His Doc Martens set a clipped pace down southwest sixteenth street. "There's a few mega churches in West Des Moines that encourage parishioners to proselytize to the homeless. Once a week a carload of Christians will

CHAPTER 22

set out to bring the lost sheep back to Jesus. But in all their talk they forget that the homeless are human beings not just reeds to be bent to their will. They act like it's all a big fucking game. Give a homeless man a loaf of bread and a Bible and score one for the Lord." Red rose up his neck and flushed his cheeks and ears. Otto threw his arms up like an NFL referee signaling a good field goal. In all his indignation, he sounded like a born again preacher.

The men crossed Martin Luther King Jr. Parkway. The four-lane artery was a newer addition to the downtown area marked by bike trails on each side and wide landscaped medians. Rudy marveled at the changing cityscape of Des Moines. Recent national polls and magazine articles named Des Moines one of the wealthiest cities in the US as well as a great place for young professionals. City planners were quick to reinvest tax revenues to improve the historic downtown area. Developers gutted old industrial buildings and installed luxury lofts. Bar owners and restaurateurs clambered to build in the Court Avenue district. While the capitalists raced to make money and move the downtown area forward, companies moved operations and headquarters out to the western suburbs in search of cheaper rents and larger plots of land for endless parking lots.

Otto and Rudy continued on their course down Sixteenth Street, passing a power station and a large, abandoned industrial complex. The road ended and they crossed from the street to a wooded patch.

"Where are we?" Rudy asked.

Otto pointed ahead, beyond the large stand of cottonwoods. "The Des Moines water treatment plant and levy are just over there. This used to be a Ford Factory."

"Ford made cars in Des Moines?"

"Once upon a time."

They were closing in on the Raccoon River. During flood years, the levy and treatment plant were ground zero for protecting the city's water supply.

They cut across the abandoned parking lot and trekked between buildings. Within a hundred yards of entering the deciduous forest, they came upon a collection of shanty structures. The framework of these homes cobbled together from downed branches, repurposed lawn tarps and plywood. Rudy was astonished at the creativity and ingenuity reflected in these dwellings. The more impressive homes could have been one of the outbuildings or old chicken coops on his parent's farm. Although the structures were scattered among the trees, a small ring of makeshift chairs circled a communal fire pit dug into the ground.

At the far edge of the hodge-podge camp, a large, canvas Coleman tent was set up under several tarps strung up around trees. A pristine guitar case with a rose etched into the PVC exterior sat in a canvas camp chair outside the shabby tent.

"Where is everyone?" Rudy asked.

"Looking for odd jobs, scavenging for bottles and cans or panhandling for money."

A skinny African American man clad in clean jeans and multiple layers of bright fleece ducked out of an elaborate structure. The walls were constructed from discarded wooden pallets and lined with Tyvek house wrap presumably stolen from a construction site. The house even had a functioning door fashioned from a busted screen door covered with a heavy wool blanket.

"How you doing, Robinson?" Otto asked.

Robinson set down a long-handled ax and the two men embraced. Rudy wondered if Robinson understood that the eighty-eight on Otto's hand stood for Heil Hitler. Robinson eyed Otto's neo-Nazi tattoos. His mouth twitched before he covered his displeasure with a gap-toothed smile.

"Can't complain." The man shrugged his small, but powerful shoulders. His deep, bass voice had a lilt of bayou roots like John Lee

CHAPTER 22

Hooker reincarnate. Rudy could see Robinson starting life as the son of a sharecropper and living a life similar to the famous bluesman. "Woodpile's getting low. Gotta chop everyday to keep everyone warm." Robinson rubbed his stubbled chin and looked to the darkening sky as the wind rose. "Storm's blowing in."

Rudy glanced into Robinson's house through a window covered by a torn screen. He spied a rope bed covered in blankets. On the nightstand he spotted several titles of the beat authors.

"Who's your friend?" Robinson asked and nodded toward Rudy.

"Cowboy's looking for a friend of his."

Rudy wondered why Otto didn't refer to Abby as his girlfriend, but he handed Robinson the flier.

"Jack Kerouac said, 'The prettiest girls in the world live in Des Moines,'" Robinson said as he admired Abby's photo. "This one's no exception."

"Have you seen her?" Rudy asked.

Robinson shook his head. "Afraid not."

"Rose got anyone staying with her?" Otto asked.

Rudy shifted from foot to foot anxious to keep moving. Hide and seek wasn't a game to be played idly, speed was key.

"She's like a little kid bringing home every stray in the neighborhood. Last one she brought home stole Ernie's hooch, so she's under strict orders to mind her ps and qs."

"Thank you for your time," Rudy said. His chest deflated and his shoulders sagged. He turned to hike out of camp.

Otto shook his head in a way that only Rudy would notice, so he turned around.

"How's Sterling? Ain't seen her around much lately," Otto said.

"Weather's been good. Little too good if you ask me. Like Father Winter's got a trick hiding up his sleeve."

Both men paused and looked at the western horizon with narrowed eyes like they were waiting for the sky to change colors from gray to purple.

"Sterling's been good. That old girl'll out live us all."

"You all ready for turkey day? You need anything?" Otto asked.

"Naw," Robinson said, waving his arm in a dismissive manner. "I scored one of them big turkey fryers on one of my dumpster diving trips out west. You ever had fried turkey?"

Otto smiled and shook his head. "I'm a vegetarian."

"By choice?" Rudy asked, his eyebrows rose in a look of disbelief like he'd seen the Easter Bunny run through camp.

"Keeping my temple clean," Otto said and rubbed his belly.

Robinson slapped him on the back and laughed.

Rudy grew tired of listening to the men's idle chit-chat. "Do you know of any place else we should look?" he asked.

"She meth around at all?" Robinson asked.

Rudy squinted and looked from Otto to Robinson and back.

Otto smiled, his teeth could have been an advertisement for an orthodontist. "He's asking if she does drugs."

Rudy felt like a naive buffoon. "No. No drugs."

"You better pray it stays that way," Robinson said and handed the flier back to Rudy. "There's a dozen pimps in the city that would love to turn her out."

Again Rudy felt the pain in his chest and the familiar tingling in his arm. He massaged his chest and shoulder. The talk of pimps and prostitutes made the fluttering anxiety in his chest worse.

"Cowboy, give him your backpack."

Rudy shucked his pack and handed it to Robinson. The man unzipped the bag and riffled through the contents.

"Thanks, man," Robinson said. "Mighty kind of you."

"You got any other ideas where to look for the girl?" Otto asked.

"The usuals." Robinson cracked open a granola bar and took a bite.

CHAPTER 22

"Bus station, food pantries, the skywalks and flophouses. Might also check out the motels on fourteenth."

"Thanks for your help." Otto shook Robinson's hand and motioned for Rudy to begin the trek back out of the woods.

Chapter 23

Men from the YMCA Supportive Housing Campus stood at varying distances down Ninth Street. Several smoked, some fidgeted with their tattered overcoats and others stood like statues dedicated to the disenfranchised, but none of them talked or interacted. On the other side of the street, women scurried down the block leaving their office jobs and headed for their cars parked on the southern reaches of downtown.

Abby preferred to keep her ostrich head in the sand and oblivious of mankind's perversions. Predatory and uncivilized, men on one side of the street set to pounce while their quarry ran from tree to tree with heads bowed in fear. She imagined Rudy escorting her down the street, guiding her away from puddles and opening doors.

Rose and Abby strode down the male side of the street. Several men nodded a greeting, two even said Rose's name like she was a local celebrity — famous among the destitute. Rose walked with head held high against the freezing rain that misted around them. Abby felt like she was walking down the high school hallways with some of the popular girls. For some reason, this put her at ease like popularity equated to security, but it also made her yearn for the banality of school. Abby longed for fourth period chemistry or even fifth period physics. She'd even welcome the horror of gym class. But routine made her easy prey as she considered Aidan stalking the high school hallways.

CHAPTER 23

"Where you from?" Rose asked.

"No where."

"Come on now," Rose said with a whine. "Secrets don't make friends." Abby fidgeted with the bottom of Rudy's sweater as she might play with the hem of a too short sundress. "I'm from a small town about an hour from here. And you?"

They crossed a major four-lane road and hiked the bike trail paralleling the thoroughfare.

"Shiprock, New Mexico." Rose's face twitched as she said the name like it caused her physical pain.

"What's in Shiprock?"

"Not much." Rose shrugged her slender shoulders.

"Why'd you leave?"

"I already told you about dirty uncle Sal." Rose flipped a cigarette from a pack of American Spirits. She showed the pack to Abby. "I know they're racist, but I think it's funny."

Abby didn't understand the reference, but knew Rose expected her to laugh. She complied with a weak giggle as they walked along a road between two abandoned factories.

"I decided I'd had enough of uncle Sal's secret basement fun time. I stole two hundred dollars from my job working the drive-through at That's a Burger and ran off with my boyfriend."

"What happened then?" Abby hung on each of Rose's words.

Rose was easily the most interesting person Abby had ever met in her short, sheltered life. The most curious person in her high school was the twit that wore a different silk flower in her hair everyday.

At the dead end, Rose finished her smoke, rubbed the butt out on the bottom of her sneaker and put it into a plastic bag in her hoodie pocket. From the dead end sign, they tramped across a field to a wooded area.

"We drove to Denver to stay with his aunt or sister or someone. Anyway, I left when he started hitting me. Didn't want to end up another cliche like my mom. You know the idiot woman that repeats the pattern of abuse, leaves home to escape the violence only to find someone worse."

They followed a narrow path through the bramble and crossed into a clearing under a canopy of trees.

"You're safe here," Rose said, indicating their surroundings. "It's better than family and no dirty uncle Sal."

Abby looked around the camp, focusing on the line of five-gallon buckets set-up at the tree line as a latrine. A few small tents and makeshift shelters filled in a clearing around a dugout fire pit.

When Abby looked beyond the stand of nude trees surrounding the camp she spotted Terrace Hill. The governor's mansion sat up on a bluff overlooking the confluence of the Des Moines and Raccoon rivers as well as the expanse of downtown stretching toward the capital building. At the far end of the camp a man pushed a rusty wheelbarrow of firewood.

"Rose," he said and waved her over.

Rose frowned and trod over to the man like a child expecting a scolding. Abby held her breath to listen in on their distant conversation while the man eyed her with suspicion. Rudy's wool sweater was damp from the walk and smelled like a farm animal.

"You bring home another stray?" he asked.

"She needs help and I don't need another lecture."

Rose waved Abby over.

"Red, meet Robinson. Our tribal leader."

Robinson wiped his hand on his dirty jeans and accepted Abby's offered hand. His palm felt like soft, warm leather. He was a small African American man with a large presence.

"Hello, sir," Abby said and accepted the offer of his handshake. He clasped her tiny hand in both of his in a gesture both warm and pragmatic.

"It is a pleasure to meet you," she said.

CHAPTER 23

The two-hand shake held her in place while he surveyed her, tilting his head side to side. His hands were rough and callused from a lifetime of labor.

Robinson smiled broadly displaying every gleaming white tooth in his head, but his eyes remained transfixed on Abby. When their eyes met there was a moment of recognition.

"Two rules." Robinson held up two crooked fingers. "Don't be trouble. Don't bring trouble. This isn't paradise, but it is our home."

Abby glanced around the cottonwoods that surrounded the peninsula. The trees leaned in sheltering the camp and dampening the noise from the nearby arteries leading commuters into downtown or out to the airport. The canopy above acted as an umbrella deflecting much of the freezing rain. In the fatal game of hide and seek she was playing with Aidan, this *was* paradise.

Chapter 24

Rudy and Otto hiked out of the cottonwoods and followed the line of the Raccoon River back to Martin Luther King Jr. Parkway and connected with the Meredith Bike Trail.

Rudy waited for Otto to explain the flophouses and motels Robinson mentioned. When it became apparent Otto was content to hike without words, Rudy burst forth with the questions swirling in his mind.

"Why doesn't Robinson stay at the shelter?" Rudy asked. He had to shout over the rumbling of the city's sand trucks and snow plows rolled out of downtown dispatched to the major arteries.

"Shelters get overcrowded. There's fights and gang activity."

Rudy stopped in his trudging and turned back to look at Otto. "There are gangs in a shelter?"

"Gangs have a recruiting field day in a homeless shelter. Gangs give men a sense of belonging, a sense of family. Bangers offer a way out of the shelter and off the street."

They crossed over the Raccoon River and used the trail to cut back under the bridge they'd just traversed.

Rudy shook his head.

"What's the matter, Cowboy?"

"Gangs and pimps in Des Moines. You and Robinson talk about it like it's a weather report." Rudy wasn't as intimately acquainted with the city as Otto or Robinson, but the two opposing personalities of Des

CHAPTER 24

Moines weren't lining up.

"Gangs and pimps are the realities just like the weather report. No city in the Bible belt is without a dark side."

They crossed under the MLK Bridge. The roar of cars passing overhead was deafening but faded fast. When Rudy looked up, he spotted several bedrolls tucked into the spaces where the road above met earth.

"Why'd you tell Robinson that Abby was my friend and not my girlfriend?" Rudy stepped around piles of trash and debris encroaching on the trail.

"Most homeless women are trying to escape an abusive relationship. If I told Robinson that Abby was your lady, he'd assume you gave her a reason to hit the streets. Out here people trust friends far more than family or lovers."

Rudy tightened his scarf around his neck. The two bridges spanning the river's elbow at the low-lying flood plains created a wind tunnel. The breeze coming off the Raccoon reached its icy fingers under Rudy's every layer and massaged his pale skin.

"It's fucked up. But the people we are closest to are the ones that can cause the most pain," Otto said.

Rudy paused to regain his bearing and catch his breath. This short hike was no more strenuous than most of his daily chores on the farm, but he was winded, fatigued and his muscles ached.

"How do you know I didn't hurt her?" Rudy asked.

"You walked into the shelter like John Wayne saunters into a saloon looking to scare up a posse." A cloud passed over Otto's placid face like the past rolling over on itself washing him in misery and regret. "I've known bad men. Evil men. And you're not one of them."

They headed down a sharp slope next to the river and under the Fleur Drive Bridge. Otto wandered around under the bridge looking up into the ledges of the overpass's structure. Stuff was shoved into those ledges, but no one hid there.

"Ever heard of The Order or David Eden Lane?"

Rudy shook his head.

Otto recovered his tranquil demeanor as the stress dissolved from his face, tense shoulders relaxed and his fisted hands opened. "Lane was the founder of the neo-Nazi movement in the United States. Like I said, I've known very evil men. My dad helped David Lane run his publishing company."

Rudy studied Otto to see if he was pulling his leg, but the man's expression wasn't hiding a grin and his cheeks weren't puffed out like he had a mouthful of bullshit.

"I was born and raised to be a white supremacist and pass my genes on to an Aryan woman and stop the Zionist conspiracy. I was David's prodigy, his most devoted pupil until he was arrested in eighty-five. I was eighteen when they took him away." Otto's eyelids drooped and the corners of his mouth pulled down into an expression of deep sadness.

"What'd you do then?" Rudy asked the question but wasn't sure he wanted to know the answer.

"I was fucking brainwashed. I knew it wasn't right but I didn't see a way out of the life. My mom encouraged me to take multiple wives to have more children and keep the Aryan bloodline alive. I wasn't buying it. She brought home women for me, most of which were coerced or drugged.

"I left Idaho and moved to Denver. I got high one night, drove into the Five Points neighborhood and robbed a liquor store. I left the family and the life. Used the money to move to LA."

The answer surprised Rudy in its simplicity, although he was certain much of the story had been whitewashed over. "How'd you end up working for the shelter?"

"I took up with a bad crowd in LA, got hooked on meth and ended up in rehab. Turned my life around, got a drug counseling degree and here I am."

CHAPTER 24

Rudy paused in his thoughts. Rudy kicked at the pile of trash blown against a bridge support.

"Wanna know the most fucked up part of this whole damned thing?" Otto asked with a snort.

"Nazis, meth addiction and polygamy aren't enough?" Rudy asked.

Otto tilted his head to the side conceding Rudy's point. "A few years ago, I did one of those DNA ancestry tests. Took a swab of DNA from my mouth and sent it in. Turns out I descend from ancient Israelites."

Rudy shook his head and furrowed his brow in confusion. Aside from being a hotbed of ethnic and religious tensions, he knew little about Israel.

"I'm an ethnic Jew." Otto rocked back on his heels, tossed his head to the sky and cackled to the falling rain. His whole body jiggled and shook with him. "I'm fucking Jewish."

Rudy watched the man laugh without sharing his mirth. His emotions were a tumbled mess and he didn't know how to respond. Too much had happened. He rocked back and forth on his feet and rubbed the center of his chest where his upset stomach seemed to be burning a hole through his ribs.

When Otto recovered from the giggles, he glanced around the corner of the pedestrian trail looking for something or someone. While Otto's biography was intriguing, it wasn't getting them any closer to Abby.

"Why are we wandering around under this bridge?"

"There's some guys you should talk to," he said turning to face Rudy. "Come on."

Chapter 25

Aidan strode past an abstract sculpture of a head of wheat that was an assault on the senses, like the artist – or rather, welder – was drunk at the acetylene tank. He wandered into the homeless shelter expecting to see nuns or monks given the Franciscan moniker, but the reception desk was empty. He followed the noise into a small cafeteria to find a handful of people cloistered around a television in the corner watching a local news personality standing outside his parents' house. His senior photo filled the flat screen tv. Although the picture was taken two years ago, there was little resemblance to the man he'd become, the man he'd constructed from the 140 pound weakling. He ducked back out the way he came before anyone noticed him or recognized him from the photo on the flat screen.

At the entryway he noticed two rubber door stoppers and scooped them up in one fluid motion as he returned to the outside world. He tucked them into his hoodie pocket. Back at the garish sculpture he scanned the parking lot and spotted the Cadillac as it glistened with a thin layer of ice. He flipped the hood of his sweatshirt up and stalked toward the car. As he marched passed a battered and rusted out Ford Escort, he snapped the antenna off and bent the tip to a 45-degree angle.

At the Cadillac he didn't waste any time looking around. Fortune favored the bold. If he looked suspect then someone would be suspicious. He jammed the door stop between the door and jam wedging it deep in the rubber gasket. A few inches closer to the door hinges he stuck the other stop into the widening gap pushing it down with the palm of his hand. He'd gained an inch of clearance and slid the busted antenna into the car angling for the unlock button.

After missing twice and swearing under his breath, he hit the mark and slumped into the car. Even if he didn't already know this wasn't Rudy's car, the proof was in the stench. It smelled like a woman – fresh laundry, lavender and femininity. Additionally, a pair of earrings sat forgotten in the cup holder and a box of tissues sat in the backseat within easy reach of the driver. Women paid attention to such creature comforts in their cars, while men chose to focus on engine size.

There was nothing of Rudy's in the car aside from a stack of fliers bearing Abby's face. He found a Sharpie in the center console and made some art of his own.

Chapter 26

The traffic was a deep rumble as cars poured out of downtown, some headed home, some for flights to distant holiday celebrations. Rudy trudged along behind Otto as they left the Fleur overpass and headed toward the next viaduct. Three men stood in a loose circle under the bridge.

"Men who have spent time inside the system don't like the rules and regiments of shelter life. These guys are the nicest felons you'll ever meet."

Rudy scratched his head. "You talk about Des Moines like it is Los Angeles or Detroit."

Otto laughed. His chubby belly shook like he was the jolly fat man himself. If only Rudy could sit on Santa's lap and wish for an early Christmas miracle.

"Why are you laughing?" Rudy asked. Anger flushed his cold cheeks and crinkled his brow.

"Calm down." Otto lifted his hands up as if to surrender. "Iowa is at the heart of the meth trade and I-80 is a prime drug trafficking highway. The black and Mexican gangs from the coasts have smaller units here in Des Moines, helping traffic the drugs out of Iowa and funnel them to the coasts."

"So, Iowa is the hub of a supply chain?"

"Yeah. Something like that. It don't take a fancy business degree to

CHAPTER 26

figure that out. After NAFTA was signed into law, a lot of manufacturing jobs were shipped to Mexico for cheaper non-union labor. Without high-paying, low-skill jobs, meth became big business. Instead of using the drug to stay awake while pulling a double shift on the factory floor, they use it to stay awake to cook more crank."

"I'm sure George Bush Senior didn't see that one coming," Rudy said.

"You had to notice that Newton is self-destructing now that Maytag is closed."

Newton, a small town between Grinnell and Des Moines, was once a manufacturing hub boasting the world headquarters of Maytag. Since Maytag sold out to Whirlpool, the town now boasted the highest unemployment in the state. The factory workers that used government resources for career retraining either left the area or commuted to Des Moines. The deserted homes of Maytag employees were now host to meth labs and grow rooms like a miniature Detroit.

Otto stopped and pulled a bottle from his backpack. "You're going to need this."

Rudy took the flask-sized bottle of Jameson Irish Whiskey and studied it for a moment before sliding it into his coat pocket.

"I call them the three wise men. Don't know much about them. They must live around here, but I have no idea where. If they lived up there..." Otto pointed up to Terrace Hill, the governor's mansion that overlooked them from the bluff above. "We'd all be much better off."

"They just hang out here by the river?"

"Sure." Otto shrugged as if it all made sense in his world.

They crossed from the bike path onto the floodplain of the Raccoon River and under two viaducts carrying commuters into downtown or out to Des Moines International Airport. The thunder of tires and engines was deafening. After a few minutes, the roar of traffic on the bridge faded like someone turned down the volume.

The three men greeted Otto with smiles and handshakes, while they eyed Rudy with weary resignation. The men looked like brothers: same resigned look, graying hair and sloped shoulders. Rudy differentiated them by outerwear: camouflage, wool overcoat and layered sweatshirts.

"What's the topic of the day?" Otto asked.

"We were discussing the decline of the American family." The man paused and looked Rudy over from head to toe. "Maybe farm subsidies would be a more appropriate topic."

The men remained in a tight circle and Rudy continued to talk hoping one of them would step aside to let him in. Rudy felt like a dog left out in the cold scratching at the door to be let in.

"Cowboy, you got a farm?"

Rudy bobbed his head in affirmation.

"You got cows?"

"No, sir."

"Jesus. Don't call me sir. I work for a fucking living."

"Cattle aren't environmentally sustainable nor profitable. We rent out our pastures in the winter for other farmers' cattle to graze."

The men all looked down at their coffee mugs at the same time. Otto motioned for Rudy to keep talking by twirling his finger in a circle out of the sight line of the men.

"It's cheaper to buy a cow from the meat locker than raise my own. We raise corn, beans, chickens, goats and just enough hogs to feed my family."

The man in the camouflage jacket lifted his arms to the surrounding river and floodplain. "If you was to make this land sustainable, what'd you do?"

Rudy looked around. While this was a ridiculous exercise, he needed their help.

"I'd rely on quick growing veggies like onions and radishes. With the threat of floods, I'd stay away from long-term crops like corn or tomatoes or beans. A goat or two for milk and a good laying hen. The

CHAPTER 26

right animals and crops it doesn't take much land to support yourself."

"If only we can plant cigarette trees and get the goat to piss Johnny Walker," Wool overcoat said. The men chuckled in unison.

"Wouldn't that be the life?" another one said, with smoke rolling out of his crooked nose.

The men shifted and allowed Rudy to enter their circle.

"What you need from us, Cowboy?"

Rudy looked at Otto and considered his words. "My sister is missing. Wondering if you've seen her."

Each man gave the photo a long look and frowned. The mood shifted from jokes about farm life to reality.

"She get tired of collecting eggs and run off?"

Rudy chewed on his mouth and kicked at the loose gravel.

"You sure she ain't hiding at her boyfriend's place?"

Rudy tried to clear his throat but the phlegm wouldn't budge from its resting place on his vocal chords.

"No boyfriend," Otto said.

One of the men pulled a stainless steel flask from his back pocket and took a long pull before offering it around the circle. When it was passed to Rudy, he looked at Otto for instruction. Otto gave him a tiny nod. Rudy tipped back the flask allowing the foul liquid to touch is lips without taking it into his mouth. He thought of Bill Clinton's infamous lie about not inhaling. The noxious whiskey scent filled his palate and he sputtered.

The men laughed at him. Wool overcoat slapped him on the back. "You'll get used to the burn."

Rudy laughed. "I hope not."

"If we see your sister, we'll let Otto know," Camo guy said. All the men nodded their agreement.

Without guidance from Otto, Rudy slipped the small bottle of Jameson whiskey from his coat pocket and handed it to Camo guy. "Thank you for your help."

Rudy and Otto made their way back toward Martin Luther King Jr. Parkway as clouds roiled and turned overhead.

"I gotta ask," Rudy said. "Why are you helping me?" Self-pity blew over him like wind blowing off the river pelting him with drops of freezing drizzle.

"You've asked me dozens of questions. Let me ask you one first."

"Fair enough."

"Why Abby?" Otto asked.

Rudy's eyebrows furrowed.

"You're in love with her, right?"

"Yeah," Rudy said without hesitation.

"Why her?"

"She's the most beautiful person I've ever met. The more I get to know her, the more amazing she is."

"What makes her so beautiful?"

"She has the faintest freckles on her eyelids and she has this..." He paused and looked off into the distance. "Sadness."

Otto squinted at Rudy with a knowing grin.

"A sadness so deep and sincere that it breaks your heart. She thinks she hides it under her clothes and behind her bookishness. All I want to do is take it away, because when she smiles nothing is wrong with the world. Her joy is so complete."

"Shit, son. We gotta get you a guitar. You'd make a killing in Nashville." Otto laughed and his belly shook.

"When you're done mocking, wanna tell me why you're helping me?"

Otto paused in his march back to the shelter and turned to face Rudy. "You're the American dream. Everything I wish I could've been if I hadn't been born into the Nazi life."

"Look. I don't need your bullshit."

"You're like John Wayne and little Opie Cunningham all rolled into

CHAPTER 26

one. Who wouldn't help Opie find his missing dog or help the Duke bring justice to the West."

It'd been a long time since someone spoke to Rudy like he was a little kid too big for his britches. It happened a lot when he first took over the farm, but the men at the farm bureau and feed store soon took him seriously.

"Look at me. I'm covered in tattoos that spell hate."

"One says, 'hat.'" Rudy said trying to make light of the conversation he started.

"You noticed that."

"Hard to miss."

Otto shrugged. "Either way. Happily ever after is not in my future. If I can help someone else, that's the ballgame."

They passed by the old Ford factory again. Des Moines had been able to reinvent itself after the decline of manufacturing, but watching cars roll off an assembly line in Des Moines would have been awesome.

"There's no kids," Rudy said.

"School doesn't let out until tomorrow," Otto said.

"I mean there are no young people on the streets."

"The average population of Iowa is old," Otto explained. "Median age is something like forty."

"But I haven't seen a single teenager. The TV leads me to believe there's more kids on the streets."

"Iowa has a decent juvy system and the foster care system is at least a generation ahead of other states. There's a good safety net in place for kids in this state. Most kids that run away because they feel misunderstood usually go home in a day or two. More determined runaways leave the area for someplace warmer. These are pretty mean streets in the winter."

Rudy danced in place and kicked the base of the wheat sculpture. "I gotta keep looking."

"Well, Cowboy. It's getting late. I gotta close up shop for the night, but you call me if I be for any help on Friday."

Rudy nodded and looked to the darkening sky with a deepening frown.

Chapter 27

Garrison dropped his keys into the empty fishbowl by the backdoor. The bowl once held Sarah's Siamese Fighting Fish. She loved that fish intensely for about a week, but it lived on for a year unnoticed and neglected. Nancy repurposed the bowl, as she did with all things. Nothing stood idle in their house for long without finding a new crafty purpose: clothes became quilts, old jewelry became wind chimes and broken dishes became mosaic flower pots.

Peanut butter cookies, his favorite, cooled on an embroidered tea towel on the kitchen island. Janis Joplin sang the blues from Nancy's sewing studio on the floor above. He stacked a few cookies in his hand, grabbed a glass of iced tea and headed upstairs to his den.

At the top of the stairs, Sarah's door stood open wide. She was perched on her rumpled bed facing the door and thumbing through a family photo album.

"Whatcha looking at?" Garrison asked.

"Pictures of Vicky," she said and smiled, but the corners of her eyes turned down. "Before the drugs."

Garrison handed her two cookies and set the iced tea on Sarah's nightstand. He sat on the bed next to her. She spread the photo album across their laps.

With a bright smile and missing front teeth, Vicky's sweet innocent face looked up from the page. She sat in front of a festive Christmas tree showing off her new Barbie dolls, while her baby sister drooled down Nancy's shirt.

"You were too young to remember this, but Vicky was convinced you were going to grow up into a Barbie doll." Garrison reached over and played with Sarah's long blonde and lavender hair.

"Vicky wasn't much of a feminist, was she?" Sarah asked.

They both laughed and Sarah leaned her head into Garrison's chest.

"What was she like?" Sarah asked. "All I remember are the drugs and the fights."

Garrison flipped through album pages until he found a picture of Vicky and Sarah sitting on top of a slide. Sarah clutched a doll as Vicky held her.

"You remember this?" Garrison asked pointing at the photo.

Sarah shook her head and munched on a cookie. Catching crumbs in a cupped hand before they spilled onto the photo.

"You were obsessed with this Strawberry Shortcake doll, carried it everywhere. We were on vacation, driving through South Dakota heading for Yellowstone. We stopped for a picnic lunch, you two played in the park, before we headed west again.

"We were on the road for an hour before you realized that Strawberry Shortcake wasn't there. You left her on top of that slide. Oh God, how you cried and begged me to go back and get her. I swear you cried for hours."

"I don't remember that." Her brow was furrowed as she searched her father's face.

"That night we stayed at this little shit bag motel in Jackson, Wyoming. We ran over to the K-mart to get snacks for the next day. We lost Vicky in the store. Looked for her everywhere. We were telling a store manager what happened when she showed up with a new Strawberry Shortcake doll in her hands. She bought the new doll with the allowance she'd been saving for a cowboy hat." Tears welled in Garrison's eyes.

CHAPTER 27

Sarah closed the photo album and set it aside while she bounded out of bed and rooted around the bottom of the closet for a minute and came back with the well-loved doll tucked under one arm. She set the doll on Garrison's lap.

"How you doing, Daddy?" She sat back down next to him on the bed and wrapped her arm around him. "You look worried."

He kissed the top of her head. "Wishing I knew where Abby was," he said. "What's she like?"

"What's the word I'm looking for? I learned it for the ACT. She's out of place in time." Sarah paused and look at the ceiling. "I got it! She's anachronistic."

"How do you mean?" Garrison asked.

"It's like she stepped out of a 1980s Brat Pack movie. Super preppy clothes, no cell phone, sheltered, naive but super smart. Like Ivy League, going to save the world someday kinda smart. But she's really quiet. She doesn't talk much in class, but you know she knows all the answers, but it was like she did not want to be a know-it-all."

"What about Rudy? Is he a good guy?"

"I never thought he had any interest in girls until he started dating Abby. It wasn't like I thought he was gay or anything. I thought he'd grow up to be like a bachelor farmer, just him and his farm." She paused. "They're an odd couple. But he really loves her."

"How can you tell?" Garrison asked.

"They went to Homecoming together this year. You should see the way he looks at her. I can't explain it. He never took his eyes off her. It must be something to be loved like that. I hope somebody looks at me that way someday."

"He's got to get through me first." Garrison sat up straighter and puffed out his chest.

"Daddy!" she squealed and slapped his shoulder.

They sat in silence for a few moments before she said, "Thanks for talking to me like this."

"What do you mean?"

"It's like I'm consulting on a case." She smiled. "You had enough respect for me to come to me. I think that's pretty cool."

Garrison felt his tear ducts prickle again. Hearing his daughter say he was 'pretty cool' was better than any Father's Day card. He cleared his throat and tried to push those thoughts aside.

"If I learned anything from Vicky, it was to be quiet," Sarah said. "She fed me candy so I wouldn't tell you her friends were over when she was babysitting. She'd slap me when I was too loud. She taught me to be silent."

"That's why you didn't talk," Garrison said. Each year of preschool and early grade school, the teacher would call him and his wife with concerns that Sarah wouldn't talk. These concerns didn't subside until Vicky was deep into her addictions. "What does that have to do with Abby?"

"It took years to unlearn the lessons Vicky taught me," Sarah said. "What did Abby learn from Aidan?"

Garrison pulled his daughter into a sideways hug, his arm wrapped around her slender shoulders with Strawberry Shortcake between them.

Chapter 28

Rudy's eyes drooped as he struggled to keep his eyes on the blacktop leading into town. He's stopped at every truck stop and rest area along I-80 between Des Moines and Grinnell. He posted the missing fliers everywhere he could: bulletin boards, restrooms and next to gas pumps. He rubbed his eyes and took another swig of bitter gas station coffee topped off with four packets of sugar. The acidic drink reignited the heartburn in the center of his chest.

He pulled on the road leading to his parents' farm. Headlights flashed in his rearview and approached at a rate of speed inadvisable on the poorly maintained country road. The SUV swerved to the side like it was going to pass him. Instead of allowing the aggressor to run him off the road, he pulled into his grandparent's driveway. The SUV continued down the road in a roar of engine and dust.

Maybe Garrison was trailing him like he was in pursuit of a suspect. Maybe it was Aidan trying to push him into a ditch. He was certainly crazy enough to try it. But as he sat in the driveway, he decided the encounter was nothing more sinister than drunk kids out for a joy ride before a day of forced family togetherness.

Jon and Edith's house sat on one hundred sixty acres of prime farmland. Large white wrap-around porches stood in contrast against red brick walls even under the waning moon. The huge live oaks flanking the large house begged for children to hang from their branches with maybe a tire swing or treehouse. It was the kind of house where cheery Christmas stories took place.

Jonathan Edwards started farming this plot of land after returning home from the forgotten war in Korea. His enterprising and industrious wife saved all his income from running mine wire for the field artillery battalion as well as her meager wages in a Folgers coffee tin under quilts and Pyrex bakeware and hand embroidered linens in her hope chest. When Jonathan returned home to Iowa after finishing his obligation to the Army at Ft. Bliss, Texas, Edith had saved enough for the down payment on the farmstead.

Rudy scrambled out of the car, grabbed Abby's backpack and strode to the front porch that greeted the long driveway. He fingered the chains that suspended a rustic swing and imagined long afternoons spent on the swing with a good novel and a pitcher of lemonade.

Cinnamon, vanilla and lemon-scented furniture polish culminated into a familiar and comforting scent. The house smelled the same as it always had, like his grandparents were just gone for the night rather than disappearing to the beaches of south Texas until June. The overworked radiator ticked in an otherwise quiet house.

The weeks before they headed south, grandma dedicated her time to rearranging every piece of furniture so it felt like she was coming home to a new house each summer. The redecoration was figured into the family's farming schedule after the harvest and before winterizing the barns and outbuildings. The Edwards men reported to Nana's house promptly at nine each morning before the Chevy Silverado and Airstream hit the highway.

Tonight Rudy was thankful he'd already learned the new furniture arrangement as he negotiated his way through the darkened house. Without turning on a single light, he made his way into the guest bedroom he and Abby shared the night before. He flipped on the bedside lamp and searched the pockets of her coat: an embroidered handkerchief,

CHAPTER 28

a ticket stub and useless pocket lint. Although he wasn't sure what clue hid in her coat, he'd hoped for something more substantial like an old movie where the hardened detective with a heart of gold finds an address or phone number in the damsel's trash. But this wasn't a movie and nothing was going to be that easy.

He was unaware that he was crying until he tasted the salt streaming down his face. The night before, Abby laughed as Rudy fumbled with her buttons. The flaps of her oxford shirt splayed open exposing the front of a pink lace bra and a thin line of white flesh from sternum to navel.

She looked up at him and smiled — pale pink lips hitched to one side in a smirk. Her eyebrows raised and eyes widened which sent tiny crinkles skittering out from the corners of her eyes. Rudy loved those little lines.

He drew in a deep breath in the hopes he'd calm his galloping heart. He parted her shirt and caressed her stomach with his fingertips. Abby moaned and buried her face in this neck, her lips fluttering over his collarbone like a dozen butterflies kissing his goose pimpled flesh. After her shirt hit the floor, she reached for his belt and fumbled with his buckle.

It was going too fast. Too many of his friends could barely recall their first time or they recounted it as a hot, bumbling mess in the back seat of dad's car. That wasn't what he wanted for himself and it certainly wasn't what he wanted for Abby.

She left go of his waistline when he shifted back on his heels. Her mouth parted and her brow furrowed like she had done something wrong. He kissed her cheek as a way of reassurance. She took his forearm in her hands and stroked his skin from wrist to elbow adding pressure with each pass. She cupped his elbow and lifted his extended arm until it rested on her shoulder. She continued her massage up his arm to his biceps and triceps.

Then his hands drifted to her chest. He stroked the crescent mounds of flesh swelling above the cups of her bra. Rudy heard the breath catch in her throat as he slid a single finger under the lacy restraints. Her erect nipple felt like a tiny marble perched on her soft skin.

His spinning head and churning stomach returned him to the empty room. He pulled off his Ariat boots, flipped off the lights and settled on top of the bed quilts using her coat as a blanket. From his position he could see out the bedroom's bay window overlooking the adjoining farms illuminated in the moonlight. The corn and bean fields rolled seamlessly from his parent's farm to his brother's small acreage to his grandparent's lot. At the eastern edge of the farmland a small house sat on a forty-acre plot. He hoped to acquire the Vander Linden farm before the end of the year.

Under his business plan, they would combine all the acreages into a single corporation that supported the three families. The key to this success was diversification. Corn, soybeans, goats, chickens, wild turkeys, prairie land and a few hogs. The crops supported the animals and the animals fed them through all seasons. The addition of the small farm would allow them easier access for the tractors and combines as well as an access road to the land they rented. It would also allow Rudy to move out. In charge of one of the largest farms in Poweshiek County, he was tired of mom nagging him to clean his room.

Rudy fantasized that he and Abby would be happy in the new house. He'd allow her to fix up the house anyway she chose. He wondered how she'd transform the space to make it her own, but he didn't care what she did with the house's modest rooms as long as she was there to brighten the space. But the fantasy faded as he thought about her heading off to Stanford next fall.

He'd never mentioned this plan to Abby. He didn't want to scare her with his plans for their future. Didn't want to alarm her with talk of a wedding in the restored prairie and children playing hide and seek across the thousand combined acres. But that didn't stop his mind from creating an idyllic future for them. He clung to his waking dreams to lull

CHAPTER 28

him to sleep.

* * * * *

Aidan was thankful that he didn't blow up this house as he pulled the Jeep around to the garage. It served him well the first night and since he'd forgotten to turn down the heat the cottage proved a warm respite.

He nestled into his bed of moldy drapes with every muscle in his body weary and aching. He hadn't done anything taxing in the last twenty-four hours so he wasn't sure why he hurt so bad. Maybe the fatigue was a physical manifestation of his frustration. Now that he'd set his plan in motion, the waiting and searching was excruciating. If only he'd been more patient and calculating the night before and waited for Abby to return home. If he'd just waited for her, this would all be over.

He surrendered to sleep imagining Rudy crying into the ashes of Flynn's smoldering house and a pile of Abby's bones.

Chapter 29

The flashlight turned miner's lamp cast fidgety light circles on the thin nylon walls of Rose's tent. Although she'd only slept a few hours in the trunk of Daddy's car, she was wired and anxious. A stack of battered paperbacks filled the corner of the tent nearest her makeshift pillow devised from a folded blanket in a tee-shirt pillowcase. Authors she'd never heard of: Carlos Castaneda, William Gibson, Russell Davis and W.C. Jameson. She picked up "End of All Seasons" by Davis and thumbed through its pages hoping to get lost and fall asleep in another world.

Rose rolled over next to her. "Oh God. Don't read that one," she said.

Abby fingered the colorful cover.

Rose plucked the book from Abby's hands and tossed it toward the bottom of the tent. "That guy's an asshole." Rose handed her a smaller, thinner book. "Here check this one out."

Abby cracked open Jon Krakauer's "Into the Wild" and tried to follow the tale of another lost soul wandering the world but her racing mind kept her rooted to the tiny peninsula in the middle of Des Moines.

She cloaked herself in a sleeping bag and tent and prayed to whatever God might be listening that Aidan wouldn't find her. The thin, nylon walls offered little protection from him or the elements. She'd kept Rudy safe by drawing the danger away from him, but she was now racked with pangs of guilt knowing that her mere presence endangered this small

CHAPTER 29

band of people just trying to survive.

She remained frozen much of the night staring at the tent zipper, expecting it to split open and her brother appear. The tent reminded Abby of hiding in her closet. She collected blankets and pillows from the linen closet and constructed a nest for herself among her shoes and below her shirts hanging in color order. She retreated to this space when life overwhelmed her with emotions she didn't know how to handle.

Abby's terror didn't rise from loud, arguing voices but from silence and veiled threats conveyed in glances between father and son. She'd always known that she was the chosen child, the apple of Daddy's eye. It was her brother that suffered torment and torture in dark, hollow places beneath the house she'd once considered home. His screams and tears carried through the ductwork and leaked from the walls.

Hours ago, she'd been floating on a cloud. Released from Rudy's loving arms she felt light as a balloon buoyed by love rather than helium. Now primal fear and adrenaline raced through her veins. She rediscovered a desperate, screaming fear she felt long ago after stumbling across her brother's tortured body in what she thought was a game of hide and seek. Abby hadn't been able to access that memory until now. She curled under his arm and shoulder to help him up, but his bloody feet would not support his weight even though he weighed less than his petite sister.

Abby told herself that he fell while trying to reach the sugar cookies mom kept on the highest shelf, but somewhere at the back of her mind she knew better. The red ribbons of flesh hanging from his soles could not have come from a fall. After she found her brother that day, she hid in her closet for weeks. Through childhood she developed a gift for self-delusion, her mind convincing her heart and soul that nothing was wrong. She didn't know what was worse her self-deception or her mother's addictions. Maybe the vodka and Valium cocktail were a fate that waited for her when the current course of duplicity stopped working.

Aside from the pounding of her heart and Rose's soft snores, the camp remained quiet as any winter forest. But she wouldn't give into the temptation of thinking that her pursuer wasn't circling: a fox stalks silently, an owl is quiet until talons pierce the flesh of prey.

Before ditching the car in the parking garage, Abby's survival strategy relied on movement. She drove her father's Volvo in endless circles through upscale West Des Moines neighborhoods, through the Eastside streets of shotgun shacks and strange, fetid smells of corn and livestock processing. Although environmentally unfriendly, the constant motion comforted her. But the Volvo was out of gas and she was out of cash. Attempting to sleep in Rose's tent felt like a last resort before surrendering to her fate and to the slaughter.

Motion equated to safety. Movement was security. Her current stationary status did not equal emotional safety. Without distraction, she had too much time to dwell upon the inaction of her past. She knew, but did nothing. She saw the scars on his frail body, but said nothing. In her silence, she was as guilty as Daddy. She failed her brother. This was her penance. She should surrender and allow him to string her up from the nearest tree or light her up like a roman candle. If she wasn't going to submit to his violence, she should find a new hiding spot away from other people.

She wouldn't surrender to tears. Although they stung her eyes, she wouldn't let them win. Crying meant purging and she had to hold on to every drop of pain to fuel her anger.

In her short, sheltered life this was the first time she'd slept outside the confines of her own bedroom. Instead of thinking of herself as doomed for death, she tried to reframe the thought as a grand adventure. She wasn't a coward in hiding rather an explorer seeking a new outpost in the wilds of Des Moines. Abby floated in and out of consciousness imagining she was on an expedition across the US with Rose and Chris McCandless by her side.

Chapter 30

Rudy pushed through the back door of his parents' house and was comforted by the smell of home: laundry tumbling in the drier, pies cooling on the breakfast table and the vanilla candle mom lit when cutting onions.

Exhausted, Rudy slumped onto a bar stool at the kitchen counter, opened a loaf of French bread and began tearing it into half inch pieces for his mother's stuffing. This was his one contribution to mom's annual Thanksgiving feast.

Mom either possessed car radar or uncanny hearing. She knew if a car was coming before it touched the gravel of their driveway. She knew he was home and was probably preparing a litany of questions and barrage of guilt. Dad, however, chose to get answers from his wife rather than asking.

Sounds of dragging boxes and dropped trinkets filtered through the ceiling and announced Dad's annual pilgrimage into the attic to dig out the Christmas decorations.

The vintage Pyrex bowl soon heaped with little bits of bread and he laid his head on the cool granite countertop and closed his eyes. The images of Des Moines' darker places and marginalized people played on a loop behind his eyelids like a twisted drive-in movie.

"Oh thank, God," Mom said. "You're home." Flannel pajama pants and Grinnell College sweatshirt were her standard uniform after she woke at three to put the enormous bird in the oven. "Where have you been?"

"Looking for Abby."

"That's what the police are for." She put a hand on her slender hips and wagged a finger in his face. "You realize your mother's been worried sick about you. Took off in my car and I had to learn about Abby's family from the goddamn news."

"I'm not the one you need to worry about," Rudy muttered without raising his head from the cool counter.

"Listen mister." She threw a towel at him. "I'll worry about you until the day I die and you can bet your boots I'll be in heaven worrying about you, too."

"You sound pretty confident about that heaven bit."

"Don't you start with me," she warned.

She rounded the corner toward him as quick as she could on stumpy legs. Rudy flinched expecting to be pummeled by her tiny fists. Instead she wrapped her arms around him squeezing him so tight he thought his eyes would pop out.

"I was gone for a day." He held up one finger to further illustrate his point. "One day. Not a week."

She pinched his chin between thumb and forefinger. "There's two dead bodies and Abby's missing." She let go of him and walked over to the fridge shaking her head the whole time. "There are things a mother should never have to say."

"You really think I want to be searching homeless camps and under bridges looking for my girlfriend?" He massaged the waxy scar on his chest trying to work out the tension he felt since Garrison showed up on the farm. The invisible strings that held his heart in the center of his chest dissolved in the flood of grief. His heart – the strongest, but most fragile muscle in his body – fell into the pit of his stomach.

"Is that where you've been?"

CHAPTER 30

Rudy put his head down on the counter and rubbed his clammy hands on his legs to quell the tremors. His left arm went numb and he stopped rubbing. Sheila put her hand on his back and for the first time Rudy felt the flop sweat gathering between his shoulders.

"You're shaking," she said as she stroked his upper back. "Are you okay?"

He tried to shrug her off swatting at her hands, but she wasn't deterred. She wrapped her arms around him from behind in what he initially thought was an awkward hug. But she rested her ear on his back and felt his wrist for a pulse.

"Come on, Mom," Rudy said. "I'm fine."

"No, you're not. You're pale and your eyes are dilated."

"I'm fucking tired," he said and swatted at her again.

"We're going to the hospital."

"Seriously, Mom. I'm fine. Just need to rest."

Rudy stood from his bar stool, but his stocking feet slid on the tile floor and he stumbled. Sheila caught him on the way down and wedged her shoulder under his arm.

"Richard!" she yelled.

Dad's boots clomped down the stairs and ran into the kitchen. He paused at the door eyes wide.

"Get me the aspirin." Her voice rose two octaves from alto to shrill and reverberated off the cabinets.

Dad's eyes grew wider as he looked from wife to son and then disappeared.

"I'm done arguing with you." She whispered in his ear. " We're going to the hospital."

Dad returned a moment later — hard leather soles scrambling across porcelain tiles. "I'll get the car."

"I'll go, but you don't have to carry me," Rudy said.

She dug her fingers into his ribs and guided him out the backdoor to

Richard's waiting car.

Chapter 31

As the hour hand ticked closer to noon, Aidan strode out to his Jeep, leaving the farmstead for what he hoped was the last time. He was rested and more determined. Thus far he failed to find Abby and finish his mission. Poking around Des Moines wasn't getting him closer to his sister. Other than Rudy, Abby didn't have any close friends. She preferred books to people, needlework over gossip and the piano over needless chatter. She didn't have a social network to help support her in this perceived time of need.

He imagined her terror when she found Mother dead in her bed or walked in on Father laid out on the floor with every orifice violated. The thought of her long sustained scream of terror gave him goosebumps as he warmed his hands on the Jeep's heat vent. He might have spared her life to watch her face. Hindsight wasn't just twenty-twenty, but the very impetus of regret. He should have waited for Abby to get home before he started Father's torture, strapped her to a chair and let the princess watch her king get dethroned.

I will always put the mission first.

As Aidan passed the spot where he'd killed the goat an enormous Golden Eagle rose up from the field while a trio of vultures circled overhead. The eagle made him smile like it was fate's way of letting him know he was on the right track.

At the road's curve he noticed the Edwards' Caddy barreling down the driveway. It cut the corner too tight and fishtailed onto the road kicking up dust and gravel and dirt. Three heads bounced back and forth as the car righted its path: mom and Rudy in the backseat, dad behind the wheel.

Aidan consider following – maybe someone found Abby – but the eagle sighting told him it was something different.

After the sedan crested the hill and joined the blacktop to town, he pulled down the driveway. At the backdoor, he walked right in. Country folk didn't believe in locks. Although his stomach ached with hunger pains, he skipped the buffet laid out on the kitchen table and climbed the back stairs in search of Rudy's room.

He strode past a small table with the marble chess set and the pieces paused mid-game. He was more interested in the shrine to Abby on top of the dresser. Photos of the couple, ticket stubs and other mementos of their relationship lined the pitted and worn wood. What a sentimental fool. Aidan pulled open the top drawer expecting to find a doll with locks of Abby's hair glued to it, but instead found neatly folded boxers and wool socks. He found nothing, not one clue. To calm himself he recited the soldier's creed.

On his way out of the bedroom he paused at the chess table and plucked up the carved marble, white queen and tucked it into his pocket.

At the bottom of the stairs, he could no longer resist the savory aromas wafting out of the kitchen. He didn't know which to eat first – the pies or the cookies – so he shoveled both into his face by the fistful. At the refrigerator he used his hands to scoop mouthfuls of potato salad, coleslaw and seven-layer dip into his mouth.

After not eating for several days, everything tasted amazing. The handfuls that didn't make it into his mouth plopped to the floor and smeared the top of his boots but he was too consumed to care. He washed everything down with a can of Old Milwaukee. When his gut began to revolt against his gluttony, he finished a second beer and walked out to

CHAPTER 31

his idling Jeep. He left the fridge and backdoor ajar.

Chapter 32

A large hand reached under Abby's deep, warm nest of blankets and shook her. She yelped and covered her face to fend off the coming assault but the beating didn't come and the resulting quiet was broken by a high, trilling laugh.

"Wake up," Rose said. "It's the best day of the year!"

"What time is it?" Abby rubbed her eyes and pulled at her face as she sat up.

"Almost two. You were out like a light, sleepyhead."

Rose's face glowed with the joy of a child waking to Santa's bounty on Christmas. Her round cheeks were flushed with anticipation rather than the chilled air and her dark eyes turned up at the corners where they met deep laugh lines.

"Get up!" Rose bounced on her knees with each word.

"Do you have some clothes I could wear?" Abby asked.

Rose considered her for a moment before nodding. "My jeans'll fall off you," Rose said and dug through a pile of clothing on her side of the tent. "But these might work." Rose handed over folded denim and a heavy green sweater.

Abby wriggled out of her chinos and set Rudy's sweater to the side. She changed into Rose's clothes and slipped on her loafers.

"You're kidding me with those, right?" Rose asked pointing at Abby's shoes. The pristine loafers looked out of place in the drab surroundings.

CHAPTER 32

"Here." Rose handed her a pair of boots that saw their best days a decade ago. "Try these on."

Abby pulled off her shoes and tossed them to the corner of the tent. The boots were at least two sizes too big. Rose handed her a pair of thick, balled up socks. She crawled out of the tent after Rose. She then posed for her new friend like a silly bride in a romantic comedy. The sweater hung down to her fingertips and the bibs dwarfed her.

Rose giggled and knelt down in front of Abby. She rolled and cuffed the bottom of the pants and the sweater sleeves in a very sisterly moment.

When they crawled into the tent the night before, the camp was empty and quiet. It now buzzed with activity. It looked like a redneck family reunion: an oil fryer large enough to hold an enormous bird, a table laden with foil pans full of traditional Thanksgiving sides. South of the communal fire ring, card tables were lined up and draped in worn and tattered blankets.

Abby took a seat at the far end of the table. She pulled a quilt off the table onto her lap and watched the commotion. From her vantage point, she saw the whole camp as well as the trail to downtown. Rose danced around the fire chatting with each person in turn while supervising the seasoning of the enormous bird: more garlic, less oregano, Sterling's allergic to cayenne, kosher salt, none of that iodized crap.

A woman emerged from one of the shanties. She surveyed the camp and smiled at Abby. She approached Abby, floating over like a ghost – less walking, more gliding like a legless apparition returned to haunt the world. The illusion was bolstered by the woman's loose and billowy layers.

"Whatcha doing all the way over here?" she asked and settled into a lawn chair next to Abby.

"Feeling useless."

"Just relax," the woman said. Her voice low ans whispery like she was casting a spell. Enjoy the festivities."

Abby chewed on her cheeks as she considered the woman's dismissal. "I feel crazy and useless like the bit of sand they put in a hula hoop. No real purpose other than pleasant noise."

"Oh, honey." The woman reached over and patted Abby's hand. "Everyone's a bit of sand. Besides, I imagine insanity comes with its own vocabulary and metaphors."

Abby continued to pull the tissue off the inside of her mouth as her fingers played across the quilt's top until she found a place where the seams spread apart and batting poked through.

"Sterling," the woman said and offered her hand with a slender wrist full of bangles. "You must be Red."

Abby gave a weak smile and nod.

Sterling reached over and twirled a strand of red hair in her hand as her smile broadened. "Very appropriate."

Rose handed Abby a plastic party cup full of warm, mulled wine that tasted like liquid holiday cheer: cinnamon, oranges and vanilla. The first sip caused her to sputter, but the next gulp warmed her cheeks and the tips of her ears. The three women sat in silence sipping wine and watching the fire burn.

Robinson pulled up a folding lawn chair next to them and took nips from a battered, stainless steel flask while taking in the scene.

"Where you from, Red?" Robinson asked. "You plan on staying long?"

Abby stared down into her cup. The sickly, sweet smell tweaked her nose but the magic liquid warmed her from the inside. "I'm not sure," she said and drained her glass.

"Not sure where you're from? Or how long you stayin'?"

"Both," Abby said.

"What's with the questions?" Rose asked.

Sterling clucked her tongue and said, "Let the girl enjoy her beverage and be thankful for the small blessings."

"Fair enough," Robinson said. He lifted his hands into the air.

CHAPTER 32

Rose and Sterling had an easy relationship and communicated without words in brief glances and small gestures. Abby was jealous of their ease and comfort. They were quick to laugh and seemingly had few cares beyond the weather and enjoying each other's company.

The more Abby tried to adopt their demeanor the more her mind raced and revved her anxiety. Her neck and shoulders ached from tension. She pulled her shoulders down and tilted her head side to side stretching the muscles in her upper back.

The wine warmed her tummy. It also pulled at the corners of her mouth, forcing her to grin.

Rose refilled their cups and leaned back. She lit a cigarette, but blew the smoke away from Abby. She smoked with one hand and played with Abby's hair with the other.

Robinson moved to the other side of the fire, but Abby felt his eyes on her most of the afternoon. Maybe he'd seen her picture on the television or in a newspaper. Maybe this wasn't the place for her. She wasn't reassured when Rose got up and disappeared from the fire circle.

Abby should have driven farther. Instead of using her pocket change on soda and snacks that first morning on the run, she should've put the money in the gas tank and gone somewhere warmer. PBS showed a documentary on the Austin music scene a few weeks ago. It looked like a nice city. She could play the keyboards and join a band. She was aware that her daydreams were naive, but allowed herself the simple delusion. No one else needed to suffer or live in fear because she was too chicken shit and self-absorbed to save her own brother years ago. She celebrated the day he packed his Jeep and left for Dartmouth. He'd escaped on his own and she was relieved of her obligation.

Rose returned with her guitar in hand. She dropped a half-moon tambourine into Abby's lap with a wink. She flipped the guitar strap over her head and shook her hair out of the way like she was about to take center stage of the Ryman Auditorium and rock Nashville. She strummed a few times and adjusted the tuning pegs. With long, nimble fingers splayed over the fret board, she started with "Sweet Caroline."

Halfway through the first chorus the whole camp sang along. A few members of the camp disappeared and returned with instruments of their own: a harmonica, a ukulele and a five gallon bucket turned drum.

Although drunk on friendship and wine, Abby kept her eyes on the trail leading into camp waiting for Aidan to arrive.

Chapter 33

After a morning of staring at his whiteboards and yelling at state troopers to find the Flynn vehicles, Garrison was glad to be home.

He held Nancy and Sarah's hands as their arms circled the small dining table laden with their Thanksgiving meal. The rich, savory smell of roast turkey breast and stuffing lifted the cloud of the Flynn family tragedy and helped him focus on the moment.

"And bless this food for the nourishment of our bodies and souls. In your name we pray," Garrison said.

"Amen."

With his fork, he layered cranberry sauce, then Nancy's famous snowy white mashed potatoes and finally a thin sliver of the beautiful, golden bird. In his mouth he balanced and weighed the flavors until his palate proclaimed them in perfect harmony.

The shrill ring of the telephone pierced the serenity of the moment. Sarah eyed her father. Garrison looked at Nancy. She sighed. He finally nodded to Sarah. She rose from the table and answered the cordless extension in the front room.

"This is your best turkey, yet. What did you do different?" Garrison asked trying to distract them both from the impending bad news. Good news knocked on the front door, while bad news came in an unexpected phone call.

"Daddy, it's Mr. Edwards." She covered the receiver and added, "He sounds really upset."

Nancy reached over and squeezed his hand before he got up and took the phone from Sarah.

"Hello," Garrison said

"Rudy's had a heart attack," Richard said in a rush of words.

Garrison's mouth dropped open. Rudy wasn't old enough for a heart attack, maybe it was something else like drugs or a panic attack.

"How's Sheila holding up?" Garrison asked.

"She's not." Richard choked on his words.

"We'll be there."

Garrison returned the phone to the charging cradle and rubbed his temples. For five precious moments he'd been present with his own family before being pulled back into the darkness of the surrounding world.

"What's going on?" Nancy asked, her hand over her heart as she anticipated bad news.

"How would you feel about taking this to go?" Garrison asked, indicating the table.

* * * * *

The hospital hallway hummed with the dull buzz of machinery and the low, soft voices of those caring for the sick. Richard and Sheila huddled on a sofa in the visiting area. Sheila's face was red and tear-stained. Richard stroked her hair and kissed her forehead.

Nancy set the picnic basket she carried on a nearby chair. She withdrew a tablecloth a draped it over the coffee table and retrieved Tupperware dishes of their dinner and a bottle of chardonnay. Sheila shook her head and buried her face into Richard's chest.

"Today is about celebrating our blessings," Nancy said and patted

CHAPTER 33

Sheila's hand. "Dig in."

With Richard's urging, Sheila sat up, wiped her eyes and helped herself to a paper plate.

"What'd the doctors say?" Garrison asked as he cracked open the wine and divvied it into four plastic cups. He recognized the inquisitive tone he used during interrogations and he tried to change his tone.

"Not much." Richard scratched his head. "No heart attack. A slight arrhythmia due to exhaustion and overwhelming evidence of an overprotective mother."

Sheila's head snapped up, her dour expression replaced with tightly drawn lips as she glowered at Richard. "He needs Abby," she said and poked Richard in the chest.

"You know I taught Abby embroidery," Nancy said. In her infinite wisdom, Garrison's brilliant wife changed the subject.

Sheila looked up from her turkey and gave Nancy a feeble, crooked smile. "She gave me a needlework sampler for my birthday a few months ago. It's beautiful. You taught her well."

"Have you seen her backpack?" Sarah asked before cracking open a can of Diet Coke and diving into the plate balanced on her knees.

"Rudy's been carrying it around the last few days," Sheila said.

"Her dad called to set up the lessons with me. He was insistent that ladies should be well-rounded: tennis, piano and needlepoint. He was very peculiar about it."

The conversation hit a natural lull as everyone ate in silence for several minutes.

"None of us will understand what happened it that house," Garrison said.

Nancy sighed. "I hate it when you say cryptic shit like that."

Richard jerked his head asking Garrison to join him down the hall.

"Excuse me," Garrison said. He put his plate down and joined his friend in the hall.

"Caught your press conference the other day." Richard's scorn and disappointment was unconcealed in his voice.

"Yeah," Garrison said. "How'd I do?"

"Thought I was watching SportsCenter." Richard settled into an armchair down the hall from the ladies. "That press conference was like watching you read out of a baseball cliché book."

"You know why baseball players speak in clichés?" Garrison asked

"Is that rhetorical?" Richard sat with his legs wide, chest thrown out and poised to pounce.

"Baseball is actual poetry in motion. It's hard to wax lyrical about that so they resort to clichés."

"Jesus," Richard said. "I suppose you think police investigations are poetry in motion."

Garrison laughed. "Not remotely. Clichés satisfy the public. They are comforting and have the added benefit of not answering the question."

Richard crossed his arms against his chest. "How 'bout you drop the double speak and tell me what's really going on?"

Garrison hesitated.

"Don't give me that police business horseshit." Richard's voice rose to a shout. "That's my son in there." He pointed toward the ICU room.

Garrison flopped into a seat facing Richard. His shoulders rolled forward and his eyes fixed on the tile floor. "I saw evil this week. I walked into its home and took inventory." Garrison paused. "Those parents deserved everything Aidan gave them and more."

"You can't seriously believe that?"

Garrison met Richard's eyes issuing a warning not to challenge him on this point.

"That boy had thousands of opportunities to get help." Richard rolled up the sleeves of his dress shirt and displayed well-defined forearms as he clenched his fists. "Aidan's the villain, not the victim. He crossed that line Tuesday night."

CHAPTER 33

"I'm not saying he isn't guilty as hell, but you didn't walk into that basement and see the literal torture chamber they built. That shit'll haunt me for years."

Richard's eyes narrowed as he cracked his knuckles, like he was getting ready to fight Garrison as a surrogate for Aidan. "I didn't see the basement, but I've met Abby."

Garrison nodded.

"She grew up in the same household and she hasn't gone off the deep end. She may be scarred but she's not homicidal."

Garrison rubbed the gray stubble forming on his chin and moved to massaging his temples.

"Abusive parents often focus their rage on the child they most identify with, a way of projecting their self-hatred onto a surrogate."

The men studied their shoes and the tile floor for a while listening to the women laugh and banter.

"Thankfully, there's nothing wrong with Rudy's heart other than a worried mother, but that won't be true if you don't find Abby."

A doctor with deep circles around her eyes approached the women. Richard and Garrison stood and rejoined the group. "Rudy's resting. I gave him a sedative to help him sleep. Given the circumstances." Her hands twisted inside the pockets of her white lab coat. "I'd like to keep him here overnight. He admitted to having chest pains over the past two days. While that might be a stress response, I'd rather be safe."

Chapter 34

Saint Peter Manor offered multiple levels of care from rehabilitation to hospice services for Grinnell's aging population. Although the building had all the trappings of security, the staff worked much harder to keep the residents in rather than keeping the public out.

Aidan slid in through an open window. One of the orderlies or nurses must use the small supply room as a smoker's nook because an ash can tumbled off the sill as he pulled his leg into the room. He paused for a moment listening at the door to the hall trying to determine if he tripped an alarm. When he heard no one, he slipped into the hallway. Thanksgiving wasn't a busy holiday at the nursing home.

As he strolled down the hall, he peeked his head into an occupied room. A man slept in the adjustable bed, his wrinkled skin pulled into an expression of a perpetual scream. The old guy in the bed looked like he stood at death's door and death turned him away with one bony finger. By luck or trick of fate, Aidan had climbed into the hospice wing. No noisy residents and no visitors and staff to cause problems.

The television blared a mindless sitcom about a dysfunctional family with an endless laugh track. Aidan figured the television volume had less to do with entertaining the resident and more to do with distracting visitors from the coming reaper.

A tray of bland, soft food sat untouched on the bed table. Aidan grabbed

CHAPTER 34

the pudding cup and ducked into the adjoining bathroom. He didn't risk the time to take a shower, but washed up using the sink. He was starting to see the benefits of his jarhead haircut. Two swipes of hand soap over his head and he was clean without the benefit of ten different man-scented products marketed to make him more desirable and masculine.

He used his fingers to scoop the pudding into his mouth. Although he binged at the Edwards' house he was still hungry, he required a massive calorie load to maintain his physique. Everyone in Grinnell was on the lookout for him, so he couldn't stroll into Casey's General Store and order a taco pizza.

He stood beside the old man's bed, devoured the applesauce and dry toast, while the TV daughter explained to the overprotective father why she broke curfew. He'd like to hear Abby's excuse for breaking curfew: study group, late night shelving books at the library, too much time playing patty cake with loverboy. She didn't deserve to die easy at the end of a noose. Fire was too merciful. He wanted – needed – to wrap his hands around her neck and extinguish her life for himself.

He pulled a pillow from behind the old man's head and slipped the case off. He peeked into the deserted hallway then made his way toward the nurse's desk. Glancing into every room along the way, the patients each had identical trays of food. No Thanksgiving feast for the toothless and invalid.

The last door before the nurse's station was a small break room with a microwave and fridge. He peeked around the corner to see the staff gathered around a potluck dinner in the community room watching the Lions lose yet another football game. He nipped into the break room. He pulled open the refrigerator door, grabbed a four pack of Red Bull, several cans of Mountain Dew, a half-eaten ham sandwich and a handful of fun-size Snickers bars. Once his pillowcase bag was full, he moved to the coat rack. He dug through several coat pockets before he came out with a set of keys. He pulled the Ford key and electronic key fob off the ring and returned the rest of the keys to the pocket. He needed the car, no reason beyond spite to take all the other keys.

He snuck back down the hall to the supply closet, slithered out the window and back into the settling dusk. Time to find Rudy.

Chapter 35

Rudy opened his heavy eyelids with considerable effort. He blinked a few times to clear his eyes, but the drugs made everything fuzzy, like looking through the sheers in the living room. IVs ran out of both his arms and a tube ran from his crotch down his leg and off the bed.

Voices rose from somewhere in the cold room. A woman with a vaguely familiar voice said his name in a shrill squawk. Rudy scanned the room for a source when he spotted the television and his senior yearbook photo. The Des Moines news anchor reported live from outside the Flynn house still surrounded by crime scene tape. He wondered if the news anchor was allowed to go home for a few hours to enjoy the holiday or if she'd set-up camp in the news van. Strange thoughts undoubtedly influenced by the drugs flowing to the IV stuck in his arm.

"I should've blown it up," Aidan said as he stepped from behind the privacy curtain. "Burned the motherfucker to the ground. I had all the fuel I needed. Just needed my sister. Wouldn't have been complete without her blistering and dying in that fire."

Aidan's hulking frame filled Rudy's vision. During graduation two years ago, Aidan had been scrawny and weak—like a sapling stuck into the ground without water or care. Now he resembled a Bur Oak with massive limbs.

Rudy tried to sit up in bed, but the various tubes kept him confined.

His arms were unable to support his weight and his elbows crumpled as he tried to push himself up.

Aidan pulled a rock from his pocket and put it on the tray table positioned over Rudy's bed. It took him a moment to recognize the white queen from his chess set. Aidan had been in his mom's car and now his bedroom. Panic rose and his sedated heart boomed to life in his chest, but he was frozen, unable to call out for help or even sit up.

"According to the white board at the nurses' station, you had a heart attack. A cardiac event they're calling it." Aidan paced the small room. "They should really work a little harder to protect patient information. Seriously. A fucking heart attack? What are you, like fifty?" He loomed over him smiling. His eyes lit up in maniacal glee and his lip curled into a snarl of contempt.

"I'm here for observation," Rudy said. Tried to defend himself, but his voice cracked, not from emotion, but dehydration.

Aidan loomed over him, his face red and glistening with sweat. "Abby's curfew is ten. What the fuck were you doing out so late?"

Rudy flailed trying to find a way to sit up or find a way to be less vulnerable than being held in a prone position and nearly naked.

"Where's my sister?" Aidan asked.

"I don't know."

"Where's Abby?" His voice rose to a shout. Aidan pulled at the collar of his Dartmouth sweatshirt like it was choking him.

Rudy pursed his lips and shook his head.

Aidan loomed over Rudy. His new muscular build looked all wrong like he pulled on a muscles suit. His dainty hands on the He-Man body didn't add up.

"Why Abby? What did she ever do?" Rudy asked slurring all the words together.

"Nothing.." He smiled and his eyes widened and looked crazed like pictures of Charles Manson. "She did nothing"

CHAPTER 35

Rudy wanted to understand Aidan's motives – however irrational – but was also afraid to engage or enrage the psycho. "That makes her guilty?"

Aidan leaned over the bed. He grasped Rudy's jaw between thumb and forefinger forcing their eyes to meet. "Did you know? Did she tell you that the old man beat and raped me almost daily?"

Rudy glared back without answering.

Aidan started flexing his hand alternating between wiggling his fingers and balling his fist so tight the knuckles turned white. "Did you fucking know?"

"No," Rudy said. With great effort, he reached up to push Aidan away, but missed the mark and struck air.

Aidan reached back and pulled the sweatshirt's hood over his head and then slammed his fist into Rudy's chest. Pain shot across his sternum drawing his shoulders and legs forward to collapse around the initial injury and guard against the next blow.

Alarms sounded from the equipment next to him as well as from the hallway. As he sputtered air, Rudy glimpsed Aidan turning left into the hallway as two nurses scurried in from the right. He pointed but didn't have the breath to raise any alarms other than the blaring monitors.

Chapter 36

Garrison rolled over on the couch as newspapers and files crunched under his weight. He wiped away the drool from his mouth and sat up. He'd fallen asleep on the sofa while reviewing the evidence from the Flynn's wine cellar turned torture dungeon. A twisted bit of logic in the middle of the night told him that understanding the crime would help him understand Aidan's next victim: Abby. It was the same logic he used when he reviewed Vicky's copied case file yet another time – as if understanding the pimp's motive in beating Vicky to death would help Garrison better understand his estranged daughter. He knew his logic was flawed but he clung to it, nonetheless.

He rubbed the sleep from his eyes. Sarah was nestled on the love seat opposite him, wrapped in an afghan and waiting for Dad to wake up. He stood up and started stacking files trying to clean up his mess and to hide the more gruesome crime scene photos. Sarah didn't need to suffer from the same nightmares that had plagued him for three nights.

"Hey, Daddy." Her voice was low and throaty.

"Morning, baby," Garrison set the pile of papers on the end table and sat back down to face Sarah. "What time is it?"

"Three."

"What are you doing up so early?"

"We're going shopping."

"At three in the morning?"

CHAPTER 36

"It's Black Friday."

Garrison nodded. "Greed fest." Black Friday was the one family tradition his contempt and cynicism exempted him from attending. His idea of a big shopping trip was two Amazon packages in the same day.

She pulled the blanket up over her shoulders and stuffed two fingers in her mouth, a disgusting habit lost since childhood.

Garrison crossed to the armchair, sat on the arm and pulled the blanket from her mouth. "What's going on?"

"When Vicky went missing, how long did you look for her?"

"She ran away in April. It was actually Maundy Thursday."

"How do you remember that?"

"I washed her feet at Mass." Garrison remembered holding Vicky's tiny feet with blue painted toenails. He looked away as fresh tears filled his eyes. "After she ran away, I checked up on her for months because I knew the area where she was staying. She disappeared at the end of October."

Sarah rocked back and forth in the chair comforting herself.

"I don't remember a lot, just mom crying into the turkey she set on fire."

Garrison recalled the deep, smokey smell of charred turkey as his wife lay sobbing on the small kitchen rug that ran the length of their tiny galley kitchen in the Chicago suburbs.

"They found her the week before Thanksgiving." Garrison stroked her cheek.

They leaned against each other for minutes before Sarah spoke again, "Daddy, you gotta help Rudy."

"I'm trying to." Garrison waved his hand and indicated the files.

"I mean you gotta help him find Abby."

"I knew what you meant." The threatening tears spilled down his cheek.

"What would you do if it was me? If I was missing?" Sarah didn't wait for an answer. "You wouldn't stop. You'd tear apart the entire state, turning over every rock just like you did for Vicky."

Garrison glanced up the stairs to Vicky's photo on the wall.

"You gotta help Rudy." Sarah touched her palms to her father's chest in a pleading gesture. "Will you do that for him?"

He wiped the tears from his face and said, "I'll help him."

Garrison stood and hugged his daughter as Nancy walked in. Her velour tracksuit and cross-body purse were a tribute to shopping efficiency. Nothing would stand between her and a great price on a Michael Kors handbag or new sheets.

"Are you ready?" she asked.

"I gotta get my shoes," Sarah said.

"Wear something comfortable. We'll be walking."

"Yes, mama."

"What are you up to today?" Nancy asked as she turned toward Garrison.

"Gonna go see Rudy."

"You're going to help that boy, aren't you?" Although posed as question, it wasn't a request but a demand. Whoever said that men rule the world didn't live with these women.

"Before you leave, you should know that I don't need anything. I have more socks and underwear and dress shirts and khaki pants than any other man on earth."

She ran her pink tongue and blew a raspberry at him. "You ruin all my fun."

"I don't think that's true," he said pulling her into an embrace.

"You be good today." She wagged a finger in his face.

"I'm not the one with the credit card," Garrison said.

She blew another raspberry at him before heading out to the car.

Chapter 37

Aidan waited in the shitty Chevy Malibu he'd stolen from the old folks' home. He hid his Jeep in the back parking lot next to the rusted out Crown Victorias, Oldsmobiles and other old lady cars forgotten by negligent family members and dementia patients.

He tossed another Red Bull can into the back onto a pile of empties. He sat outside Grinnell Regional Medical Center all night waiting for his sister to come comfort her boyfriend but she never showed. After last night's threat, Rudy wouldn't wait long. Dressed in Wranglers and cowboy boots, he was a man of action and a man of honor. He'd hit the dusty trail soon and Aidan would follow.

Aidan flexed his right hand, wiggled his fingers and hoped the pain would shoot out of his nail beds. He'd strained his hand performing surgery on his mother. The pain summoned a smile. It was the result of a job well done. He'd carved off his mother's unspeaking lips and unhearing ears and dropped them into her glass of water on the nightstand. His favorite part of this chore was slicing out her unseeing eyes without piercing the orbs. Proud of his work, he carried her eyes into his father's study so that she might finally witness the torture. When his mother expired, he felt a warm surge of energy enter him, giving rise to his loins and arousing all his senses. It was like the first drink of water after a week in the desert choking on sand.

Father's death didn't offer such a gift as his heart stopped as a result of prolonged torture, rather than a single violent action. Although this lack of energy surge frustrated him, he looked forward to dispatching his sister. The resulting gift from her death would be overwhelming. He wanted to be touching her skin when her soul kissed his.

He smiled until his cheeks ached. Those were probably the only muscles he'd been unable to transform in the student fitness center. He intended for his body to be only a small part of his great becoming — the first step. His transformation from emaciated weakling to the chiseled body of a Greek god had taken too long and he was growing impatient in his great quest.

I am an American solider. I am a warrior. I will always place the mission first.

Classic literature told him that every hero and championed warrior must overcome adversity through a number of trials, but he was impatient to skip to the third act.

The trip home for Thanksgiving was meant only as a prelude – a prologue – to the unfolding of his mission during winter break. The long drive from Hanover to Grinnell offered too much time to fantasize and imagine each eventuality. He was so worked up by the time he pulled his Jeep into his parents' driveway that he thought he might explode.

When he came in the back door his mother fussed over his high and tight haircut and the body acne that had spread to his neck. She was too stupid or stoned on Xanax to even comment on his new physique.

She sent him away to the grocery store with a long list. When he stood in line for the cashier, his favorite teacher, Mr. Burnett, was ahead of him and didn't recognize him when Aidan handed him a dropped coupon. He'd spent hours after school in Mr. Burnett's calculus class.

Aidan now wondered if he should be proud that his transformation had been so complete that even his mentor, the man that wrote a glowing recommendation to Dartmouth, didn't recognize him. The unforeseen benefit of his new physique was no one would recognize him so he could

CHAPTER 37

stalk his prey in plain sight.

Raindrops plinked off the windshield. He ran the wipers to clear the glass when he noticed Investigator Gordon enter the hospital. His father would roll over in his grave knowing the police had been in his house – that is if his unclaimed body wasn't already cooling in a drawer at the State Medical Examiner's Office. The old bastard hated the police and forbid his children from contacting the authorities, even in an emergency. He wasn't sure if Father harbored a genuine distrust of the police or if it was a ruse to keep the authorities from uncovering his extracurricular activities hidden in the white room under the patio.

Maybe he could still burn down the house before more people learned what happened to him in that room. Did the cop know? Had he discovered the hell hidden in the wine cellar? Worse than the actual abuse would be the world knowing his shame.

I am an American solider. I am a warrior. I will always place the mission first.

His mission was evolving: kill Abby and torch the house before his shame was revealed.

Chapter 38

Rose crawled into the tent, her dark eyes bright in the flat, gray light. When Abby rolled over, Rose offered her two hard-boiled eggs in a flimsy plastic bowl. The strong stench of sulfur invaded her nasal passages and her stomach churned. She waved off the eggs.

"Morning," Rose sang.

"Need quiet." Abby mumbled from under a mountain of blankets. Her head pounded like the bass drum during band practice, thumping a regular rhythm.

"Come on, we've got work to do."

"My head." Abby rubbed her temples and massaged the bony arches over her eyes. She ran her tongue along her top teeth trying to strip the fur off. Her mouth tasted like she drank an entire carton of expired orange juice.

"Baby girl's got her first hangover." Rose's laugh pierced Abby's eardrums and made her head throb.

"It's just a headache," Abby said.

"Here drink this." Rose handed her a bottled sports drink. "It'll help."

Abby's head spun when she sat up. The first sip hurt. Her teeth seemed to wince in pain when the electrolytes and sugar washed over sensitive enamel.

"Oh my God. This is terrible." Abby closed her eyes against the bright daylight.

"You think that's bad? My uncle Jorge used to make this horrible hangover cure. Tabasco, black pepper and Sprite spiked with vodka. He drank it all the time." Her lips hitched to the side in a crooked pucker. "Now that I think of it, that might have been his drink of choice rather than hair of the dog."

Abby curled her lip in disgust.

"Drink up," Rose said. "We have real work to do."

"That sounds ominous."

"It's not all fun and games," Rose said as she rummaged around the bottom of the tent. "We gotta prep for the storm."

Abby had never prepared for weather other than a change of wardrobe. The way Rose acted made Abby think of news reports of people looting Home Depot and grocery stores preparing for the "storm of the century" which came every other year. The house on Broad Street stood for over a century, withstanding tornadoes, blizzards and every other manner of extreme Iowa weather. The tent, however, could be flattened by a stiff wind.

Rose clambered back out of the tent. Gray light filled the space like the gloom of the day liquefied and splashed over every surface. Abby wanted to scrub the gray from her skin before it soaked into her soul. As she pulled on her jeans and Rose's boots, rain began to plink off the canopy over the tent. When she scooted out of the tent she was greeted with sprinkles too small to register on her skin, but felt like pin pricks. She did a quick survey of the camp and trail looking for her brother. She pulled on Rose's stocking hat and stuffed her dirty hair into it. She longed for a shower, but safety came before hygiene. Above all else she needed to help the community that sheltered her.

Rose pulled a small camping hatchet from a leather sheath and hefted it. "I'm going to teach you to survive in the wilderness using only a hatchet," she said. Abby squinted her eyes at the worn tool and doubted her friend. Survival required more than a dull ax.

As Rose led them away from the tent, Abby stumbled over one of the tent pegs and fell flat on the hard-packed ground. From her crumpled position she pointed at her feet, "They're too big."

"You'll grow into 'em." Rose winked before pulling Abby to her feet. "I'll give you some extra socks before we leave."

"Leave? Where we going?"

"We're staying at the shelter tonight. Sterling's in line to get us beds."

While the idea of sleeping in a bed was appealing and access to a shower sounded like heaven, she was leery to spend time in public. After two nights in camp, she felt safe here ensconced in the cottonwoods far removed from everything she'd ever known or where anyone would expect to find her. Maybe another night. One more night and she might be ready to step back into the world: back through the looking glass.

They rounded the fire pit and Rose grabbed the wheelbarrow.

"How long have you been here?" Abby asked.

"About five months. The spring floods receded in May. My first tent was destroyed when some gutter punk that was crashing with me fell asleep with a lit cigarette. We dug out the fire pit in June."

"Why is the fire ring dug into the ground?"

"So people driving by don't see the fire and call the police." They trekked beyond the borders of camp and into a place where the trees crowded each other. "We don't need to advertise that we're here and get harassed by the city."

Rose set down the wheelbarrow and picked up the hatchet. "You don't wanna chop down a new growth tree because it has a long life ahead of it and greenwood smokes more than it burns." She twisted a small branch off a sapling, stripped back the bark and pointed at a vein of green inside the twig.

Abby focused on the branch and nodded like she was learning a complicated chemistry formula, although this was far more exciting than anything taught in her high school classes. Over the past week, she'd discovered that she thrived on pragmatism and practicality. Survival wasn't an abstraction or theory buried in a library book. Without the resources purchased with her father's money or without the help of her kind hearted new friend, she'd be hanging from her brother's noose.

"You wanna look for an older growth tree that's either dead or unhealthy. Like this guy." She patted the trunk of a small Cottonwood. Half the upper boughs were nude while a side branch retained shriveled, desiccated leaves brown with age. "This part of the tree is dead." She pointed at the portion holding on to foliage from seasons past. She handed the hatchet to Abby. "Taking down this one is good for the environment. It'll give more light to the healthy trees around it."

Abby held the ax head in her left hand while she fondled and explored the handle with her right. She ran her thumb across the blade testing the edge.

"It isn't sharp," Rose said. "It's all in how you wield it." She circled the tree running her fingers along the bark. "Examine the tree and the area. Which way do you want the tree to fall? Are there knots in the way?"

Abby ran her fingers over the wood.

"Give it a try," Rose said.

With hatchet in hand, Abby felt powerful. She swung it at the dead tree and yelped with glee as it buried itself in the wood and chipped the bark. Adrenaline and dopamine rushed through her veins and she felt alive for the first time in days.

With Rose's instruction, Abby worked at chipping away bark and meat of the tree in a triangle. Although her hands and arms ached from the labor, Abby kept swinging.

"That's good," Rose said as she tapped Abby's shoulder.

Abby wiped sweat from her brow. Work felt amazing. She grinned as she rubbed her throbbing hands together.

"Let's take her down," Rose said.

Together they pushed the top of the tree toward the chopped side. After a couple good shoves, the tree toppled. Abby squealed and lept in the air in triumph.

"I did it!" Abby shouted. "We did it!"

Abby hugged Rose in an almost tackle. Rose guffawed and returned the forceful embrace.

Chapter 39

"These gruesome murders have shocked and outraged this quiet Iowa community."

Rudy listened with his eyes closed grasping at the last moments of rest before fully working and giving into the pain pulsing through his chest.

The morning national news had picked up the sensational story of the Flynn's family's violent end and Iowa's largest manhunt.

"I'm standing outside the Flynn home three days after the bodies of Aideen and Ciarnan were discovered after a mysterious 911 call. Aidan Flynn, the son of the victims, is wanted for questioning. According to sources close to the investigation, Aidan Flynn is considered armed and extremely dangerous."

"Jesus, they call that journalism?" Garrison asked from somewhere nearby. Rudy's eyes flew open, unnerved that once again he wasn't alone in the room. "Speculation followed by conjecture, wrapped in unnamed sources. What a crock of shit." Garrison said to the television. "Whatever happened to Katie Couric? She was a classy dame. Blondie might be a local girl made good, but she's a nitwit."

"They mentioned me last night," Rudy said.

"You should have watched a little longer. Nancy Grace thinks you helped plan the whole thing."

"Sorry I missed my fifteen minutes of fame, but I had a visitor." Rudy tried to sit up but winced from the IV in his hand when he put weight on his arms. Instead, he reached for the remote and allowed the bed to do the work for him. After a quick search of the room, he determined that the chess piece was gone. "Aidan dropped by."

Garrison hopped up for his chair and approached the hospital bed. "He was here? Why didn't you call anyone?"

"Aside from being chained to this damned bed and high as a kite, he fucking sucker punched me in the chest, then ran out like a little bitch. Nurses thought I was having another heart attack and sedated me."

"What did he want?"

"Abby."

Rudy dropped the bed rail down and swung his legs over. He tucked the flimsy gown between his legs and tested his stocking feet on the floor. "He wants to kill Abby." Rudy pressed the call button. "His eyes. They were wild and crazy, like when my uncle Doug got back from Iraq."

Garrison nodded then steepled his fingers in front of his mouth. "Do you know where she is?" Garrison asked.

"I have an idea."

The nurse entered the room. "Look who's awake." She opened the blinds and took his vitals. "You're doing much better."

"When can I get out of here?" Rudy asked.

"That's up to the doctor." The nurse sighed and crossed her arms across her festive scrubs.

"I'm ready to go, so let's get him in here." Rudy paced within the reach of the IV tubing.

"She does rounds at noon."

The clock above the door read twenty before eight.

"I'm leaving in fifteen minutes," Rudy said. "Can you remove these?" Rudy indicated the two IVs restricting him to bed.

"I can't remove the IV without doctor's orders." She put her fisted hands on her hips and blocked the doorway.

CHAPTER 39

"Can you tell me how to do it?" Rudy asked.

"Do I need to get security in here?" she asked and crossed her arms over her chest.

Garrison stood, parted his jacket to reveal the badge on his belt and positioned himself between Rudy and the nurse. "I don't think that'll be necessary."

Rudy pulled the IVs from his arms and held a cotton swab to the sites.

"If you need him to sign AMA forms, you should bring them," Garrison said.

The nurse turned on her heel and stalked out. Garrison and Rudy turned to face each other.

"Shouldn't you be keeping me here and telling me to stay out of police business? Isn't that what they do in the movies?" Rudy asked.

"If I thought that'd work, I'd give it a try." Garrison laughed.

Rudy stood and adjusted his gown. He swayed on his feet for a minute. He closed his eyes until regaining his equilibrium.

"Your mom brought a bag." Garrison indicated a closet. "You know she'll have my balls if anything happens to you."

"Yours won't be the first set she's collected."

Rudy rifled through the knapsack his mom brought for him and pulled on two undershirts, his favorite blue western shirt and a clean pair of Levis.

"There's a guy at a homeless shelter in Des Moines. He's a little weird at first, but he's been helping me."

"Why do you think she's in Des Moines?"

Rudy pulled Abby's backpack from a cubby in the hospital closet, withdrew her notebook and opened it to her research notes. He pointed to a smiley face in the margin next to the name of a homeless shelter and a star next to Otto's name.

"She was researching battered women in the homeless shelter. She even talked to Otto."

Rudy closed the book and returned it to the elaborately embellished backpack.

"Weather's supposed to get bad tonight," Garrison said and pointed at the weather report muted on the television. A red swath cut across Iowa and much of the Midwest on the graphic indicating six to twelve inches of snow in the next day.

"Weather happens. Can't change that," Rudy said.

Rudy sat on the edge of the bed. He pulled on his battered work boots and looked at Garrison with his eyes squinted with determination. "I'm starving."

Chapter 40

Snow fell and melted as Garrison pulled into the parking lot of Principal Park. The minor league baseball team ended their losing season months prior, but the small restaurant in the skybox level remained open year-round. They called Otto on their way into Des Moines, but he couldn't meet them until eleven so they stopped for breakfast.

Getting out of Garrison's Ford Explorer, Rudy noticed two Bald Eagles trolling the Des Moines River for fish. He paused and watched the huge birds glide over in broad circles. When he was a boy, seeing an eagle in the wild was uncommon and good luck. Although the birds were now a fixture along Iowa's waterways, he still considered them a good omen.

They took a seat near the windows overlooking left field and dozens of geese huddled in center field.

"Why'd you pick this place?" Rudy asked.

"Where else you gonna get this view and a fifty cent cup of coffee?"

Two dozen Canadian geese broke through the light dusting of snow as hundreds of webbed footprints revealed the grass.

"Could you answer some questions for me," Garrison said after they ordered breakfast. "These aren't going to be easy."

Rudy nodded into his coffee cup.

"Was Abby abused?" Garrison asked in a whisper.

Rudy laughed. "Dr. Flynn worshiped her and gave her anything she ever wanted. He was over-protective for sure. Controlling, too. Wouldn't teach her how to drive."

"Wait." Garrison cocked his head. "Didn't her mom drive?"

"Her mom was sick or something. Abby said she never left the house."

"Was Aidan abused?"

Rudy leaned back in his chair and gazed out the window searching for the right words. "We were in gym class together junior year. Everyone's required to shower after running the mile. I wasn't looking or anything, but some things are hard to miss and harder to forget. Aidan's got scars everywhere. Across his back, down his legs, even on his dick." Rudy shivered like a draft rushed over him, but it was the memory of those scars that scared him.

Garrison shifted in his seat.

"There's something else."

Garrison leaned forward encouraging him to go on.

"I'm not one to party. Can't stand watching a bunch of jocks playing beer pong and talking shit about their girlfriends who are in the next room discussing the latest trends in lip-gloss. It's a strange scene.

"Well, I went to a Halloween party at the Mendez farm a few years ago. Everyone was drunk, sitting around a bonfire, telling ghost stories. Aidan chimed in, started telling a story about a man that constructed a torture chamber to control his young son. The old man beat and mutilated his son. Aidan went into too much detail. Really freaked everyone out. It was was pretty fucked up."

Garrison shook his head and squinted out the window.

"Aidan kept playing with the fire, adding more lighter fluid and daring people to jump the flames." Rudy paused and sipped his coffee. "There was something in his eyes. This crazed look. I saw that look again last night."

"Why didn't you tell someone?" Garrison asked.

"What was I supposed to say? I think Aidan's a little nuts and he's got some nasty scars. No one would've listened to me. Besides, Aidan used to be the size of a toothpick. A stiff poke in the chest would've knocked him over. Now he looks like a Batman action figure but more ripped."

"We haven't been able to get a recent photo." Garrison leaned over and rested his forearms on the table.

"He's fucking huge. There's no way that shit's natural."

The waitress returned with plates of eggs, hash browns and sausage. "Need any ketchup or hot sauce for your eggs?" she asked.

"No ma'am" Garrison said.

Garrison pulled a small baggie from the inside breast pocket of his coat. He dipped his fingers into the bag and sprinkled red pepper flakes on his over-easy eggs. Garrison bowed his head and exhaled into his dry, white toast. "I love this place. No one does a better breakfast in Des Moines, but why do they serve the toast dry? Can't they smear a little butter on it while it's still warm?"

Rudy looked out at the window at the tarp covering the infield. A Christmas tree marked each of the bases while Santa watched from the press box. The looming holiday was unwelcome without Abby. At the bottom of his sock drawer was a velvet box from Bill's Jewelry Shop with an emerald necklace waiting for Christmas Day. He longed to see the gem sparkle next to Abby's porcelain, freckled skin.

"What happened in that house?" Rudy pierced his fried eggs and played with the runny yolks. "I need to know what Aidan is capable of."

"Son, I've been in some sort of law enforcement since I was your age. Military Police, Chicago P.D. and now Poweshiek County. I've never seen anything like this." Garrison pulled a file from his messenger bag. He withdrew a few eight by ten photos, examined them for a moment and put them face-down in front of Rudy.

"Not even in Chicago?"

"In Chicago, I mostly worked gang neighborhoods. Kids shooting kids over nonsense. This was personal." Garrison dumped another two packets of Stevia into his coffee mug. "The FBI name is a family annihilator—killing his entire family in meaningful ways. That's worse than any gang shooting."

Rudy flipped over the photos. The first one was a wide shot of the room Rudy discovered when he'd snuck into the Flynn home. The next two photos were close-ups of torture devices. He turned the photos back over and gazed out at the ballfield. Rudy closed the file and looked back at the ball field. More raptors circled the river just over the blank scoreboard along the right field wall.

Garrison sucked in a deep breath, pursed his lips and considered Rudy for a long minute.

"I've been calling it White Hell," Garrison said and gathered the photos. "If Satan exists, his room is painted the same shade of white as those walls."

"I've seen it," Rudy said and took another bite of bacon.

"You what?"

"I snuck into the house after you left the farm the other day."

"Fuck!" Garrison voice rose and a few patrons looked over. He pursed his lips and moved his hashbrowns around the plate with his fork squeaking under the pressure of his utensil. After his hash browns turned into mashed potatoes, his breath smoothed and his anger dissipated.

Rudy reached across the table and pulled the fork from Garrison's hand. "Did Dr. Flynn torture Abby?"

"From everything I've learned in the past two days, Aidan was his only victim." Garrison added cream to his coffee and watched the white swirl with black until the coffee was a uniform light brown.

Rudy excused himself from the table. In the men's restroom, Rudy ran cold water over his wrists to cool the flush rushing over his body and burning his cheeks. The water splashing against his pale forearms felt like liquid bugs scurrying over his vulnerable skin.

He splashed his face to chase away the boogeyman in his mind. But the

CHAPTER 40

monsters weren't just in his head. They lived. They'd taken on human form of flesh and bone and blood to torment him or more likely to torture Abby and Aidan.

Rudy faced himself in the mirror and tried to gaze into his own dark brown eyes. He punched the flimsy paper towel dispenser. Although dented, it retained its mirror finish without a scratch. Most of the damage was to his wrist rather than the dispenser. He shook his head and snatched up several paper towels. He patted his face and arms dry. Mementos of the team's winning seasons lined the bathroom walls. In his youth, the term 'farm team' fascinated him. He wondered why all the triple-a affiliates weren't tucked into the fields and pastures of Iowa. Like someday he'd be riding in his dad's truck on the way to the feed store and come across the Yankees' starting lineup getting ready for spring training in Mr. Vander Linden's back forty.

Back in the dining room, Garrison was chatting with an older man with a shock of silver hair and an oversized sports coat.

"Why you ever joined the Army is beyond me. You had real talent. Hell, you could've gone all the way," the man said as Rudy approached the table.

"Well, thank you, sir," Garrison said. His face grew redder by the moment.

"You still throw the old hard ball around?"

"Naw." He looked at the ground, his face crimson.

Rudy sat back down.

"You ever see your old man pitch?" the older gentleman asked Rudy.

Rudy opened his mouth to correct the older man, but was cut off.

"This old boy made a knuckle ball look pretty," he said. "Isn't that right, seventeen."

Garrison flashed a sheepish grin.

"I'll let you boys get back at it," the man said. "Good seeing you, Gary." He limped away to a table in the corner with the waitress following him.

"Knuckleball?" Rudy asked.

"I played a season in the minors before college," Garrison gulped the last swallow of coffee and pointed at the older man. "He owns the team. Eats in here almost every day. You name a high school prospect from the last fifty years and that man can rattle off his stats." Garrison laughed. "Seventeen was my high school number." He gazed out at the pitcher's mound, a gray hump rising above the snow like a whale resting in the shallows. His eyes narrowed to slits as he recalled a brief moment from his glory days.

"We should go," Rudy said. "Otto's expecting us."

Chapter 41

Abby held the hatchet between her knees, while she rubbed her hands together to warm them. She double-checked the rim of her stocking hat for fly-away hairs, before setting back to work breaking down the tree they felled. The hatchet made her feel powerful, even invincible. It also gave her the courage to ponder her predicament, to consider – maybe for the first time – the nature of her family.

"Do you think people are born bad?" Abby asked as she added a log to the wheelbarrow.

"Getting a little philosophical for this early in the morning," Rose said. She loaded a few more pieces of kindling into the wheelbarrow. She twitched her head indicating they should head back to camp. "There's a big difference between surviving and being evil. Snakes aren't born bad it's a survival instinct."

"Yeah, but snakes are gross."

Rose laughed. It sounded like the high trill of a flute. "Snakes only attack when they need food or if they are threatened. They aren't malicious."

"So you're saying we're all snakes?" Abby asked.

"Something like that." Rose picked up the wheelbarrow and headed back to camp at a fast clip.

"But some people are malicious. Some people are—"

"Assholes." Rose laughed again. "Tell me about it."

They dumped the wheelbarrow on to a larger pile of kindling near the fire circle. Rose sorted the wood into stacks. Abby tucked the hatchet into the hammer loop on her borrowed overalls. The weight of it comforted her and relieved her anxiety.

"In my experience, assholes are made, not born," Rose said. "Survival either makes you hard or softens the edges."

Abby sat on a nearby lawn chair and looked up at Rose like she was the teacher and Abby the pupil at the school of hard knocks.

"From the time I left Shiprock I was hell-bent on killing myself, either provoking my boyfriend into beating me or by my own hands." She lifted her sleeves to display thin scars running up her wrists and forearms.

Abby touched her inner thighs unconsciously tracing the scars she'd put there. She never considered them self-destruction, but rather self-expression: a ritual to purge emotion.

When Rose finished sorting wood, she dropped into a camp chair next to Abby. Rose watched as Abby stroked the blade of the hatchet.

"When I left Denver, I hopped a train I thought was headed for California. I fell asleep and woke up in Des Moines with a railroad bull standing over me. That son of a bitch beat me so bad it took a month at Broadlawns Hospital before I could talk again."

Rose turned and lifted the back of her hair to reveal a jagged, waxy scar that ran from the base of her neck to above her ear near her temple.

"Funny thing," Rose said. "When I woke up, I didn't know where I was or who the president was, but I knew every chord on my guitar. If that son of a bitch wanted to hurt me, he should've smashed my guitar." Rose dropped her long, black hair and smoothed it over the scar. "It took almost being killed to learn that I wanted to live."

Abby drew her thumb down the hatchet face feeling each nick in the blade. "My brother wants to kill me," she said. The confession lifted a weight off her like the words were wings rather than a death sentence.

"I'm sure that's not true," Rose replied with a dismissive tone. She

CHAPTER 41

stacked larger pieces of firewood in a square with twigs and rolled newspaper in the middle.

"No, really. He hung a noose over my bed."

Rose looked up from the wood pile. "That's fucked up."

"Yeah." Abby stared into her lap. "I didn't help him when our dad was beating him."

"You're serious?" Rose asked.

"Wish I wasn't."

"Could you have stopped it?"

"I should've tried."

Chapter 42

The shelter was hopping with twice the usual volunteer staff. Cafeteria-style picnic tables no longer filled the mess hall. They were replaced by rows and rows of cheap office armchairs with numbers scribbled on the back with black marker. Rudy didn't check-in with the busy front desk, but headed to the administrative offices at the back of the building.

"Hey, Otto," Rudy said walking into the big man's storeroom turned office.

"You weren't fucking around were ya, Cowboy?" Otto asked indicating a stack of newspapers strewn across his desk. Abby and Aidan's faces looked up from the newsprint pages. "I saw your picture on CNN this morning. You really are John Wayne."

Rudy shook his head. It wasn't the chase that made John Wayne famous, but rather the triumph in the third act.

Garrison and Otto looked each other up and down both estimating the other man like cage fighters about to get into the ring – calculating strengths and weaknesses.

"This is Garrison Gordon," Rudy said.

"Chief Gordon? Like in the comics?"

"James Gordon was the police commissioner, I'm the county investigator," Garrison said, offering his hand to Otto.

"Isn't that essentially the same thing?"

CHAPTER 42

Garrison chortled with laughter. "I don't associate with super heroes. They tend to be a lawless bunch."

Otto pointed at Rudy. "He might look good in a cape and tights."

Rudy's cheeks flushed hot for a moment. Rudy was concerned the law man and former Neo-Nazi wouldn't get along, but his worries were assuaged by their joking banter. Then he decided to redirect the conversation. "Have you heard anything from the wise men or Robinson?"

"Not a peep." Otto's frown pulled all the creases on his meaty face down at the edges to mimic the line of his mouth. With his sad brown eyes, he looked like a bulldog without a bowl of kibble. "Tonight'll be a good time to check in with everyone. I expect we'll be full with the weather rolling in."

"You said you might have a few other places we could look," Rudy said.

"I know of a few rocks worth kicking over."

Otto stood and turned to one of his supply shelves and retrieved a scrap of black cotton. He turned and tossed it to Garrison. "You'll need this."

Garrison unrolled the fabric and held the Slipknot tee shirt to his chest. "How many of those tee shirts do you own?" Rudy asked.

"My friend's brother-in-law used to drive the tour bus for the band. He got me a good deal on a box of extra larges." Otto winked at Rudy.

"Is this really necessary?" Garrison asked as he held the tee shirt by the tips of his fingers as he might hold a smelly diaper bound for the trash.

"You look like a cop," Otto said.

Garrison looked down at his attire, laughed and peeled off his button down and sweater. The tee shirt hung like a tent over his Patagonia undershirt.

"Off-duty or not, no one trusts a cop," Otto said.

"And who doesn't trust a Slipknot fan?" Rudy asked.

Chapter 43

Garrison and Otto strolled into Java Joes, a locally-owned coffee shop a block from the downtown bar district. Upon entering, Otto shook hands with a skinny, nervous kid at the large coffee roaster inside the front door.

"Gary meet Jared," Otto said.

Full of manic energy, the kid nodded at Garrison and prattled on about the latest shipment of Ecuador Aces. Green coffee beans spun inside the roaster while Jared paced in front of huge jars of roasted coffees for sale. Another clerk came over and took Otto's two-quart Stanley thermos.

They stepped away from the roaster and took a seat at a nearby table. From this vantage point, Garrison could see the whole coffee house as well as those entering and exiting.

"So what's the story with that kid?" Otto asked, pointing his thumb back at the SUV parked outside where they left Rudy explaining his hasty hospital discharge to his mother on the phone.

Garrison glanced around for prying ears. The multitude of voices, occasional coffee grinder and steaming milk created a dull cacophony. Intermittently Garrison could hear Elvis trying to get the cellblock jumping over the sound system.

"His dad's a good buddy of mine. Fun-loving, outgoing guy and totally unsuited for the solitary life of a farmer, but Rudy has a natural gift for the business. He took over the family farm when he was just fourteen. He

CHAPTER 43

put it in the black within a year. Now it's the largest farm in the county." Jared opened a valve and filled the cooling bin with beans crackling and smoking hot. The air filled with the sweet, fruity scent of coffee like they were swimming in a French press.

"Rudy's a good kid. He was a nationally ranked chess player when he was like ten. Then he turned his attention to farming."

"Sounds like a focused guy," Otto said. "What about this girl we're looking for? Anything I should know that I can't learn from CNN?"

"Haven't had much time to watch the talking heads discuss my case, but there's a lot we haven't told the press." Garrison, again, glanced around the café. "Abby's a scared and confused girl on the run from a psychopath."

"Is he really that dangerous? The picture they keep showing on the news he looks like a twig."

"I talked to his roommate. Aidan joined the school's ROTC program and takes it very seriously. Turned into a dedicated gym rat. Might even use steroids. I guess he's just massive now."

Jared opened a door and the beans dropped into a large plastic bag. The clerk returned with Otto's thermos.

"The roaster," Otto said and pointed at Jared. "He's not destitute by any means, but he's got this weird ethos. Believes material possessions are an affront to humanity. He lives in an abandoned warehouse, doesn't want to own anything that he can't carry in a backpack."

Otto stood up from the table and approached Jared. "I'm looking for a friend and wondered if you knew of any new squats in the city."

Jared's shoulders sagged. "Come on, dude."

"You know I'm not going to get anyone in trouble. Just gotta find my friend."

Jared relented and wrote down several addresses on a napkin.

Chapter 44

Rose used a broken broom handle to set two metal teakettles on the smoldering fire while Sterling prepared a French press with coffee grounds. Rose wiped the soot from the kettle off her hands onto the legs of her overalls.

Sterling rose from the picnic table and crossed to her home on the other side of camp. Her waist-length dreadlocks shook as she strolled.

Abby assumed her usual spot next to the fire in a canvas camp chair with a blanket draped across her lap. Her hands explored the quilt top until they again found the tattered seam between blocks. She ran each finger across the soft fabric. Although she kept an eye on the trail into camp, she'd grown more comfortable in her surroundings. Having the hatchet at her side eased some of her worry, but didn't entirely release the knot in her stomach.

She tucked her mouth and nose into the collar of Rudy's sweater she wore over her borrowed clothes. It no longer smelled like Rudy, but was fouled with the salty, acrid scent of body odor. Mrs. Edwards' homemade laundry detergent smelled like heaven – an endless clothesline of sheets flapping in the wind on a cloudless day. Making cleaning products seemed like a much more pragmatic skill than tennis or needlepoint or piano or all the other ladylike hobbies her father insisted upon.

She ached for long, hot bath with an excess of body wash and bubbles. She'd trade her father's useless Volvo for the Neutrogena Hand Cream on her nightstand. She'd sign over her inheritance for haircut and manicure. She didn't consider herself to be prissy or fussy, but how did people go without bathing for weeks at a time.

"I had four younger sisters back in Shiprock." Rose laughed, her eyes focused on the distant skyline. "Five girls in one tiny house. Can you imagine?"

Abby shook her head. Her home or former home, was a hulking, lonely place. Even when everyone was home, it was still devoid of life. Even though she and Aidan were siblings, she often felt like a only child.

"It was chaos." Rose pulled at a strand of Abby's hair and twirled it between her fingers. "But you wanna know what I miss the most?"

"What's that?" Abby asked.

"Doing their hair in the morning. They'd line up like I was running a salon out of my bedroom."

Abby giggled. Once a month, she was driven to Salon 802 and given the full treatment: hair cut, conditioning treatment, eyebrow waxing, manicure and basic pedicure. At first it was a fun adventure, then it became a chore and another exercise in Dad's control. He dictated the haircut and clear nail polish.

"Could I do your hair?" Rose asked.

Abby fiddled with her ponytail and greasy hair. "Sure."

Rose scurried over to her tent and returned with a brush and hair elastics wrapped around her wrist.

Abby continued playing with the frayed quilt. Such a shame that someone's hard work fell into disrepair.

"Do you have a sewing kit?" Abby asked.

Rose shook her head and looked up to where Sterling stood outside her house. Three days in camp and Abby came to think of Sterling's shanty constructed of discarded plywood as a home. With the owner's presence it contained as much warmth as Rudy's parents' farmhouse. "Hey, you got a sewing kit?" Rose called to Sterling.

The woman held up a finger and ducked into her tiny house. Shuffling and soft scrapes indicated she was searching for something. She returned holding a cigar box.

"Will this do?" she asked, handing the box to Rose, who passed it to Abby.

Abby flipped open the lid to find multiple packets of needles, wooden spools of Clark's thread, a few skeins of embroidery floss and a tarnished pair of gold stork scissors. She smiled with the reminder of a quieter and simpler time in her own life as well as the decades this sewing kit lived through.

"Found it a few weeks ago." Sterling said. "Glad someone'll get use out of it."

Rose stood behind Abby, pulled back her hair and brushed it out in preparation for braiding. The pull and tug of someone playing with her tresses was therapeutic like a massage.

Abby pulled out a brown skein of thread and a crewel needle. She set to work repairing the frayed quilt seam. Instead of using a simple slipstitch, she opted for the more elaborate double featherstitch, which looked like little bird tracks across the surface of the simple nine-patch block. An idea struck her as she tied off her brown thread. She loaded blue thread onto her needle and set to work creating a blue bird at the end of the brown tracks. Sterling and Rose chatted about camp gossip and the brewing storm while supervising Abby's work.

"Damn, girl," Sterling said. "Where'd you learn to do that?"

Rose braided Abby's hair back in thick rows and rolled the rest of the hair into a topknot.

Abby shrugged. "My dad made me take lessons."

"Your moms didn't teach ya?" Sterling asked.

"She didn't leave the bedroom much."

"She sick?"

"Vodka and Valium."

CHAPTER 44

It was the first time she admitted mother's drinking and drug problem. She never even talked about it with her father or brother and was too ashamed to tell Rudy the truth of Mother's ailments. She wasn't embarrassed for herself but for Mother. Aideen was quite the looker and proper lady in her day. In recent years her teeth rotted, her pale skin was marred with the telltale broken blood vessels of her addiction. Her once lustrous hair hung limp and dull from malnutrition.

Sterling studied her for a moment. "Lemme guess. Irish Catholic?"

"Irish. Not so much Catholic."

Sterling sighed in disapproval. "It should be more criminal to give booze to an Irish Catholic woman than selling it to a minor."

Abby completed the satin stitching on the second bluebird and started outlining the third. She tied off her thread from the third bluebird. "Here you go. Good as new."

"Better than new," Rose said. She ran her long fingers across the embroidery. They inspected her work as an art historian admired a Rembrandt or Renoir. "That's amazing."

Useful. She was becoming useful. Her lessons in embroidery weren't a waste of time or a frivolous pursuit. "Got anything else that needs mending?" she asked.

Chapter 45

They pulled up in front of a burned out church on the eastern edge of central Des Moines. The Full Gospel Baptist Church was a brick shell with boarded up windows and doors, while most of the yellow painted trim was marred with black soot.

"Years ago, it was an actual church," Otto said. "Several down on their luck parishioners paid a small tribute to sleep in the sanctuary. One of the guys that slept here was upset about cockroaches and set the place on fire.

"In the end, the church was a tax shelter and a scam. Four years of court battles and no one knew what to do with the building. The city's declared it a nuisance, but the owner's in prison for assaulting a woman with a baseball bat."

Otto led them into the alley behind the church.

"Each year the city tries to evict the camps and squats by threatening arrest and seizure of property. And every year the city council looks like a bunch of jackasses without a legal leg to stand on."

"What about places like this?" Rudy asked.

"Although they can legally evict the squatters, the city usually leaves them alone. The populations that take over buildings like this actually improve the structures."

Otto pointed at a newer staircase. The treads constructed from pine two by six planks were not worn like the rest of the building.

CHAPTER 45

The old church looked burned out from the outside but as Otto lead them through a makeshift plywood door and down a set of stairs into the church's basement. Instead of soot staining the walls, they bore a fresh coat of graffiti art.

Upstairs in the main sanctuary, new rudimentary walls were constructed to create rooms. The walls were covered with fliers of concerts at local bars, more graffiti and Salvation Army oil paintings personalized with stylized dinosaurs and aliens.

Rudy pulled a spare tack off a poster and hung up the flier of Abby while Otto and Garrison wandered the labyrinth of hallways looking for an occupant.

"It's more like a dorm than any of the flophouses I've seen," Garrison said.

"Unlike drug dens or flophouses most squats have stricter rules than any dorm I was thrown out of in college. And that's saying something." Otto began knocking on doors. "Tenants are required to have a job and contribute to building improvements. Drugs are not tolerated."

A woman with a shock of dyed blue hair and an artist's case turned the corner. Her breath caught when she saw the men.

"Hey," Otto said. His booming voice was now quiet and diminutive. "I'm from the Franciscan shelter downtown. Can you help me with something?"

The woman smiled displaying a mouth full of crooked teeth. "Ya'll helped me when I first got here."

"We're looking for this girl," Garrison handed her a flier.

"She in trouble?" she asked.

"Danger, not trouble," Rudy said and stepped forward.

"Haven't seen her." She frowned.

Rudy nodded and dropped his head. "Thank you for your time." His shoulders slumped forward as he headed back the way they came.

"Give us a call if you see her," Garrison added.

The men clambered down the back steps, ducked under loose fencing and stumbled out onto the cracked, uneven pavement.

"There's another squat a few blocks away." Otto said. He scratched his head, wiggled his lips in consideration and looked at Rudy. "It ain't a nice place."

Rudy nodded as he considered Otto's warning.

Otto led the way through the snowy streets several paces ahead of them. The snow falling on the sidewalk covered the thin layer of black ice from sleet earlier in the day. Rudy stepped off the sidewalk in favor of the grass. The uneven texture offered better traction.

Garrison put a meaty hand between Rudy's shoulder blades. "Son, we've got to keep looking."

Rudy gazed down at his feet and nodded.

"We're looking for a needle in a stack of needles and we're going to take some wrong turns."

"I understand that." Heat rose in his cheeks. He resented the investigator for telling him things he already knew. Garrison's gift for stating the obvious was condescending and annoying.

"You gotta have faith we'll find her," Garrison said.

"Are you fucking kidding me right now?" Rudy turned cat quick and grabbed Garrison's arm. "Quit telling me shit I already know." Rudy pulled away from Garrison and stumbled after Otto as they walked past ramshackle houses lining the Eastside streets.

* * * * *

Hot, dry air rattled through the Chevy's dusty air vents melting the fat snowflakes that fluttered across the windshield. Aidan watched as the trio of men clambered out of the SUV but for the first time in days Rudy wasn't carrying Abby's ridiculous bag. As they turned into the alley behind a dilapidated church, Aidan ran over to the Explorer and tried the

CHAPTER 45

doors to no avail.

He shucked his hoodie and held it up to a rear window where Rudy rode as passenger. Using the sweatshirt to muffle the sound, he rapped the window his folded pocketknife. Inside the Ford, he snatched the backpack and left the white queen chess piece on the seat.

Although his mission was to kill Abby, tormenting Rudy was petty and altogether satisfying.

Chapter 46

They rounded the corner on another block on their trek away from the squatter's church into an Eastside neighborhood. The long blocks featured the modern equivalent of shotgun shacks separated by narrow driveways. Most front yards featured a small fenced-in area, some even boasted 'beware of dog' signs warning passersby of the Chihuahua resting on the stoop.

Rudy was hit with a wall of stink, like a bloated bit of roadkill cooking in the hot summer sun. The back of his tongue revolted and pulled back into his throat to gag him. He bent double and wretched several times without vomiting.

"Welcome to the Eastside," Otto said.

"What's that smell?" Rudy asked, holding the top of is hand under his nose trying in vain to block out the stench.

"Rendering plant."

"Jesus, that's terrible," Rudy said. "And I drive past a hog confinement twice a day."

Otto paused in their march into the working class neighborhood and pointed at a house. A realty sign lay toppled in the yard next to a knocked-over mailbox. A battered screen door leaned against the home's asphalt shingles. The door's hinges hung askew from the aluminum frame while the screen hung in shredded ribbons. The front porch sagged with gaps in the railing like a smiling drug addict. On a block of eyesores, this home

CHAPTER 46

stood out.

Otto stalked up the walkway, up the stoop and through the front door like he owned the place. The big man paused at the threshold and waved for them to follow. Rudy entered the house looking for a reprieve from the rendering stench but the house had its own funk.

The matted shag carpet appeared brown but deep divots where the furniture stood for decades revealed the carpet's true green color. Three limp bodies lay in a pile on a futon covered in mysterious stains Rudy didn't want to consider. There were six legs, otherwise he couldn't tell where one person started and another ended in the tangled mess of limbs, hair and clothes.

Burned spoons and insulin syringes littered the glass-top coffee table along with glass pipes, condoms and aluminum foil packets. The kitchen reeked like someone took a shit on the linoleum floor and lit it on fire – which was a real possibility as a huge, black scorch mark marred the kitchen floor.

The men searched the house in silence using hand signals. Garrison motioned that he'd search down the hallway. Rudy followed Otto into the kitchen. Bottles of drain cleaner, bleach and rubbing alcohol lined the cracked and peeling Formica countertops. Rudy wondered if the maid had taken the decade off or if he was missing a crucial part of the puzzle.

Otto pulled open the basement door and jumped back like he was bowled over by a stiff wind. The strong scent of cat piss filled the room.

"Get the fuck out," Otto yelled and ran from the room.

"Holy shit!" Garrison covered his nose and mouth.

Otto and Garrison both grabbed Rudy by the shoulders and pushed him out of the room. They ran out of the house and didn't stop until they were a block away.

"What the fuck was that?" Rudy asked through heaving breaths.

Otto pulled out his phone and dialed while Garrison tried to regain his breath from the short jog.

"I'm calling to report a meth lab at the corner of ninth and Harrison," Otto said. "Yeah, I'll hold."

"A meth lab? Are you fucking kidding me?" Rudy kicked at a pile of snow and paced the sidewalk. "We went to look for my girlfriend in a goddamn meth lab?"

"The Eastside is home to multiple generations of hillfolk from the rural counties of Iowa that moved to the city in search of better jobs," Otto said. "A lot of people on this side of town think of Wal-Mart as a promising career opportunity if they can't get a monthly draw check from Uncle Sammy. Given a fistful of dollars, they'll turn a blind eye to the drug den next door."

"Cold as shit out here," Rudy said. He jumped up and down trying to get his heart rate up.

"Here," Garrison said and offered his keys. "Might be better if your not here when the police show up."

Rudy's hand hovered over the keys and he scowled at Garrison.

"Your face has been all over TV. Police will hold you here for an hour asking irrelevant questions," Garrison said.

Rudy snapped up the keys from Garrison and stalked off toward the Explorer. He pulled up the collar of his coat to shield against the snow. The breeze was picking up speed and shifted out of the north.

Rudy kept his eyes on the twisted and canted sidewalks as he hiked several blocks before spotting the Explorer. Teeth chattering in the blowing snow, he jogged the last block to discover the back window smashed. He glanced around the quiet street expecting to find Aidan watching from a distance, but he wasn't there. Rudy strode to the broken window and peered around the gummy glass. The white queen sat on the seat as if the say, "Checkmate."

He flung open the door and hopped into the seat as the safety glass crunched under his weight. Abby's bag was gone. Not under the seat,

CHAPTER 46

not in the cargo area, it was gone. He jumped out of the car, crossed the street and flopped down to the curb. He rubbed his thumb across the marble chess piece.

"What the hell happened here?" Garrison asked as he approached. His voice held an accusation as if Rudy broke the window in frustration.

"Aidan," Rudy said. He didn't look up from his shaking hands.

"Son of a bitch." Garrison crossed to his Ford and surveyed the damage. He used a gloved hand to sweep the glass shards onto the already littered road verge. "Did he take anything?"

"He stole Abby's backpack." Rudy help up the chess piece. "He left this."

"What's that?" Otto asked.

"The queen from the chess set in my bedroom. My grandpa gave me this set when I graduated high school. He carved the pieces himself."

"Holy shit," Garrison said and slapped his meaty hand to his forehead as sirens rose in the distance.

Chapter 47

Bett's Military Surplus was a small squat, brick building on Army Post Road set among pawn shops, low-rent lawyer offices, used car lots, three diners advertising Des Moines' best tenderloin and near the dilapidated Fort Des Moines Provisional Army Officer Training School. Snow accumulated in small mounds at the corners of the building and in the gutters.

"Soldiers and squads are the foundation of the decisive force. They must be organized, equipped and trained with superior lethality."

His Dartmouth hooded sweatshirt and fatigue pants were no match for the approaching storm or the battle ahead. He needed to resupply. He'd driven past a Walmart and a Target in favor of this tiny retailer. While Gore-Tex and other performance materials may have been better choices in this weather, he preferred to wear something manufactured for battle, sewn with threads of honor.

The musty shop was half an hour from closing so efficiency was of the utmost importance, out of courtesy and the clerk would remember a customer that made his stay open late on a snowy day.

Carefully constructed model airplanes hung from the ceiling over rows of shelving laden with a hodgepodge of items: camouflage hats, tactical helmets and key rings embellished with bullets.

The older gentleman behind the glanced up from his F-16C Falcon model. "Help you find something?"

CHAPTER 47

"I'll let you know," Aidan said as he wandered the racks of hanging clothes.

From a row of boxes, he picked out long, waffle-weave underwear, from hangers he pulled down a heavy winter coat and insulated bib overalls.

"May I set these here?" he asked and dropped his arm load of clothes on the glass case next to the cash register.

"Want me to bag these up?" the clerk asked.

"You can put it in here." Aidan threw an Army-issue rucksack on the counter. He went back into the shelves, picked up two pairs of gloves and a fur-lined winter hat.

"Anything else I can get you?" the clerk asked as he keyed each price into the battered cash register.

"How about a decent pile of flapjacks?"

* * * * *

A few patrons hung around the Kozy Kitchen in the hour before the dinner rush. Three men sat scattered around the cafe, sipping coffee at booths around the kitschy establishment. Antique bake ware and tin signs decorated the walls.

A perky peroxide blonde well beyond retirement age greeted him with a smile and sad eyes.

"How many?" she asked.

Aidan looked to the doorway behind him and back at the woman. "Just one."

"Booth or table?"

"How about that one?" Aidan asked, pointing to a booth next to a large plate glass window overlooking the parking lot and Southeast Fourteenth Street.

She slapped a menu on the table. "Coffee?"

"Sure."

Cheap, faux wood paneling flanked the walls lined with art salvaged from a thrift store dumpster. The light fixtures looked like they were rescued from a 1970s bowling alley. The booths were upholstered in either avocado green vinyl or vivid, plush animal prints. A glorious velvet painting of fat, strung-out Elvis overlooked Aidan's corner booth next to the window.

Aidan sat next to the drafty window and set the menu aside. Although he didn't allow himself carbs often — not since the transformation — today would be an exception. He was getting closer to Abby. A dull thrumming from the bottom of his gonads signaled his journey was reaching climax and a carb indulgence was the least of his worries.

"What can I get for you?" The perky blonde was back with a carafe of coffee and her order pad at the ready.

"Tall stack of flapjacks."

"Flapjacks?" She picked up his menu and tucked it under one flabby arm. "Where you from?"

"Not from around here," Aidan said.

The waitress knew what he wanted and was just trying to make conversation, but he wasn't interested.

"Pancakes. I'd like some pancakes." He couldn't hide his annoyance.

"Buttermilk or whole grain?" she asked.

"Just good ol' fashioned pancakes and a side of bacon."

"Whatever you say, sweetheart." She turned on her heel and stalked off.

Aidan was glad the terrible decoration cluttered all the walls, leaving no room for a television. He was loath to see his yearbook picture on CNN again or hear any more bullshit theories about his motives.

Aidan riffled through the backpack trying to determine what was so precious to Rudy. He snatched up the notebook and began reading the mindless drivel of his sister. Her entries vacillated between school notes,

CHAPTER 47

observations about her classmate and love poetry that was naive at best. He skimmed the entire journal, flipping the pages until he found her research notes about the homeless in Des Moines. Unlike the rest of the journal, the margins were filled with doodles of hearts and smiley faces, which he would have expected on the poetry pages. Thinking about and researching the destitute made her happier than waxing lyrical about Rudy. He now understood Rudy's focused search and could hunt on his own.

The pancakes arrived. He smothered them with half a stick of butter and most of the bottle of syrup. He drifted away on a river of carbohydrate bliss.

His mission had changed again, but as a soldier he adapted. In his mind he reviewed where he'd been and his next possible move. He finished his pancakes and headed out into the growing storm.

Chapter 48

Rudy stretched out across the Explorer's expansive backseat and closed his eyes. They'd passed through the first circle of hell and were about to descend into the second – from a meth lab to the lesser whorehouses of the Des Moines area. He needed a moment to collect himself.

Pushing the last days out of his mind was like pulling back a curtain to get a better view of the world beyond the plastic covered window. He focused on the darkening horizon looking for a bright spot of hope among the squall.

The Grinnell Public Library was quiet as tomb. The modern library was built with prairie style flourishes: repeated lines, large banks of windows, a flat roof and integration with the surrounding prairie landscape. Louis Sullivan and Frank Lloyd Wright would, however, disapprove of the prefabricated bookshelves and manufactured furnishings. A faint musty odor of decaying paper filled the air, which made Rudy long for the old Stewart Library a block away. The library of his childhood where he first discovered his lust for knowledge was now transformed into the Grinnell Area Arts Council.

Most days the library bustled with staff and patrons, but the combination of the late hour and pouring rain kept most people at home. No one worked the circulation desk or the children's section. Rudy wandered the stacks before he found someone reshelving books in the tall mystery

CHAPTER 48

shelves at the back of the library. She balanced on tiptoe on the step stool to reach the upper shelves.

"Excuse me, ma'am," he said.

Rudy assumed he was addressing an older woman because of her professional attire: black pencil skirt, green silk blouse and patent leather flats. He was speechless when she turned around. Her hair looked like fire leaping from her freckled face. The color wasn't red nor was it orange.

"Sir, may I help you?" she asked. When he did not answer, she said again, "Sir?"

"I'm looking for some books," Rudy said.

She smiled and her green eyes sparkled like emeralds catching the light. "I think you may have come to the right place. I could be wrong, though." She set her armload of books down on a nearby cart and turned back to him. "Were you looking for something specific?"

Rudy shook his head in an attempt to shake his brain awake, but she mistook his gesture.

"We have blue books and red books but I just ran out of green books. You'll have to come back next Thursday if you want a green one."

Rudy smiled and shook his head. "Sorry. A little distracted."

"Shiny objects?" she asked, a broad smile spreading.

"No. Not exactly." He unzipped his jacket as his whole body flushed. "I ordered some books on sustainable farming through interlibrary loan."

"Follow me." She turned and headed toward the front of the library.

He trailed her to the checkout desk. Prior to this he'd never understood guys that bragged about a woman's legs, but watching her heart-shaped calves flex and contract with each stride changed his mind. In addition, her long hair bounced and bobbed above her waistline calling attention to her pert ass.

"Your name?" she asked as she sauntered behind the desk.

"Rudy Edwards."

She shuffled through several sheets of paper, nodded to herself and disappeared into a backroom.

Rudy ran through every romantic comedy movie he'd ever watched — which was limited – looking for an easy way to ask her out, compelled to get to know her better. Yet the movies made it look so organic — the conversation would open up a door the Lothario could effortlessly walk through. He didn't see any doors opening up for him in this situation.

"Here we go," she said as she returned with a stack of books and academic journals. She began filling out paperwork. "These are due back in two weeks and cannot be renewed since they were borrowed from another library. I certainly hope you enjoy 'Academic Journal and Research in Agricultural Science'."

Rudy winced. She must have thought he was a nerd or a hippie reading volumes about sustainable farming. He signed the form she put in front of him. "Where's the regular librarian?" he asked.

"Are you dissatisfied with the service today?" Her face fell.

"Just curious."

"She ran to the post office to flirt with Mr. Personality before we close. I'm covering for her."

Rudy's smile widened. He thought he saw his door of opportunity peek open. "Mr. Personality?" he asked.

"You know. The postal clerk on Saturdays. Talks in a monotone. Won't crack a smile. I swear that man wouldn't know a joke if it jumped up and bit him on the funny bone."

Although jubilant inside, he forced his mouth into a frown in mock outrage. "He's my dad."

"You can't be serious." Abby reached up and covered her mouth. Her freckles faded as her face grew crimson.

"No, really."

"Oh my God. I'm such a jerk." Abby paced behind the desk, wringing her hands and biting her lower lip.

CHAPTER 48

"Would you consider having dinner with me as an apology?" he asked. He wasn't going to wait for the door to creek open — he kicked it down instead.

"He's really your father? No lie?" she asked.

"'Fraid so." Rudy leaned toward her.

"I can leave as soon as Suzanne gets back from flirting with your dad."

"So that's a 'yes'?"

Abby nodded. Her face was so flushed with embarrassment that her freckles were now indistinguishable.

It took him a month to realize that Abby wasn't flirty with anyone else and that he was the sole recipient of her charms. With anyone else, she was reserved and withdrawn.

Rudy dropped off to sleep as the Ford rolled and bumped over Southside streets on a mission deeper into the underworld.

His phone buzzed in his pocket. He rubbed his eyes and pulled his cell phone from his jacket. His realtor's information popped up on the caller ID.

"Hello?"

"Rudy. It's Dan Fox. Just wanted to let you know the Vander Lindens accepted your offer on the farm."

"That's good news." Rudy's voice cracked as he choked on the news he'd have his own home. "That's really good news."

He stared down at his phone. He wanted to share the news with Abby, wanted to call her and start making plans to move in but that wasn't going to happen. Panic grew more acute and fluttered in his chest like he'd had too much caffeine. He massaged his chest and prayed he wasn't heading for another hospital stay.

Chapter 49

The Explorer cruised down Southeast Fourteenth, the main thoroughfare of Des Moines' Southside. They passed dozens of used car lots, scrap yards, multiple pharmacies and several ethnic grocery stores. The busy, four lane road was a bevy of white trash shopping hubs.

Garrison slowed and pulled into The Buena Vista Motel, a small motor inn. A tall privacy fence separated the squat building from the road and prying eyes.

"We don't need to stop at this one," Otto said.

"Why not?"

"Let's just say, they cater to a different clientele."

An older man stepped out of a room and pulled the hood of his parka over his shiny bald head. His brow wrinkled and upper lip raised in a look of disgust.

"What sort of clientele?" Garrison asked.

"I've only seen older men with little boys getting rooms here."

Rudy gawked out the window at the run-down motel like they were passing the scene of an accident, his face agape with conflicting horror and fascination.

They continued down the road and pulled into the next motel. The sign for the A-1 Motel advertised air conditioning, color televisions and boasted American ownership. They pulled up to the office.

CHAPTER 49

"What the hell are we doing here?" Rudy asked.

Otto turned in his seat to look at Rudy. "Most people only come to the Southside to worship run-down cars or get some decent Italian food."

"And we came here to scope out the whorehouses?"

"Why don't you stay in the car for this one?" Garrison said.

Rudy remained in his reclining position in the backseat while Garrison and Otto hopped out. He lifted his hand and gazed at his ragged nails. Since meeting Abby, he began a routine of taking care of his hands to keep them soft and presentable for her. He sat up and searched the console for a nail file but found a tube of Mary Kay hand cream buried under maps and various ephemera. He rubbed lotion into his cuticles and the webs of his fingers.

Outside, the low-hanging swirling clouds touched the motel's pitched roof running down the length of the dilapidated building. White exterior paint peeled in long ribbons next to the royal blue trim and doors.

Inside the office Otto and Garrison argued with the clerk while he shook his head the whole time like a Parkinson's patient. Their voices drifted out of the office and through Rudy's cracked window.

"Bachelor party?" the clerk asked in a thick Middle Eastern accent. He stroked his dark, well-groomed beard.

Otto shook his head. "We're looking for your newest girl."

The clerk's smile faded to a sneer. "I don't know what you're talking about."

"Don't give me that shit. You know exactly what I'm talking about," Otto said, his voice steely as he poked a thick finger in the clerks face. "Which room?"

The clerk looked down at his reservation book and frowned with his chin jutting out. "The boss isn't around. I can't do anything without his approval."

A young woman in an oversized camouflage jacket materialized from the back of the motel. She led an older, graying gentleman by the hand.

Her brilliant red hair glowed against the gloomy background.

Rudy bolted from the SUV leaving the door ajar as he ran toward her. "Abby!" he yelled.

The redhead hustled faster for the door of room seventeen while she fumbled one-handed with the enormous motel key ring. She froze in the doorway with her head bowed to the floor.

The old man dropped her hand, threw several bills from his pocket to the ground at her feet and ran off, his soiled trench coat flapping in the wind. The redhead shook her head, entered the room and slammed the door without collecting the balled up bills on the ground.

Rudy stared at the door for what felt like whole minutes until Garrison put a hand on his shoulder. His hand slid down Rudy's shoulder to his elbow trying to guide him away from the room. "She's not here, but the guy told us about another place down the road." Garrison pulled on Rudy's arm. "Come on."

Rudy pointed at the door and opened his mouth to speak but gave into Garrison's tugs on his arm and allowed himself to be led back to the SUV.

"Jesus, kid. You alright?" Otto asked. "Look like you seen a ghost."

Rudy nodded and crawled into the back seat. He had seen a ghost.

Chapter 50

Abby huddled under a blanket next to the dwindling fire watching the flames lick the graying wood. Rose sat next to her puffing on a stubby brown cigarette with the faint scent of cherries and vanilla.

"You're coming with me," Rose said. "Sterling stood in line for an hour to get us beds."

"You said you hated the shelter," Abby said. She would stay in the camp not only to avoid being discovered by Aidan, but also to prove to herself she could survive one night on her own. If Rose could survive a lifetime on the road with only her wits and guitar, then Abby could survive one night in a tent.

"Anything's better than freezing to death."

Abby rolled her eyes at her new friend and turned back to the fire. Rudy told her, "weather happens." Although his mantra seemed dismissive and glib at first, especially for someone making a living off the land, it proved much more profound. Abby was incapable of controlling the jet stream but she could prepare for the coming storm.

The time to be passive was over. Whatever happened, she had to be ready.

"It's supposed to drop below zero tonight. You've got to come with me."

"I'm safer here," Abby said. She rose and added a log to the fire. "It'll be dark soon. You should go."

Rose sighed, stubbed out her smoke and stood. She wrapped her arms around Abby enveloping the smaller girl into a deep embrace.

"I won't be able to sleep a wink knowing you're out here," Rose whispered into Abby's ear.

"Go. Get warm. Have a bowl of soup for me."

Rose nodded. "Good night, sweet girl." Rose kissed her cheek and pulled away.

"Good night."

Rose hoisted her guitar case and strolled to the edge of the clearing. "I'll see you in the morning." She called back over her shoulder.

Abby returned to her perch next to the fire. She was now the sole inhabitant of the camp. She wrote herself into the hero's role of a post-apocalyptic science fiction novel. She felt like Robert Neville doomed to wander the world alone in Richard Matheson's *I Am Legend*. Unlike Neville, she welcomed the solitude. She needed private moments without Rose fawning over her or Robinson taking inventory of her every move.

She closed her eyes and relished the warmth of the fire on her cheeks and breathed in the smoky air. She could still smell the faint vanilla odor of Rose's cigar among the burning leaves.

Rudy's pale and placid face flashed in her mind. The image of him with a baby goat tucked under one arm flooded her consciousness like a broken levy. His remembered laughter washed over her, but she refused to let loose the tears pulling at her lids.

She squeezed her eyes against the cold and wished she was enjoying the warmth of the hearth at the Edwards' farm, curled up on the plaid sofa facing a crackling fire. Rudy would play with her hair while she rested her head on his lap. But she made the decision not to bring her brother's brand of psychosis to their door. Her life was small and insignificant – no matter what her father thought – and she was unwilling to put the Edwards' in danger for her sins.

CHAPTER 50

She opened her eyes and rocked back and forth on the lawn chair trying to comfort herself as she would a crying baby. In her rocking, a glint shining off the hatchet blade caught her attention.

She snatched up the hatchet and cradled it on her lap and caressed the cold metal blade. She ran her thumb across the blade's edge. It wasn't as sharp as her pocketknife and it bore many deep nicks and burrs. This blade would not serve her purposes. The flame grew as it swallowed the newest log down into the belly of the fire as it changed from red to yellow-orange with a blue base. An idea sparked in her mind.

She balanced the hatchet over the rock fire ring and held the handle with the toe of Rose's boot so the blade hovered over the blue flame.

Although she didn't have her backpack and cutting kit, she craved emotional release. She needed to cry and surrender to the deep well of anguish and swim in the depths of her guilt.

After several minutes of anticipation, Abby pulled the hatchet from the fire. The handle was warm in her cold, bare hands and heat radiated from the blade.

She slid up her left sleeve, which proved to be quite a task. Each layer was larger than the one below it: her Cuddle Duds base layer under an oxford shirt under Rose's sweater under Rudy's cardigan. With effort she revealed the flesh of her forearm. She hated her pale freckled skin. It always looked like she was covered in red mud. She wanted to scrape off all those red marks. A scar was the least of her worries.

She inhaled and drew the blade down her forearm. The pain was searing and satisfying. The hot metal didn't draw any blood, which was part of her usual ritual, but it did unleash the emotions she tried to push away.

The tears came in violent waves of wailing sobs like an undulating ocean before a tsunami. She cried for her indifference toward her brother's plight. She cried for the life she'd never have with Rudy. She even cried for the loss of her dead parents. Her screams of anguish and grief echoed off the trees and shanty houses.

Under other circumstances, in the privacy of her bedroom, she would prep her inner thigh with iodine, then cut herself and weep as the blood flowed. The cut was a timer on her sadness. Once the blood stopped, she cleaned the wound with peroxide, bandaged herself and moved on with life. A ceremony to cleanse grief and self-doubt.

Without blood and no timer, she cried until her eyes ran dry. The burn left a long white, blistered welt that stood out next to her red, burning flesh. She cut the inside of her thigh because no one would ever see it and the scars were nearly invisible. Rudy didn't mention them the other night when she stood before him naked. Her arm, on the other hand, would draw attention. She didn't like hurting herself in such a visible and noticeable place, but she had little choice. She wasn't about to drop her pants here in the open.

The burn cooled quickly in the frigid air, although it seemed to make her colder. Relieved of some of her burden, she pulled the blanket over her shoulders again and returned to watching the fire.

Chapter 51

Outside the next motel, Rudy leaned against the SUV and gathered himself in the growing squall. Find Abby, punish Aidan, live happily ever after. These eight words became his mantra and he repeated them when he felt his focus start to slip and hope fade.

A woman crossed the slick parking lot in clunky heels. Her peroxide blonde hair pulled into a high and tight bun and the long petite frame and peculiar grace with each movement she could've been a ballerina, but the brocade corset and fishnet stockings betrayed her true profession. She carried a bag from the chain pharmacy across the street and a carton of Camels. Through the plastic grocery bag he could see a can of generic Cheese Whiz, a box of saltines and a two-liter of Mountain Dew.

"Howdy," Rudy said with a nod. With effort he kept his eyes on her face rather than showing her the disrespect of ogling her shapely and lithe body.

"Hello, Cowboy," she said and stashed her groceries behind her back. She ran the tip of her pink tongue along her bottom lip. The movement was meant to entice Rudy, but it made him uncomfortable. Such overt, sexual gestures always made him feel awkward.

"You look cold," Rudy said.

"Not that cold," she said. She opened her lightweight fleece coat to display her bountiful breasts swelling over the bounds of her corset.

"Let's get you inside," he said.

A slow smile spread across her lips displaying a mouthful of cracked, crooked teeth. "Yes, please."

She took his hand and led him to a room beyond where Garrison and Otto unsuccessfully knocked on doors.

* * * * *

Abby flipped a cigarette from Rose's pack of American Spirits and stuck it in her mouth. She wasn't sure how to hold it between her lips so she tried different configurations but each one left her feeling more idiotic. She looked around and searched the tent floor for a lighter. When she found the disposable Bic, she clambered out of the tent and strolled toward the dying fire. On the walk she tried holding the smoke different ways – between her fingertips, at the crook of her fingers, between thumb and forefinger. Again, nothing felt right.

A few kids at school smoked and they made it look kind of cool and illicit, but they weren't the people she hung around. Rose made it look sexy with her long, tan fingers, full lips and she often touched her tongue to the filter like she was kissing a lover.

After several tries, the Bic's reluctant wheel spun and sparked. She held the flame to the tip of the cigarette but it wouldn't light. She sighed in frustration.

To avoid killing the flame again, she blew all the air out of her lungs, flicked the lighter to life and lit the cigarette. She sucked the noxious smoke into her mouth and coughed. Although she hadn't brushed her teeth in days, this tasted worse.

When she recovered from coughing and sputtering, she looked at the offending cigarette gripped between two small knuckles. She considered squashing it out of the ground but she was determined to figure it out like it was a physics or calculus problem.

CHAPTER 51

She lifted it to her lips and drew in another puff. This time she inhaled the smoke. It made her dizzy and a little disoriented, like she'd woken suddenly from a nap. She blew out the smoke and watched it curl to the darkening sky in a seductive dance. She dropped the cigarette and raked a boot over it several times until the filter shredded and tobacco flakes scattered in the wind.

* * * * *

Soft pink and red light filtered through scarves draped over shabby wall sconces and bedside lamps. As Rudy and the girl entered the small motel room, she dropped his hand and hurried around the bed to unpack her groceries onto a nightstand.

The stale stench of cigarette smoke was so strong in the tiny space Rudy could taste the cheap, toxic tobacco. Only the faintest whiff of cheap perfume over-powered the putrid scent.

Round, black cigarette burns marred every surface from the vanity covered in enough beauty products to start a salon to the martini bar set up on the dresser bolted into the floor and wall.

"How much?" Rudy asked and pulled his wallet from the back pocket of his Levis.

"One hundred for thirty minutes."

Rudy fished two hundred-dollar bills from his wallet and dropped them on to the dresser turned mini bar. He would pay for her time but not her services. The thought of her hands touching the same places Abby caressed revolted him.

She stripped off her coat and threw it on a pile of clothes in the corner. "Do you mind if I get comfortable?"

"Not at all." He didn't know where to sit because every surface looked dirty beyond cleaning. He settled into the armchair next to a rattling heater.

She pulled a sleeve of saltines from the box and tossed it on the bed. Next she retrieved a used convenience store soda cup from the bathroom, filled it half full of Mountain Dew topped with a shooter of vodka. She perched herself cross-legged on the bed, giving Rudy full view of the tiny strip of fabric covering her genitals. She swirled the processed cheese product on to several crackers and ate each one in turn followed by a quick swig of her cocktail.

"Let's cut the bullshit," she said with a saltine in her mouth. She sprayed little bits of cracker on the soiled, threadbare bedspread. "We both know you're not here to partake of the goods."

Rudy nodded.

"What do ya want?" she asked again, more insistent this time.

Rudy took a seat on the far end of the bed, facing the girl. "How'd you end up here?" he asked.

"What the fuck?" She jumped up from the bed and edged toward the door. "You're not some Jesus freak, are you?"

Rudy shook his head and looked down at the dingy bedspread. "My girlfriend's missing. Something happened. She ran away."

The girl moved away from the door, but didn't return to the bed. "You hurt her?"

"God, no." Rudy pulled a flier from his coat pocket and handed it to her. She studied it, even ran her fingers across Abby's face in a soft caress.

"Did you take this picture?" she asked.

"Last week."

"She's happy." The girl pointed at Abby's face. "Her eyes are crinkled at the corners. That's how you can tell."

"Have you seen her?" Rudy asked.

"Sorry. It's a long way from here." She held up the picture. "To here." She sat down on the bed again.

Rudy reached over to take the flier.

CHAPTER 51

"Can I keep it?" she asked.

Rudy nodded and she tucked the photo into the Bible on the nightstand.

"So how'd you get here?"

"The usual way. Dad was an asshole. Ran away from home. Got hooked on drugs. Met a man that promised to take care of me. He was sweet for awhile, then he turned me out."

Rudy looked around the room and asked, "Do you want to leave?"

"Ain't nobody gonna want me now."

They were quiet for a minute as if both acknowledging the truth.

"When you first ran away, where'd you stay?" he asked.

"Couch surfed with friends for awhile, but with my drug habit I wore out my welcome real quick. This old pervert let me stay with him for a few months if I'd clean the house naked, but that got old. Then I met Carl." She talked like she was repeating the weather report, but she wouldn't meet his eyes. Sadness pulled her features down.

"What's that?" he asked pointing at several pills on the nightstand next to a mortar and pestle.

"Oxy." She met his eyes.

"What's it like?"

"The whole world melts away like waking up from a bad dream." When she finished her row of cheese and crackers, she lit a cigarette. She balanced the Camel at the place where her too dark lipstick ended and her gums started. After a long drag, she exhaled the smoke as she might blow out a candle. "You don't wanna mess with that."

She crawled across the bed toward him until she was in his face. He thought she was about to kiss him, but she exhaled smoke into his face like a dragon begging him for a fight. "You still got hope. Don't kill it before its dead."

They both looked toward the door as voices grew louder outside followed by banging on the door.

Chapter 52

When Rudy disappeared into a room, Garrison and Otto resettled into the idling Ford. Otto lifted his Stanley Thermos from the backseat and refilled their travel mugs. Smokey ghosts of warm vapor filled the air with the intoxicating scent of coffee.

"What'd ya think he's doing in there?" Otto nodded to the room Rudy disappeared into. "Hand job?"

Garrison sputtered trying to keep the coffee from spewing out of his nose. He swallowed and recovered. "I don't think so. Poor kid just lost his virginity three nights ago. I can't imagine he's soliciting sexual favors."

The men sipped in silence. Snow fell in lacy jags, like ballerinas falling from the heavens and using the frigid sky as an elaborate stage.

"County Investigator. That takes some ambition," Otto said. Garrison could tell he was digging for a conversation and avoiding the obvious topics of Abby and Rudy.

"Work was simply a way of escaping Chicago," Garrison said

"Chicago can be a mean town. Chew you up. It spit me out twice."

"I didn't bust you, did I?" Garrison asked.

"Naw. I got ran out of town on a rail by the Black Disciples."

"That had to hurt."

"My ink doesn't engender feelings of goodwill from the darker-skinned peoples of the world." Otto tapped his tattooed knuckles on the dashboard.

"I can only imagine."

A large fist pounded on the driver's side window, pulling both men from their banter.

"What the fuck you doing here?" a large African American man yelled through the window.

Garrison didn't know how to answer the question. Tell the truth and the pimp would beat them, but no convenient lie occurred to him.

"Get the fuck out of the car!" he yelled. "Now, motherfuckers!"

They climbed out of the SUV. Garrison held on to his stainless steel travel mug in case he needed it as a weapon. When Otto rounded the back of the SUV, he carried the large thermos with the same intent.

The man's black leather trench coat hung open to display an over-sized set of matching khaki Dickies work clothes and a huge diamond encrusted cross necklace that swung with each swirling head bob.

"What the fuck you doing here?" the man asked again.

"Excuse me," Garrison said. He stepped to the side and away from the vehicle to give him a clearer path if he needed to bolt.

"Time for you to leave." He stepped forward and poked a finger into Garrison's chest.

"We're waiting for our friend," Otto said pointing to Rudy's room.

"Man, that's fucked up."

"We're not interested in your girls," Garrison said.

"So it's me you got a problem with?"

"Yeah. That's right."

"You dumb motherfucker. You know who you're messing with?" He lifted his shirt revealing a Chicago gang tattoo and reached for his waistband.

"I wouldn't do that if I were you," Otto said.

Garrison reached into his coat's inner pocket for his police credentials, but Otto put a hand on his shoulder.

Garrison forgot the badge in his pocket and lunged for the coward in front of him. He took one swing and dropped the man. When the man's limp body smacked the cracked pavement a nine-millimeter flew from his waistband and skittered across the parking lot. Garrison picked up the gun with gloved hands, ejected the magazine, thumbed out all the rounds and pocketed them. He dropped the gun and magazine next to the man. He kicked the pimp in the ribs four, five, six times before Otto wrapped an arm around his midsection and pulled him away.

"Not cool," Otto said looking down at the pimp splayed out on the ground.

Garrison pounded on the door to the room Rudy was hiding in. The girl answered the door with Rudy looking over her shoulder. Garrison reached past her, grabbed Rudy by his coat collar and yanked him out of the room.

Outside, he led Rudy to the SUV and roughly pushed him into the backseat like he'd place a suspect in the back of his squad car. The girl stood in the doorway to her room and puffed on a cigarette. Smoke poured from her mouth and nostrils like a dragon after too many battles with Saint George. Otto crawled in behind the wheel and revved the engine while Garrison dove into the passenger seat.

The Explorer fishtailed as they slid onto Southeast Fourteenth, but Otto kept it under control, allowing the speed to drop to slow crawl over a thick sheet of glass.

Once the car was under control, Otto pulled his phone from his coat pocket. Garrison slapped the phone out of his hand to the floorboard.

"What the fuck?" Otto said.

"No cops," Garrison said.

"Come on, man. I'd feel a lot better knowing that gun is off the streets."

A loud wail sounded from the back of the car.

CHAPTER 52

Otto checked the rearview for a police car or flashing lights. Garrison's heart sank into his stomach until he looked into the backseat. Rudy's head was tossed back, neck corded as he screamed to the ceiling. In all his years of witnessing the misery of the human condition, Garrison had never seen it manifested this acutely. Once the boy's primal scream faded, his hands clenched into white-knuckled fists. He held his fists to his temples in a posture of confused pain and anger. He massaged circles into his scalp until he started slamming his fists into the side of his head.

"Pull over!" Garrison shouted. "Now!"

Otto pulled into Mr. Rangoon, a Chinese buffet closed early due to the weather. The garish neon sign in the window cast their faces in eerie red light. When they stopped Garrison jumped from the passenger seat, opened the back door and drug Rudy out into the parking lot by one flailing arm.

"What the fuck!" Rudy screamed at Garrison. He shoved him, but Garrison was unswayed on his steady feet. Rudy leaned his right shoulder back, a telltale sign he was winding up to take a swing. As Rudy's fist moved past his body, Garrison grabbed the boy's wrist and spun him around pinning Rudy's arm behind his back. Rudy yelped in pain and stopped struggling.

Garrison held Rudy's arm until his breathing became less ragged and released him. Rudy stepped away and massaged his shoulder.

"He's gonna kill her and there's nothing I can do." Rudy paced on a small strip of grass in front of the closed restaurant punching his thighs with each step.

Otto stepped between them and asked, "What happened in that room?"

"I didn't fuck her, if that's what you're asking," Rudy yelled in Otto's face.

"I'm asking what happened."

"She said that hope is bullshit." Rudy's shoulders sagged like all the anger ran out of his fingers and puddled on the icy pavement.

Garrison looked over at Otto for help, but Otto had assumed the same defeated stance as Rudy. He knew from experience that losing hope was the entrance to despair on the long road into hell.

They all sat in silence for several moments while wind buffeted the car like a maniacal mother trying to rock a baby to sleep.

Rudy turned toward Otto. "I asked for your help not a tour of hell. Fuck this town!" Rudy said. "Why in the hell would you live here?"

"Decent music scene. Lots of minor league sports," Otto said.

"And the rest of it?"

"Ninety-nine percent of the people who live here would never know there's a meth lab down the street or hookers frequenting their favorite gas station."

"Bullshit." Rudy spat the word like it was a swig of bitter coffee.

Chapter 53

Driving the five miles from Mr. Rangoon back to the shelter took an hour as thick flakes of snow fell over a thin layer of black ice glazing the road. No one spoke, either out of reverence for their journey through hell or to allow Garrison to drive without distraction.

Rudy stared out the window at the illuminated signage of fast food joints, used car lots and big box hardware stores. Windows glazed with ice made the world beyond the windows go wavy like they were in a submarine trolling murky waters. The world rolled by in undulating currents and tides not dictated by the moon but by the jet stream.

The abstract wheat sculpture looked like it had been dusted with glitter as it shimmered outside the Franciscan Outreach Shelter. The men hustled into the building in an effort more like skating than walking.

They filed into Otto's office and fell into the provided chairs without looking at each other. Otto flipped on the flat screen television across from his desk. The chatter of the news anchors was welcome in the looming silence.

"Can you believe this shit?" Otto pointed at the ten o' clock news. "The biggest manhunt in Iowa's history, a hundred year storm and all they can talk about is shopping."

The top news story consisted of several shots of local malls before they cut to another story about a trampling death at a mall on the east coast. Abby's life hung in the balance and the news focused on the tragic effects of rampant commercialism.

Otto turned to Garrison. "Aren't you glad you don't have to deal with that? People killing each other over cell phones and the latest toy craze."

"There was a fist fight at Walmart last year over who knows what. I swear people's IQs plummet when they walk into that building."

Rudy glanced at his watch and took another dose of medicine from his coat pocket. With a handful of pills, he caught Otto's eye. Otto nodded and reached into the mini fridge tucked under his desk. He threw cans of Pabst to Garrison and Rudy.

"Drink up, Cowboy," Otto said.

Rudy glanced at Garrison for approval.

"We're out of my jurisdiction," Garrison said. "Besides you look like you could use a drink."

Rudy popped the pills into his mouth, cracked open the can and took a long pull of lukewarm beer. He choked as one of the capsules caught in his throat.

"God made beer because he loves us and wants us to be happy," Otto said.

"But he made whiskey to keep the Irish from ruling the world," Garrison said.

"You gonna be alright to drive home?" Rudy asked. He tapped his fingers on the cool can, anxious to get home, sleep in his own bed and prove to his mother that he was all right.

"We ain't going home tonight," Garrison said. "Driving in this weather would be suicidal, if not homicidal."

Otto turned off the television. "We don't have any open beds. Ran out of beds at eight this morning and we ran a lottery for the waiting chairs. This floor can be comfortable in a pinch."

"People enter a lottery just to sit in the chairs?" Rudy asked.

"On nights that the temp drops below freezing we offer spots in our chairs. It isn't ideal but it is better than freezing to death on the street."

CHAPTER 53

Otto turned to his wall of magic tricks and metro shelving behind his desk. From a lower shelf he pulled out several sleeping bags, pillows and sleeping pads. "Not exactly five-star accommodations, but it beats spending the night in the ditch or wrapped around a tree."

Chapter 54

Aidan faced the bar and stared at the neon domestic beer signs, NASCAR plaques, an infamous picture of Babe Ruth and small placards advertising fried delicacies served in red plastic baskets. Each patron's face reflected the eerie red glow from the neon signs, each face marred by bad marriages and a life of disappointment. The bartender, a large man with "Coop" tattooed down his forearm, walked up and nodded at him.

"Vodka tonic," Aidan said.

"Got some ID?" Coop asked.

Aidan pulled a driver's license from a ratty brown wallet and slid it across the bar picture side down. Coop furrowed his brow, looked at the ID and returned it as delivered. Aidan had stolen the ID from an unlocked room at a frat party late in his freshman year.

Two men shambled into the bar, dusting snow from patched thrift store coats. The taller of the pair wore boots with bright red shoelaces like a lumberjack. Aidan recognized him from earlier in the day. Paul Bunyan might be Aidan's ticket to finding his sister. The other man donned a Vietnam veteran ball cap and wore the narrow-eyed glare of a man that had seen war.

The two men took the open bar stools next to Aidan. He considered chatting them up at first, but waited for a natural way into their conversation without appearing to be an interloper.

CHAPTER 54

"It's colder than a polar bear's balls out there," Paul said.

"Colder than a witches titty in a brass bra." Camo guy said in a slow, slurred voice.

"Cold enough to freeze the balls off a brass monkey."

Aidan took a sip of his beer and said, "Colder then your ex-wife's heart."

Both men snorted with laughter.

"Good one," the lumberjack said.

His short friend threw two crumpled five-dollar bills on the bar and nodded at the bartender. Without taking their order, Coop poured two shots and traded a five for two ones.

The acrid smell from the shots wafted toward Aidan and turned his stomach. The jungle juice from the frat's Saint Patrick's Day party was terrible, but the stench of this stuff made him think of the moonshine his roommate brought in from his father's still in Kentucky.

"So what's your story, pal?" the lumberjack asked.

"Looking for a girl," he said.

"Aren't we all?" The lumberjack punched his friend on the shoulder to indicate that he should laugh at the lame joke.

"I ate lunch at a soup kitchen on the Eastside." Aidan pulled Abby's wallet from his jacket pocket. "The girl in front of me dropped this. I've been looking for her all day to return it."

"Any money in it?"

"Never looked."

"Who says there's no honor among thieves?" The lumberjack guffawed.

The men sat in silence as Aidan nursed his beer. The bums sipped their shots wincing with each drink.

"You guys seen a pretty teenager with bright red hair and freckles? She looks like she just walked out of a mall rather than a homeless shelter."

"You're looking for a fucking unicorn. Most homeless bitches look like they fell off the back of a truck." The lumberjack threw back the rest of his drink and laughed. "You tried walking the river?"

"Not looking to jump in."

"Naw, man. There's a bunch of camps along the river."

"Homeless camps?" Aidan asked.

"Start around Seventh and Thomas Beck. Walk west on the bike path and you're bound to find several camps along the way."

"Thanks, man. Next round is on me," Aidan said and motioned for the bartender.

"Another drink for me and a round for my new buddies." Aidan motioned to the two empty shot glasses on the bar.

The bartender squinted at him until Aidan put a twenty on the bar.

"There's a great brewery along the way. Too bad it's so late. Coulda got ya good pint."

"Speaking of which," Aidan said and glanced down at a missing watch. "Don't like driving after closing time."

Aidan left the bar and scampered across the icy parking lot to his stolen Chevy Malibu. After two tries the engine sputtered to life. He shifted into drive and pulled away from the bar. He turned down Seventh Street toward the river. Halfway across the Raccoon River Bridge he hit a patch of ice and lost control of the car. The back end fishtailed. The rear driver's side tire caught bare pavement and spun the car sideways. As the guardrail flashed by the windshield, Aidan feared the spinning wheels would catch and launch the sedan over the rails into the frozen river below.

The bridge sloped uphill and slowed his glide across the invisible ice. The downtown skyline shrunk out the driver's side window. Out the passenger window, he spotted a sign denoting the T intersection looming closer and closer. Gripping the useless steering wheel, he braced for impact.

Although slowed by the ascent, the car slammed into the signpost. The

CHAPTER 54

collision hurled his head into the window, cracking it.

Once he righted himself, he pulled up his messenger bag from the floorboard, shook off the broken glass and abandoned the stolen car.

Aidan crossed the street and traversed the steep slope down to the bike path paralleling the river. Stylized, wrought iron lampposts cast pearlescent pools of light at regular intervals on the icy trail lighting his way to his sister.

Chapter 55

Abby considered her sleeping position before she crawled under the mountain of blankets. She wouldn't be able to move under the crushing weight once ensconced in the heavy bedding for the night. According to Rose, the temperature was going to drop well below freezing and Abby's plan did not include becoming a human Popsicle. She donned every piece of clothing she had and then pulled on woolen mittens and a thick beanie she'd borrowed from Rose and covered herself with every blanket in the tent. She waited as late as possible to sleep, walking several laps around the camp to kill time and wear herself out before entering the tent. It would be a long night alone in the wilderness and she desperately needed the sleep. She set the unsheathed hatchet on Rose's pillow, pulled off Rudy's sweater, rolled it up and cuddled it under one arm like a child holds a beloved teddy bear.

Two days away from the house without Dad making every decision, she was beginning to realize the full extent of her family's dysfunction. Distance allowed her to see her dad less as an overprotective and loving parent and more as the controlling, abusive monster he really was. Forbidding her from having a cell phone was about his need to control all communication. He dictated her clothes, her hobbies, even prevented her from driving.

The more she thought about it the hotter her cheeks grew like anger was burning her up from the inside. Anger was a new emotion, one she

CHAPTER 55

didn't understand, but maybe she needed it tonight as her resolve to stand up to her brother grew from a small seed to a strong tree unmoving in the gale.

She relished her first night alone, without her parents asleep down the hall or Rose snoring next to her. In a few short days, they'd become fast friends and the closest thing she had to a sister. Rose proved a better sibling than Aidan ever had. Although Abby felt safe for the night, it was time to draw the danger away from Rose and the camp. More important, it was time to stand up to her brother.

Tonight was a test: spending the night alone to prove that she wasn't the spoiled princess she was raised to be. Tomorrow a new test waited for her. She'd hike out of camp and present herself to the nearest police station. She'd stand defiant against Aidan and protect those she loved.

With great effort she turned onto her side and pushed all thoughts of her brother and Rudy out of her mind to allow the sandman easy access. She thought about decorating her dorm room next fall. Would she go with the typical preppy theme forced upon her by her father or would she choose something more modern? What would her roommate be like? Maybe she'd be like the sister she never had. Her name would be something wholesome, like Mary Ann or Kimberly or Robin.

They'd be best friends and study buddies because they were both in the pre-med program. They'd go to their first frat party together and get drunk. They'd nurse each other through the hangover with bottles of 7-Up and saltines. Mary Ann's parents would invite her over for holidays or maybe they'd go on a ski vacation to Colorado. She'd create a new family – a better one.

Abby fell asleep imagining herself zipping down the ski slopes, the wind blowing back her hair and the warmth of friendship burning in her heart.

Chapter 56

After two blocks of stumbling down the bike path, Aidan was finally warm in his snowsuit cobbled together from the surplus store. His body warmth loosened his muscles still aching from the car accident. Gusting wind pushed drifts across the path, so he followed the line of lampposts. The snow glowed pink reflecting the lights of the city.

He flexed his hand inside his gloves. He had sprained his wrist bracing against the steering wheel, adding abuse on top of the injuries sustained during the first half of his mission. The SmartWool liner gloves inside Thinsulate mittens kept his digits limber even as they swelled to fill the layers. To keep his mind off the pain, he counted his rhythm like he did during physical training runs. The cadence cleared his mind.

Four steps. Two squeezes of his fists. In through the nose and out through the mouth. Four steps forward.

I am an American solider. I am a warrior. I will always place the mission first.

After passing twelve lampposts, Aidan noticed a tent on the slope between him and the river. Powdery snow covered the domed surface except a single edge of blue tarp that fluttered and snapped in the gale.

Aidan studied the slope, trying to determine the easiest way down to the tent without loosing his footing and slipping into the frozen river below. The tent was perched on a small rocky ledge ten yards below the

CHAPTER 56

path. Sliding was his only option as snow covered any footholds.

He sat on the ground and leaned to one side. He dug his heels into the snow, shifted his weight and began to slide. The snow compacted and turned to ice under his mass. He careened down the hill until his swollen fingers caught the rocky edge and his boots hung inches from the shoreline. He pulled himself up to the ledge using the fingertip pull-up technique he perfected only two months ago to impress his ROTC chief officer.

Slumped against the hill, he slowed his breathing by counting to seven with each inhale and exhale. A low, thin whine issued from inside the tent. He thought it was the wind at first, until something bumped against the side of the tent.

"Settle down, Rasta," a whispery voice said. Aidan couldn't determine the gender of the voice.

He slipped a utility knife from his pocket, but his chubby, injured thumb couldn't work the mechanism to expose the blade. He pulled off his mittens, but was still unable to make the blade work. He stripped off the liner gloves and was at last able to expose the blade. In an economical motion, he slit the thin nylon wall separating him from his target. A small dreadlocked man sat bolt upright in his sleeping bag, his eyes wide in the gloom.

"What the hell, man?" he said. "You got the wrong fucking tent."

"Not really."

Aidan launched himself across the tent and lunged for the man's throat with both hands. Although he screamed like Ann Darrow when she saw King Kong, the man went down fast.

"Real men don't caterwaul like that," Aidan said. He punched the man in the face. The hit shot fingers of white light across his vision as pain blossomed up his arms radiating from his mangled fingers. "Don't you wanna be a man?" Instead of hitting him again, he bounced the man's head off the tent's dirty floor and knocked him out.

The Australian Shepherd began yipping and yowling at Aidan. Sitting at his master's feet with his head tilted to the heavens, Rasta's howl rang through the night like a siren.

Aidan wrapped his hands around the man's throat and pressed his thumbs into the hyoid bone above the Adam's apple. He'd learned the difference from his ROTC boxing coach. The lesson came as a warning about the difference between winning a bout and going to prison. He didn't feel the bone snap, instead a surge of energy filtered through his body like a triple espresso.

Chapter 57

Abby woke with a start. The wind screamed like a man in pain, then turned into a howl like a wild dog baying at the moon. Glancing around the tent, nothing was amiss in the dark. She returned her head to the impromptu pillow made of dirty laundry stuffed into a worn tee shirt. She closed her heavy eyelids and waited for sleep to return. Her mind drifted back to her freshman year fantasy and imagined herself meeting a study group in a cloistered corner of a dusty library.

Something large bumped into the side of the tent at her feet. Her head snapped back up and her eyes flew open while her heart leapt into her throat.

Aidan. One night alone and she was about to die.

There was a snuffling noise like a large animal sniffing around the edges of the ground tarp for spilled crumbs. Abby jumped out of the blankets and snatched up the hatchet.

"Hey, you!" Abby said, her voice inaudible above the wind. "Get away from here."

She shook her head. Her voice was small and shaky. She sounded like a frightened child hollering at the monster in the closet – a weak and feeble child. Something bumped the side of the tent once more and retreated with a series of faint footsteps.

In the resulting silence, below the sound of the howling wind, she heard similar snuffling noises around the camp. Her hand began to ache from her white-knuckled grip on the hatchet.

She pulled down the tent zipper undoing the teeth one by one to avoid making a sound and scaring off whoever was snooping around.

She peered through the screen while her breath materialized in white puffs. Silhouetted against the lights of the city reflected in the low-lying clouds, a large herd of deer scavenged the camp. A buck with an impressive rack looked up at her, the silver-yellow eye shine unmistakable in the twilight. The buck looked at her for a long moment before returning to grazing on the few tufts of exposed grass.

The presence of the animals calmed and reassured her. Animals sensed evil as part of the fight or flight response. If these deer were comfortable grazing in the camp, Aidan couldn't be nearby. As the sandman dusted her eyes with sleep, her fantasy morphed from the collegiate to a fairy tale. She was transported from her tent in the homeless camp to a gilded canopy bed laden with satin and velvet in the high mountains of the Alps, surrounded by conifers decorated with twinkle lights and protected by a herd of loyal, fierce steeds.

Chapter 58

Rudy grew tired of tossing and turning on the floor of Otto's office. His pile of thrift store blankets and hotel reject pillows was wedged between the big man's desk and a shelf of survival supplies. During his last attempt to get comfortable, he knocked over stacks of fire starters and water purification tablets.

He reached into his pockets and withdrew the day's ephemera: gum wrappers, food receipts and a packet of pills. He squinted at the small, white pills. They weren't his. The girl in the hotel, must have slipped them into his pocket in the shuffle to leave.

From what little Rudy knew of street drugs, these were neither meth nor anything more designer. They had to be prescription painkillers, Oxy or hillbilly heroin as she called it.

He'd been prescribed a cocktail of Xanax for anxiety, but these illicit white tabs tempted him more acutely. They offered an invitation to forget his plight, if only for a while. They offered an open door for him to step into a world beyond his own.

He opened the baggie and sniffed. Instead of filling his palate with the intoxicating scent of oblivion, they smelled bitter and inorganic. He dropped two of them into his palm, weighed and considered them. He placed them on his tongue, as he would put the Eucharist each Sunday. Holding them in his mouth, he waited to either drift away or muster the courage to swallow.

Bile and stomach acid rose up the back of his throat, catching his breath and gagging him. Rudy launched into a coughing fit and spat the pills out. They tumbled down his shirtfront and came to rest on the sleeping bag. Once he recovered his breath, he placed the sodden pills back into the bag, stood and went in search of water to rinse his mouth.

Although he'd looked oblivion in the face all day, even chased it down dark alleys and into society's darkest corners, pills weren't the answer, not for him.

Rudy picked up his boots and stepped out of the office in his heavy wool socks. He wasn't sure which of the big men snored louder. Otto's exhalations sounded like Darth Vader with a sinus infection, while Garrison's breaths reminded him of a whale breaching the ocean's surface for air. In the hallway with the door muffling the snores, Rudy was met with a more ferocious noise. Wind whipped across the top of the building and sounded like a jet warming up for take off. Thirst and curiosity about the weather called him into the dining area.

A woman sat near a large bank of windows tuning a guitar. When Rudy stepped to the vending machines beside her, he recognized the flower etching on the guitar and rose detailed strap.

"You live down by the river," he said, pointing at her guitar as he fed quarters into the vending machine.

"Other girls would be insulted by such a remark," she said and returned to humming and tuning.

"I'm sorry." He made his soda selection and watched as she worked the tuning knobs and hummed.

"Don't sweat it." She motioned to the window ledge next to her. "Have a seat. You're making me nervous."

He popped open the soda, took a swig and sat down. The syrupy sugar washed away the acrid taste of the pills and dulled the beer on his breath.

"I noticed your guitar the other day when I was talking to Robinson."

"And you are?" she asked with a disinterested tone.

CHAPTER 58

"Cowboy." He offered his hand. When they shook, he could feel the thick calluses developed over years of guitar picking. The same calluses he needed to develop if he hoped to play one day.

"I'm Rose," she said without looking up from the fret board. She started strumming a Willie Nelson tune. "You play?"

He shook his head and put his hands up. "Been trying to teach myself, but it's not going well."

She hummed a few bars of the song.

"Where do you play?" he asked.

"The skywalks pay better than coffeehouse gigs. Besides it's always seventy-two degrees with a thirty percent chance of rain in the skywalks. Not a bad place to spend a winter day." She smiled and adjusted the strap across her shoulder. "What are you doing up?"

Although stilted, this was the most normal and honest conversation he'd had all day. Chatting about music and weather was oddly comforting. He shrugged and frowned into his soda. "What about you?"

She turned to look at the snow falling past the window. "Worried about my friend, Red. She wouldn't come to the shelter tonight."

"Why not?" Rudy asked.

"Scared and stupid. Mostly scared. I don't know what happened to that girl but she's way freaked out."

Rudy's heart jumped against his chest wall and sucked away his breath. Red hair. Abby.

"What's she look like?" he asked, trying to keep the panic out of his voice.

Rose laughed. "Like an Irish elf. Freckles, up-turned nose and a fisherman's sweater."

"A grey sweater that's way too big for her?" Rudy asked.

Rose nodded.

"Where is she? You gotta tell me where she is." Rudy grabbed Rose's shoulders and looked her straight in the eyes to let her know that he meant business. His hands slid down her shoulders to her elbows. His fingers detected an anomaly on her chambray shirt, some raised stitching. He moved the fabric of her shirt to find an embroidered flower. Although most embroidery looked the same, he knew this was Abby's work, like she'd signed it.

"Where is she?" he demanded.

"Is she in trouble?" she asked. Her brownish-black eyes widened in fear for her friend.

"Where is she?" Rudy asked again shaking her shoulders this time.

"She's in my tent."

Rudy sprinted back to the office and paused at the door. An internal debate raged – wake the men or not? They'd helped him get this far he could make it the rest of the way on his own. Besides, he didn't want to wait for them to get ready. Rudy slipped into the office, stepped over the snoring men in his stocking feet. He tucked his coat, hat and gloves under one arm. Then headed into the growing storm.

Chapter 59

Abby shivered under the mounds of blankets. Her jaw ached from her teeth chattering all night. She thought her teeth might crack if she lay there any longer listening to the wind whip through the denuded trees. One of the tethers holding down the rainfly came loose in the gale. It fluttered and snapped against the tent like the wings of a bird chased from its perch.

Light flashed outside the tent, illuminating the small space for a moment. Her heart lifted when she thought it was the police coming to rescue her as if they heard her prayers the night before, but thunder clapped overhead.

She extracted herself from the crushing pile of blankets and quilts. She took the hatchet from Rose's pillow, pulled the leather sheath off the steel blade, unzipped the tent flap and stepped out into the squall. Six inches had fallen during her fitful night of sleep.

Abby scanned the white landscape. Under better circumstances, she relished the first snow of the season. The insulating white muffled the world's ugly noise and blanketed the hibernating land. The wind and snow masked the deer's footprints. The growing storm also provided another layer of protection between her and Aidan.

The lightning came in pulses rather than bolts, illuminating the low clouds in an eerie gray light like a strobe running low on battery. Each pulse of electricity lit up the thousands of tiny, crystalline snowflakes floating among the trees like wintery fireflies.

She wanted to gather wood, warm up by the fire and wait for the storm to pass before hiking to the police station. Most of the low-hanging branches near camp had been harvested for previous fires, so she hiked past the boundaries of camp and beyond where she and Rose collected firewood the day before. High stepping through the snow was a welcome workout and warmed her quickly.

The Raccoon River was reduced to a foot-wide creek running through the frozen river channel. In the windstorm, high limbs rubbed against each other – the resulting noise sounded like the happy squeal of a giggling baby. The sound raised the hairs on the back of her neck but she was undeterred. With the snap of a cracking bullwhip, a tree limb cracked from a high bough and crashed to earth. She would come back for this branch on her way back to camp.

She slipped off her thin gloves and started chopping off a low branch. After adding two branches to her pile, she started working on a higher branch. After two swings the branch sagged. She held it up with her left hand, cursing her small stature. She swung the hatchet again with her right hand. The blade stuttered off the frozen wood and buried itself in her left hand.

Her wide eyes watched in shock as blood blossomed around the hatchet head. She released her grip on the handle, but the head remained in the webbing between thumb and pointer finger for a split second before tumbling into the snow. She clasped the wound in her hand, but the trembling hand was too weak to hold the edges of the gash together.

Chapter 60

Aidan's pounding footfalls reverberated in his fur-lined hat and blocked out the shushing wind. The snow drifted like lines on a topographic map denoting the rifts between bike path pavement and tiered riverbank.

Aidan used the bike trail to hike the entire circumference of Gray's Lake Park. The park's namesake, Gaylord Gray, once mined gravel and sand out of the pond, expanding the oxbow into a larger lake and providing the concrete for the main runway at Des Moines International Airport two miles to the south. City planners redeveloped the area after the great floods of 1993 and added the trail around the lake.

He assumed that all planes were grounded as snow fell at an alarming rate while thunder ripped back the night and lightning exposed the morning landscape. Aidan hadn't slept since his night squatting in the farmhouse down the road from Rudy. The thrill of killing the bum wore off with exhaustion taking hold. Hiking through the falling snow proved a better workout than any ropes course or physical training regimen devised by his ROTC unit leaders.

The first clap of thunder made him jump and he yelped like a child – the same child strapped to a stockade in the backyard during a thunderstorm after seeking solace in his parents' bed.

"No son of mine is going to piss himself every time the weather turns," Father had said.

That night the storm had passed in an hour, but it felt like a lifetime as the clouds cried and boomed overhead and hail lashed his body. After that night in the stockade, he no longer feared the weather.

He had hiked for hours and found one occupied tent among dozen of empty shanties. He was running out of options as he neared Fleur drive and the end of the suggested route. His shitty stolen Chevy Malibu was wrapped around a pole waiting to be discovered by police with his duffel bag in the back. The discovery of his belongings would bring the manhunt much closer to him.

I am an American soldier. I am a warrior. I will always place the mission first. I will never accept defeat. I will never quit.

The trail turned north out of Gray's Lake Park, next to the Raccoon River and back into downtown. Across the river, a narrow strip of land jutted out into the river bend, unprotected by the levy and left undeveloped because of its proximity to the river and lake. Aidan squinted through the dawning light and heavy snowfall. Through the thick tree cover he noticed several tents and shacks. His heart leapt with the joy of a leprechaun at rainbow's end and he banished the thought of his last resort from his head.

He quickened his pace to a fast slog through the piled snow, ran where the path was protected from the wind and the snow hadn't drifted and high-stepped through waist-deep drifts.

In all his anxiousness, it took him half an hour to cross the Martin Luther King bridge and make his way on to the forested floodplain. He found the camp situated around a dugout fire pit. Only snow stirred in the preternatural silence. He ripped open the first tent and discovered a tangle of blankets and dirty clothes. Next he opened the rickety door to the nearest shack. No one slept in the primitive rope bed. He checked two more shanties with no avail.

The camp was empty. She was gone. Mission failed.

He spun around in the endless white, looking for any sign of life. His

CHAPTER 60

heart sick and out of time. A scream sounded from the woods to the south.

Chapter 61

Bundled in his heavy farm coat, wool cap and heavy mittens, Rudy left the warm confines of the homeless shelter. The wheat sculpture was unrecognizable under several inches of snow. He walked in the same direction he and Otto trekked a few days prior. The unplowed snow was knee-deep and still coming down as he trudged on. As he broke a trail in the snow, he thought of his animals on the farm and hoped his father put them all in the barn to survive the night.

A layer of ice remained hidden under the snow. The first snow of the season was always the wettest and this was no exception. His thick, wool socks were no match for the frigid snowmelt soaking into his boots.

The hike that had taken him and Otto only fifteen minutes was approaching an hour when he reached the first structure buried in the snow. Rudy had never seen snowfall like this. He'd heard his father and other old farmers talk about thundersnow like it was a mystical act of God. Trudging through waist-deep drifts as he crossed from the industrial complex while listening to thunder rumble and boom with the staccato flashes of lightning, Rudy decided Dante got it wrong all those years ago. Hell's address was more north than south: more ice than fire. Sinners needed a parka rather than sunscreen.

If adrenaline wasn't pushing him ever forward, Rudy may have stopped and reflected on the surroundings. Instead, he wiped the melted flakes from his heated brow and charged through the brush.

CHAPTER 61

As the sun rose behind thick layers of clouds the fog lifted from the trees and the lightning raced across the sky. A jagged white streak touched down nearby with a deafening crack like worlds crashing together. Rudy felt the blast of thunder in his bones like the shock and sting of defibrillator paddles.

Rudy ripped open Rose's tent. Abby wasn't there. He tore through the myriad of quilts redolent with acrid body odor. Under the third layer of blankets he found Abby's penny loafers. The loafers were her favorites and contrary to the surroundings – like a diamond in a coalfield.

The tracks leaving the tent were barely discernible in the drifting snow. Rudy followed the divots to the edge of camp where the trees grew denser. He paused in his trudging when another set of less disturbed and fresher tracks intersected Abby's. Rudy waited for the wind to die down so he could hear but even when the squall subsided the leaves remaining on the cottonwoods rustled against each other.

Past the tents and shanties, beyond the fire ring and past the land cleared of easy kindling and firewood, Abby stood in the thick underbrush. She appeared more as an apparition. Rudy blinked the snow from his eyes and looked again. Her red hair fluoresced against the grey sky and black of the hibernating cottonwoods. Another flash of lightning lit up the snow falling around her. She looked less like Abby and more like a pagan goddess summoning the weather.

He called out her name, but the wind caught his words and carried them off. He sprinted toward her, but skidded to a halt when he saw that he had not won the race.

Chapter 62

Thin, gray light filtered into the dim office through thin slats in the mini blinds tucked behind the stacked utility shelves. Garrison poked at Otto's hulking mass ensconced in the Marmot sleeping bag.

"Wake up," he said.

The man woke with loud snort like a hog waking for mealtime. "What?" he asked, sitting straight up in his mummy bag.

"Rudy's gone," Garrison said.

"Naw," Otto said and cleared his throat. He stretched his arms out in front of him and shook them like a jungle cat waking from a long nap in the afternoon sun. "He probably just went to the bathroom."

"He's gone. Coat and boots are gone, too."

"Fuck."

Watching Otto extract himself from the sleeping bag was like watching a street corner contortionist climb out of his tiny, clear plastic box. Each one of Otto's joints creaked and popped as he pulled it from the bag. When he stood, Otto shook his head to wake himself. It was an impressive display of the flexibility of human flesh as his cheeks and jowls swung at a slower rate than his bone structure, like a slow motion shot of a dog shaking off water.

In the large dayroom, a pretty young woman sat on a sofa in front of a huge bank of windows facing the Raccoon River. Low-lying clouds

CHAPTER 62

roiled and churned while snow fell at a dizzying rate like they looked out at the world from the inside of a snow globe. Instead of watching the sky falling outside, her eyes didn't blink while watching the news on a small TV mounted to the wall.

"The ugly guy on TV called it a snow squall." She said as a way of greeting. "Never heard it called that before."

"Ugly guy?" Garrison asked.

"You know, the pasty guy. Plaid suit, plaid shirt and striped tie, looks like an optical illusion." Her voice was drowsy like each word took effort and careful consideration.

"Hey, Rose," Otto said. "You seen the cowboy?"

"There was no stopping him," she said, her face full of disdain for Garrison. "He saw this and left." She pointed to an ornate flower stitched on the sleeve of her button-down western shirt.

"This looks like something my wife would do," Garrison said as he fingered the yellow threads. "You didn't sew this, did you?"

"Red did it."

"Who?" Otto asked.

"She's a new girl in camp. I took her in."

The girl tucked her lips into her mouth. Her lower jaw quivered like she was going to cry.

"Did you tell Rudy how to find her?"

She returned to staring at the television, tears trickled down her sad face. Garrison looked up at the flat screen. The news showed the same loop of yearbook photos of Aidan, Abby and Rudy over speculation about their whereabouts.

Rose pointed at Abby's picture, her jaw dropped without a noise.

"Is that your friend?" Garrison asked.

"She's really in danger? I thought it was bullshit. Just a reason to run away. I knew she was scared but I thought it was paranoia."

"Is that Red?" Garrison asked and pointed at the television.

"Yes."

"Where's Red?" Garrison asked.

"My tent."

Garrison knelt in front of her with his hands pressed together in a praying position turning his back on the weather. "Where's your tent?" Garrison asked.

Otto put a hand on Garrison's shoulder. "I'll show you, but we gotta wait for this shit to pass." He pointed out the window as a flash of lightning streaked the sky.

"Weather happens. Can't change that," Garrison said.

Chapter 63

Tears were a sign of surrender and the abandonment of all hope. She'd screamed not cried when she saw mother's mutilated corpse. She only allowed herself to cry when she ran the hatchet's hot blade down her hand, but now as the hatchet fell from the gash in her arm her resolve crumbled. When she turned to face her brother, the salty remnants of her hope etched warm paths down her cold cheeks.

Frozen in fear with the entire world at a stand still, she could hear the tears tumble from her face and hit the knit of Rose's sweater. The plink of her blood drops falling into the red puddle at her feet echoed louder than the thunder crashing overhead.

Aidan left for college a skinny, awkward boy and returned a hulking mass of muscles. His monstrous new physique lacked bolts jutting out of his non-existent neck and crude stitches creating patchwork out of his pale, freckled skin.

"Maybe you aren't quite the pampered princess I thought you were," Aidan said. His voice had a jovial quality Abby'd never heard before. It was playful and menacing.

* * * * *

Garrison grew impatient while pulling on layer after layer. He was anxious to get moving. He wanted Abby in his custody and far from the threat of her brother. Somehow saving Abby in this moment was tantamount to getting Vicky off the streets clean and sober.

He pulled on his boots and paced the floor waiting for Otto to reemerge from his office. This was a familiar position like he was back at home waiting at the front door while Nancy searched the house for a misplaced tube of lip gloss that hid in the bottom of the purse slung over her shoulder.

"Damn it, Otto," Garrison said. "Let's go!"

He perked up when footsteps arose in the hallway. Rose rounded the corner.

"I'm coming with you," she said.

Garrison opened his mouth to object then thought better of it. If Rose were anything like his wife or daughter, she'd harangue and harass him until he relented. He didn't have enough energy for a useless and losing fight.

Rose stood next to Garrison on the entryway rug. Although she must have been anxious to get to her friend, she stood still as a statue. Her quiet company calmed Garrison as much as hanging out with his own daughter.

Clad in snow pants, heavy down parka, Elmer Fudd hat and holding a kitchen broom like a wizard's staff, Otto looked like a kid anxious for a game of broomball except for the bag of kitty litter tucked under an arm. Garrison frowned at the broom, but Otto did everything with intention.

At the back of an empty parking lot a foot of snow covered the Ford. Garrison dodged the avalanche that fell from the SUV's roof and hopped into the driver's seat. Buckled in, he turned the key in the ignition, but the engine protested in a slow, coughing crank. He banged his fist into the steering wheel. Deep breath. In through the nose and out through the mouth.

Otto dropped the bag of kitty litter on to the passenger floorboard and

CHAPTER 63

closed the door. He then used his broom to clean off all the windows and hood.

Rose climbed into the backseat and settled in by snatching the utility quilt from the back and wrapped it around her like she was curling up by a roaring fire. After a few more slow turns, the engine coughed to life.

"Let's roll before another inch falls," Otto said as he climbed into the passenger seat.

"Which way?" Garrison asked.

Otto pointed him the way out to Martin Luther King Jr. Parkway. Garrison didn't touch the gas, but let the engine's high idle pull them along. Accelerating on the snow and ice would send them skittering sideways. The only other car they encountered was pulled off the road gathering half a foot of snow.

"Where the fuck are the snow plows?" Otto asked.

"The governor declared a state of emergency," Rose said. "Plowing is limited to emergency routes."

They pulled onto Sixteenth Street. At the no outlet sign, Garrison looked up from the road at Otto. This couldn't be the right way. The road cut between two abandoned industrial complexes and ended.

The sluggish speed seemed slower in the whiteout conditions. The wipers on high couldn't keep up with the blizzard. Garrison wished he had his shooting glasses or even his old pair of ski goggles to knock down the glare rising off the snow.

Garrison slowed the Explorer to a crawl and hopped the curb. He navigated around the rusted out oil drums blocking the driveway. The white blanket of snow covered any obstacles in their way. Garrison said a small, silent prayer that they wouldn't run over a nail or anything worse. This would be a hell of a place to get a flat.

"See the levy?" Otto asked pointing ahead.

Garrison squinted through the endless white to a narrow strip of raised earth curving next to the parking lot before heading into the woods.

"What about it?"

"It's wide enough to drive on."

Garrison shot Otto an incredulous look.

"Trust me. The guys from Water Works do it all the time to make repairs. You'll have to use that to get us close to the camp."

Garrison looked from Otto to the narrow strip of land. It looked like a set of elevated railroad tracks. He took a deep breath, blew it out and shifted down into first. He encouraged the SUV along the levy at a creep.

Chapter 64

Rudy ran toward Abby's shaking voice but skittered to a stop when he saw Aidan. His whole body shook with anger. Aidan shouted into the wind, his face as red as his hair above his mismatched military uniform.

Rudy hid behind the enormous trunk of a cottonwood. He needed to get a lay of the land and formulate a plan before rushing between them – study the chessboard before moving his next piece. Aidan was twenty feet away behind the tree, but Abby was at least forty feet away to the south of them.

"How did you find me?" Abby asked.

"Your idiot boyfriend led me right to you."

Abby whimpered.

Rudy edged around the tree trying to catch a glimpse of Abby. In this part of the woods, the dense trees blocked the worst of the wind. The resulting snow amounted to a mere six inches. His shuffling footsteps were muffled by the rolling thunder and wind in the high boughs.

"What'd you do to him?" Her question started as a scream, but devolved into blubbering.

Rudy had never seen her shed a tear and the sound of her sobs pulled at the center of his chest. Abby mewled like a wounded cat but the wind caught the pathetic noise and tossed it away. After four steps, he peered around the frosted trunk. She stood in a sea of blood while more of it dripped from her hand.

Without thinking or devising a plan, Rudy stepped from his hiding spot behind the tree and drew Abby's attention – sacrificing a pawn to save the queen. She dropped to her knees and reached out for him. He raised his hand to quiet her. Red dribbled down her hand on to the snow spreading the puddle of red wider. With no weapon and no plan of action, he darted toward Abby and further betrayed his presence to Aidan.

"Where the fuck are you going?" Aidan said. "Hold it right there!"

The three stood in a triangle – a perfect standoff. No one held the advantage while Abby lost more blood.

"You need to quit crying," Rudy said. "It'll make the frostbite worse."

She wiped the tears from her face. Her jaw quivered with either a suppressed sob or the cold leaching deeper into her bones.

Rudy leaned his weight onto his right foot so he could take another step with his left. He searched his brain and the surrounding landscape for some way to distract Aidan. The only answer to terror was more terror. He had to use Aidan's own twisted mind against him.

"I don't know what kind of bullshit the Army taught you, but you'll never be the hero." Rudy took a small step toward Abby. "The hero of our story is already dead."

The flush of anger left Aidan's cheeks as he turned his shoulder toward Abby to face Rudy.

"Your dad was a true genius." He took another step. "Psychological torture is much more difficult and impressive than physical. Wouldn't you agree?"

Aidan's head bob was barely perceptible on his thick neck.

"You aren't capable of that kind of torture," Rudy said.

The muscles around Aidan's jaw twitched as he clenched his teeth. "Fuck you."

"No, thanks." Rudy took another step closer to Abby. Only a few more steps and he could stand between them if it came to it. "What had your

CHAPTER 64

mom learned when you were done with her? Were you able to change her behavior in some way? I don't think so. What you did to your father may have been truly twisted but that revealed more about your psychology than his."

"You're wrong," Abby said, her voice weak but clear.

Aidan spun to face Abby. His face changed from the soft pink of a newborn piglet to brilliant red.

Rudy used the distraction to step forward again. Maintaining the dialogue with Aidan while ignoring Abby's injuries and waning condition, was taking its toll on Rudy. His hands shook and his legs wobbled.

"He's a coward," she said to Rudy while pointing a feeble finger at her brother.

"Fuck you," Aidan spat.

"You're a fucking coward," Abby said.

Abby issued a thin wail and fell from her knees to a lying position in the snow. Without gloves, the fingertips on her good hand were pale and turning blue. Rudy used his teeth the remove his mittens. Without taking his eyes from Aidan's pulsing face, he threw the gloves to Abby. He was loath to lose a layer but she needed them more than he did. Her fingers were quickly moving from frostnip to the more severe degrees of frostbite. Her eyelids fluttered closed over eyes focused on some far away place.

"Abby! Wake up!"

Her eyelids fluttered opened for a brief moment to reveal the whites of her eyes. Her body went limp as she surrendered to the darkness.

Rudy took two running steps toward her.

"Stop right there," Aidan said.

Lightning flashed, followed by a deafening boom of thunder, then a louder crack immediately overhead – closer and more powerful than thunder. Snowballs and icicles sharp as daggers rained down over them. Aidan ducked as a tree fell across the path back into camp.

Rudy used the distraction to run to Abby's aid. He wrapped his arms around her slender shoulders calling her name. She moaned in response. Her skin was impossibly cold and her already pale skin turned blue. She leaned into him but didn't have the strength to return his embrace.

They were rocketed backward when Aidan's body slammed into them. Abby crumpled under the weight of the two men. Aidan struck again and Rudy pitched forward, his head slamming into the tree Abby had been standing in front of.

Aidan slid his fingers under Rudy's stocking cap, grabbed a handful of hair and banged Rudy's head into the tree again. Brilliant white fingers of light spread across his vision before the world went dark. A moment later, or at least what he thought was a moment, Aidan rolled him off Abby's limp body and into a snowbank. An earful of snow snapped Rudy from his stupor.

Aidan gripped the collar of Abby's jacket and pulled her to a sitting position as he squatted over her. "Wake up, you fucking bitch."

Rudy's fingers fumbled on the ground searching for a handhold to help him sit up instead he touched a smooth handle of something. A hatchet. He wrapped his hand around the handle.

"Wake up." Aidan slapped her face. Unconscious, her head moved with the slap showing the other cheek.

With every ounce of his reserve strength, Rudy launched himself at Aidan, his feet failing to find purchase in the snow and he fell forward loosing his grip on the weapon. It bounced off Abby's flank and disappeared into a pile of snow.

Aidan rolled onto his stomach underneath Rudy and tried to shrug him off. Rudy flopped up and down to keep him on the ground. Rudy tried to sucker punch him in the back of the head but Aidan's heavy layers protected him from the blow.

Next thing Rudy heard was a sickening thwack, not of thunder, but Abby swinging the blunt end of the hatchet and making connection

CHAPTER 64

with Aidan's head just above his ear. Rudy scrambled off Aidan as Abby collapsed into the red stain spreading in the snow. A trickle of blood trailed out Aidan's injured ear while his face was buried in the snow.

Rudy put two fingers to Abby's jugular and found a weak but rapid pulse. He pulled the scarf from around his neck and wrapped it around her hand. Within moments blood soaked through the multiple layers of light blue fleece turning it black but he hoped the pressure would stanch the flow of blood. He then unrolled the sleeves of his wool sweater she still wore and tied the ends together. When he pulled the loop of her sleeves over his head he noticed that he was already covered in her crimson blood. Too much blood.

Aidan moaned and stirred. He reached to his ear. Rudy left him to suffer in the snow, his priority was getting Abby to medical help as fast as possible.

Rudy scooped Abby up in his arms. With the sweater looped over his neck, he wore her like a sling. Her head fell against his shoulder. She felt too light, like a hollow shell. He turned in a circle looking for the way out. He had lost his bearings when he ran toward Abby's scream.

Aidan's hand looped over Rudy's left boot, almost tripping him as he spun in a circle looking for footprints obscured by wind and accumulating snow. Rudy shook the hand off his foot with little protest. He turned toward the fallen tree remembering it cut them off the camp. He stepped over Aidan and again felt a hand on his boot. He kicked the hand away and retraced his footsteps through camp.

Light flashed up ahead, not from the sky, but from the levy. Then a horn rang through the silence. He didn't believe it at first, not until the headlights flashed again. Garrison's SUV was perched atop the levy and moving toward him at a crawl.

As Rudy hustled up the hill, the Ford came to a stop and Otto hopped out. He moved down the hill and tried to take Abby from Rudy's arms but Rudy waved him off. Instead, Otto hooked his arm under Rudy's and helped him up the hill. The backdoor opened and Rose reached out to take Abby's legs.

Chapter 65

Garrison ran around the SUV to help load Abby. He knew with one look at Rudy's crazed eyes that there had been a confrontation.

"Aidan?" he asked with his hand on Rudy's shoulder.

"He's down there," Rudy said and nodded down the hill toward the camp.

"Is he dead?"

"Don't know," Rudy said as they loaded Abby's limp body into the backseat.

Garrison looked down the slope and back to the Ford.

"I'll be back," he said running down the slope.

"What the fuck are you doing?" Otto yelled into the wind but Garrison chose to ignore a question he couldn't answer.

He followed the blood trail and footprints through the snow to where Aidan's body lay in a puddle of blood – judging by the lack of injuries the blood wasn't his.

As Garrison bent over Aidan to check his pulse, the boy reached up to touch his bloodied ear. Garrison jumped back startled by the movement.

"Help me," Aidan pleaded into the snow.

"You should have asked me that sooner," Garrison said.

Two days ago in the white hell of the Flynn torture chamber he had felt sorry for Aidan, understood the boy's motives. After watching the hope slowly drain out of Rudy and seeing Abby's broken body, he no longer felt pity, nor did he feel rage, instead a sense of duty drove him.

Aidan's outstretched hand tried to right his body and turn over to face the sky but he didn't have the strength.

Garrison hopped into the driver's seat and turned to look at his passengers. Rudy's eyes flicked from the hatchet to Garrison without asking the question.

"Everybody in?" Garrison asked.

"Go!" Rudy yelled.

Garrison adjusted his rearview mirror, dropped the transmission into reverse and urged the SUV backward.

Rose pulled the quilt from around her shoulders, shook it out and put it over Abby's limp body.

"No," Rudy said and pulled the blanket off. "We gotta keep her cold. She's lost too much blood and her body is in shock."

"What can I do?" she asked.

"Can you put her legs up?"

Rose lifted Abby's heels up onto her shoulder, using her head to hold the girl's feet between her shoulder and the seat.

Otto hovered but there was nothing to do. Nothing any of them could do but pray. Otto rested his hand on Rudy's shoulder and bowed his head.

By some miracle, Garrison navigated the levy and swung the Explorer around in the parking lot before coming to a stop. He swiveled around in the seat to face Rudy.

"It's about to get bumpy," he said. "You gonna be okay?"

"Just get us there," Rudy said.

Garrison poked Otto in the gut. "Buckle up."

Otto turned around as the Ford launched across the parking lot. Garrison righted the vehicle each time it fishtailed. He wasn't lying about the bumps either.

CHAPTER 65

None of them talked. No one hurled questions at Rudy or Garrison as they rocketed over ice and snow. None of them looked each other in the eye. To talk or acknowledge Abby's tenuous position on the edge of the abyss would push her over the precipice and into death's canyon.

Chapter 66

They slid to a halt in front of the emergency room bay doors. Otto ran inside to rouse the troops while Garrison hustled around to Rudy's door and helped him slide out of the backseat without disturbing Abby's position tied around the boy's neck. Rose moved with them supporting Abby's backside and keeping her feet elevated.

Otto returned with a platoon of nurses pushing a gurney. They extracted the girl's limp body from Rudy and Rose's grasp and ran her inside.

Standing in the driving snow, they finally looked at each other.

"I need consent," a nurse said waving a clipboard at the trio. Her scrub jacket billowed and fluttered in the gale.

"That's Abby Flynn," Garrison said pointing at the closing emergency doors. He said her name as if it should be the answer to any question.

"Somebody needs to sign this consent form."

Garrison marched up the to woman until their toes touched. "Gimme that fucking thing." He snatched the clipboard from her hand and scribbled his signature at the bottom of several pages.

"Are you the responsible party?" she asked without backing down.

"Jesus, lady. Could you give us a minute?"

Rudy looked down. Blood stained the front of his coat and shirt black. His hands smeared red. Garrison could see the knots that held the boy together starting to unravel.

CHAPTER 66

"Let's get inside," Otto said and motioned for them to go inside. He took Garrison's keys and headed for the Explorer.

Garrison and Rose stood still watching Rudy waiting for him to make the first move. He wiped his hands on his coat, examined his hands and wiped them again.

"Let's go, son," Garrison said and put his arm around him.

Rudy allowed himself to be led through the hospital doors, past the admitting desk, past the waiting room and into a bathroom. Garrison closed and locked the door behind them. He guided Rudy over to a toilet and sat him down.

"You gonna be sick?" Garrison asked.

Rudy shook his head, his eyes focused on some far off point. Garrison saw this gaze many times before on the faces of soldiers back from the bloody battlefield. Once called shell shock and now bore the clinical name of post traumatic stress disorder. No matter what bullshit label the experts slapped on it, the brain and soul needed time to adjust to the witnessed horrors.

Garrison grabbed a small metal trashcan and put it under Rudy. Rudy's head shook back and forth in a rhythmic motion, saying no over and over again.

"Gimme your coat and shirt."

Without thinking or looking up from the trash can, Rudy did as instructed. Garrison searched the coat's pockets and put all the contents on the vanity, then tucked the soiled coat and jacket into the bio-hazard bin next to the door.

Garrison look down at Rudy. Bloody handprints marred the thighs of his Levis. "I'm afraid there's not much I can do about your jeans."

Sitting on the toilet in bloody jeans and a thin undershirt, Rudy dry heaved into the trash can.

"Get it all out," Garrison said from the sink where he ran cold water over several paper towels, while Rudy continued to cough and gag into the waste can.

Garrison pulled off Otto's ridiculous Korn sweatshirt and offered it to Rudy.

Certain the purge was over, Garrison moved the trash can out of the way and squatted down in front of Rudy.

Rudy slipped on the sweatshirt, which was at least two sizes too big, but covered the bloodstains on his jeans. They returned to the waiting room. Garrison motioned for Rudy to sit next to Otto and Rose.

"Have they said anything?" he asked.

"No one's been out. But your friend with the clipboard has been circling," Otto said.

"I'll go deal with Nurse Paperwork," Garrison said. "Come get me, if they say anything."

Chapter 67

The emergency waiting room was empty aside from the motley crew accompanying Abby. Otto was sprawled out on the floor and snoring in great gasps and snorts. Coats, hats and gloves hung over another bank of chairs nearest the forced air heaters. They dripped to the industrial carpet squares laid out in a dizzying plaid pattern in drab neutral tones.

Rose was still wrapped in the faded log cabin quilt from Garrison's SUV while she sat with her eyes glued to the television hung in the corner. She remained motionless while local and national news anchors recounted the tragic end of the Flynn family and the manhunt of which she was now a key player. During a commercial break, she tapped Garrison on the shoulder. He snorted as he woke from his light slumber. He squinted against the brilliant white light streaming through the windows.

"All that." Rose pointed to the television. "That happened to Red?"

"Yeah." Garrison nodded. "And probably a lot more we'll never know about."

"I just thought she was a runaway. She'd slum it with me for a week then wander on home."

Garrison's eyes grew heavy and he slowly blinked with an unknowable expression like the Cheshire Cat. His head nodded a couple times like he was struggling to stay awake. Rose let him drift away.

The news came back on with three different meteorologists reading the same information over different graphics and maps and lame photos of snowy decks or patio furniture submitted by bored viewers. Rose glanced over her shoulder at Rudy. Although he was no longer covered in Abby's blood, his expression was no less haunted. He stared down at his soiled and wet jeans to the bloody handprint that looped over the toe of his work boot.

Garrison's phone vibrated on the chair beside him and stirred him back awake.

"This is Gordon," he said as he stood and walked away from the group. Rudy didn't look up when Garrison breezed past him.

Rose pulled the quilt from around her shoulders and approached Rudy. She draped the quilt over his lanky frame to distract him from the blood splatters that ran up the legs of his jeans. "You look like you need this more than I do," Rose said.

Rudy nodded but didn't meet her eyes.

"She's stronger than you think," Rose said.

Rudy whispered, "I should've protected her from this."

"No. Not really," Rose said and settled into the chair beside him.

A flush rose from around his collar, up his neck, fanned out across his pale face and set the tips of his ears on fire. "What the fuck does that mean?" Rudy asked and gave her a menacing stare.

"She was meant for this fight," Rose said and stared out the window at the dwindling snow.

"What kind of bullshit is that?" Rudy shifted in his seat and pulled away from Rose.

Rose drew in a deep breath. "She's been carrying around all this guilt. Picking it up a little piece at a time. Not noticing that the weight was beginning to break her back."

The flush was fading from his ears as his face contorted into different emotions.

"She finally set it all down to save herself and you."

CHAPTER 67

Eyes brimming with tears, Rudy met Rose's gaze. "There must have been something I could've done." His voice was a soft whisper.

"There is now," Rose said.

"What's that?"

"Don't let her pick it up again."

Rudy pulled the quilt tighter around himself and caressed the soft cotton to the small splotch of blood obscuring the careful piecing.

Garrison returned to the group and perched on a chair facing Rudy and Rose. With both hands he rubbed from the top of his graying head, down over his eyes, over his cheekbones and rubbed his mouth mashing his lips together. Rose imagined this ritual was building to bad news. Garrison cupped his hand over this mouth and popped it away like he had to drag the words out of his mouth.

"They found Aidan," he said.

Otto rolled over on the floor, snorted between snores which startled him awake. He sat upright like an old Hollywood vampire rising from the grave. He blinked twice and said, "What'd I miss?" like he fell asleep during a movie.

"They found Aidan's body partially buried in the snow," Garrison said.

"Body?" Otto asked.

"Between the weather and blow to the head." Garrison shrugged.

The group collectively looked at the floor. None of them bowed in prayer for the dead, but in thanksgiving.

"This is taking too damn long," Garrison said and marched toward the intake desk.

* * * * *

Ensconced in the huge ICU hospital bed, Abby's already petite frame looked gaunt and emaciated, although she was regaining some of her color.

Rudy sat at her bedside holding her right hand through the bed rail. Her left hand was wrapped in thick bandages from where she'd nearly severed her thumb from the rest of her digits. It took twenty-five stitches to close her up, plus ten units of blood. Although she may need surgery to repair precious tendons and ligaments, she was going to be fine, physically.

"I bought a house, well technically it's a farm," Rudy said. He talked hoping she'd respond but also to keep himself from going crazy. "The house is small and outdated, but it is a good place to start. A starter home. Needs a lot of work, but you could come stay with me until..." He didn't know what was next for either of them. He didn't want her to live in her parents' house – too sad and creepy – and there was no other family.

"Anyway. I was thinking about moving the goats over to the new place. My mom hates them and they'd be close by for kidding this spring. Strange word for birthing goats, like it's a joke."

Abby's hand twitched. He looked up at her face and her eyelids fluttered. After five hours, she was finally starting to wake up from the nightmare. She blinked several times before her eyes focused on him.

"Could we get a dog?" she asked.

About the Author

Parker O'Dwyer gained an MFA in genre fiction in the chilly climes of Gunnison, Colorado. Although she's lived and traveled all over the United States, from New York to the high country of Colorado, her writing is always connected to her Iowa roots.

She knows that monsters exist. They live down the hall, deliver pizzas, make our laws, or share your bed. But they are, undoubtedly, human.

When not writing or traveling, Parker haunts the local libraries and cafes in Des Moines, Iowa. Parker also spends her time running (slowly), listening to crime podcasts, and arguing with her cat.

You can connect with me on:

- https://parkerodwyer.com
- https://twitter.com/ParkerODwyer1
- https://www.facebook.com/parkerodwyer
- https://www.instagram.com/parkerodwyer

Made in the USA
Monee, IL
17 February 2023